Christmas 1992

Janice;

　　Hope This is mysterious
enough for you!

　　　　　　Love,

　　　　Mom and Dad

D0945277

# A DEATH
# BEFORE DYING

**A HENRY HOLT MYSTERY**

BY THE SAME AUTHOR

*The Black Door*
*The Third Figure*
*The Lonely Hunter*
*The Disappearance*
*Dead Aim*
*Hiding Place*
*Long Way Down*
*Aftershock*
*The Faceless Man* (as Carter Wick)
*The Third Victim*
*Doctor, Lawyer . . .*
*The Watcher*
*Twospot* (with Bill Pronzini)
*Power Plays*
*Mankiller*
*Spellbinder*
*Dark House, Dark Road* (as Carter Wick)
*Stalking Horse*
*Victims*
*Night Games*
*The Pariah*
*Bernhardt's Edge*

A HENRY HOLT MYSTERY

# A DEATH BEFORE DYING

## COLLIN WILCOX

HENRY HOLT AND COMPANY
NEW YORK

Copyright © 1990 by Collin Wilcox
All rights reserved, including the right to reproduce
this book or portions thereof in any form.
Published by Henry Holt and Company, Inc.,
115 West 18th Street, New York, New York 10011.
Published in Canada by Fitzhenry & Whiteside Limited,
195 Allstate Parkway, Markham, Ontario L3R 4T8.

Library of Congress Cataloging-in-Publication Data
Wilcox, Collin.
A death before dying / Collin Wilcox. — 1st ed.
p.   cm.
ISBN 0-8050-0979-5
I. Title.
PS3573.I395D44   1989
813'.54—dc20          89-11213
                               CIP

Henry Holt books are available at special discounts
for bulk purchases for sales promotions, premiums,
fund-raising, or educational use. Special editions
or book excerpts can also be created to specification.

For details contact:
Special Sales Director
Henry Holt and Company, Inc.
115 West 18th Street
New York, New York 10011

First Edition

Designed by Katy Riegel
Printed in the United States of America
1  3  5  7  9  10  8  6  4  2

This book is dedicated
to Jeff's Diane . . . and
to Diane's Jeff

# A DEATH
# BEFORE DYING

A HENRY HOLT MYSTERY

# SATURDAY
# FEBRUARY 3

10:15 P.M. Her stomach was contracting. She was drawing in her breath, about to speak. He raised his hand sharply, to silence her. Fury was a factor now. But manageable, controllable, instantly optimized. Because for now, only for now, this moment and the few moments to come, fury must be sublimated, everything in the balance, so exquisitely calculated, one instant to the next instant, one sensation to the next sensation.

These moments, yes, controlled. Calculated and recalculated. And the other word. Optimized. Yes. Delicious, that word. Deliciously descriptive.

Later, though, she must pay. She knew it, knew she must pay for what she'd almost done, the words she'd almost uttered. Her eyes told him. The illumination was enough, then: six large altar candles, calf high, six smaller candles, guttering on the floor. In their hammered gold receptacles, authentic Mayan, the candles alternated, low and high, all twelve in a semicircle. The light was metered, checked and rechecked, enough light for the camera, enough light to let her pick up her cues, yet not too bright, never intrusive.

Catching the hand signal, she had responded instantly. He would remember that she had reacted so quickly. She would see that he remembered. It would be a plus. Yes. A small plus, but nevertheless significant. Yes.

*Yes.*

They were both immobilized now, as they must be, he sitting in the carved baroque chair, she kneeling over the stone sculpture. It was an early Crawford, derivative but relevant to tonight's game, a different game every time they played. The game changed, but the rules remained the same. And she'd startled him when she'd almost spoken.

So she must pay.

She was naked; he was clothed in his silken robe, the fabric so sensual against his skin, the perfect complement to her touch when the time came, and she approached. The silken robe was a constant, yes, the single element that must never change.

Never.

With the forefinger of his right hand he touched the camera's electronic wand, the only discordant element but nevertheless essential. The videotape was his medium. Therefore, without the camera, there was no purpose, no focus.

He shifted his gaze from the crouched woman to the three-dimensional wooden collage on the wall behind her. It was a Penziner abstract, just completed, still untitled. Was the drapery around the collage correct? Should there be a spotlight? Another touch on another console would tell him. But, with his hand above the console, he hesitated. He could feel his body quickening, the first imperative. He looked from the woman, enslaved, to the low table, fashioned from rough-hewn planks, secured by hand-forged black iron studs. The stone of the sculpture, the inherent complexity of the collage, the drapery, the table, the iron studs—they were all unified. Complexity within complexity, a textural unit.

Yes.

All complemented by the naked flesh of the woman and his own naked flesh, tumid now, caressed by the soft silken folds of the robe falling around his feet as he rose from the baroque chair. Two steps between the candles and, yes, he was standing above her. As, yes, she was holding her supplicant's pose, both hands pressed to the stone, her face carefully averted. Her breasts, surely, were her premier attribute, almost perfectly proportional, contoured to fulsome perfection by the pose he'd selected, tonight's variation.

On the table lay the four flays. They were meticulously arranged fanwise, the steel-studded flay to the left, the silken flick on the right, with the knotted rope and the plaited leather between. As he moved his hand toward the table, yes, her body was slightly shifting, so that her eyes could follow his hand.

As always, yes, he first picked up the steel-studded flay, the cruelest of the four. Watching her eyes, he gently hefted the flay. Yes, the response was satisfactory, an acceptable pantomime of maidenly fear. Therefore he could replace the flay on the table, consider the plaited leather, then the rope. Finally it came down to the silken flick, as it always did, an ancient emperor's bauble, exquisitely embroidered and tasseled. Because she'd almost spoken, a transgression, he laid the flick across her shoulders, a wrist-snap, artistry incarnate. Eyes widening, pleading, she gripped the stone of the statue, knuckles white. At the second ministration she flinched, shied, drew a sharp, involuntary breath. But her eyes held steady with his as, ceremoniously now, he replaced the flick on the table. He turned to face her squarely. He stood motionless, hands at his sides. His chin was elevated, a haughty pose, momentarily frozen until, yes, he could lower his gaze, as if to finally notice her, some pathetic waif clinging to this rough stone surrounded by the golden light of the candles.

As they held their tableau, he the lord, she the cast-up wretch on this alien shore, they might be utterly alone.

Except for the camera's whir, utterly alone . . .

. . . as, yes, he stooped, knotted his fingers in the luxuriant strands of her thick hair, drew her to her feet.

In the alcove, draped in black, lit like a sepulcher, the final element of the night's creation awaited them: the bed.

Step by step, stumbling, he with his hand gripping her hair, roughly dragging her, they moved to the bedchamber. Now they were beside the bed, she on her knees, crouched, he standing erect, still with the fingers of one hand locked in her hair. The hair was done in thick plaits, according to his instructions. And, yes, she'd remembered her mark, for the camera.

And now, desperate entreaty, she raised her eyes to his. Would he forgive her? Would he spare her, just this once?

Scowling, his face as fierce as a headsman's behind the ceremonial black hood, he sharply shook his head. Entreaty denied.

Her eyes implored him.

He gripped her hair, flexed his knees. As, on cue, she gathered herself. A choreographed heave, and she lay across the bed. She lay on her back, legs drawn up, breasts heaving, a perfect pantomime of terror. As he bent over her, anticipating, she began to writhe: slowly at first, sinuously. Her eyes, wide, were one with his. In the universe, there was nothing else. As the moment lengthened his flesh lost substance, became amorphous, dissolved into pure sensation. On the rich damask of the bedspread, her fingers were widespread; the carmine fingernails, meticulously groomed, gripped the gold brocade of the spread, desperation incarnate.

With his body arched above her, their eyes consuming, flesh transcended, his fingers touched the flesh of her throat.

Sharply she drew in her breath.

Beneath his fingers, her flesh was warm. Beneath his fingertips, the pulsing of her blood was strong.

Slowly, inexorably, his fingers began to tighten.

# TUESDAY
# FEBRUARY 13

10:55 A.M. Every profession, Albert Price reflected, exacted its own particular penalty. For the cabbie, traffic was the trauma. For athletes, it was the aging process.

For him, it was the eternal push-pull of the objective-subjective, the constant necessity to remain aloof, the chronic clinician, never the friend, never the real participant. As actors must project emotion, he must project detachment. As pagan priests codified entrails, he codified his patients' tics and twitches.

And when the patient was a beautiful woman—Meredith Powell, a tawny blonde, her body radiating an electric sensuality that was all the more provocative because she sought so strenuously to suppress it—then must he be especially conscious of his role: the psychiatrist projecting the priest. Therefore, his voice must be soft and gravely modulated, his manner once removed, judiciously measured.

"We haven't talked much about your marriage, Meredith. You say he abused you." As Price paused, he automatically registered her subliminal reaction: a telltale tightening of the mouth, an involuntary wince. These, he knew, were the small, cruel barbs of memory, pain revisited.

"Yes . . ." As she nodded and looked away, Price allowed himself a moment's wayward pleasure as he noted the line of her cheek and the particular curve of her jaw. It was a wide, aristocratic jaw, tapering to a decisive chin. Greta Garbo's jaw had flared like that. And Grace Kelly's, too. The evocation: *Town and Country* covers, tweeds, vintage limousines drawn up to pillared porticos.

"But he never actually struck you," he prompted.

Drawing a deep, unsteady breath, she shook her head. "No. He—" She hesitated, forced herself to look at him directly. Would he help her, release her from the necessity of answering? No. He would only look at her—and wait.

"He—sometimes when he'd been drinking, and he wanted to—to make love, he'd be rough. But I can't say he ever actually hit me, not with his hand."

"So it was more psychological abuse, then."

She nodded.

"Meredith—" Gently admonishing, Price gestured to the tape recorder that rested on the desk between them. "Words, remember. Not gestures. We're saving on secretarial fees here." He smiled. He was a thin, wiry man in his forties. His face, too, was thin and wiry. His pale blue eyes were intense; his mouth was humorless, tightly compressed.

"Sorry," she answered quickly. Automatically Price noted the characteristic reaction: the quick, masochistic assumption of guilt, therefore blame. "Gary was—is—very smart, very intelligent," she continued. "But when he was drinking, he—he berated me. That's the only way I can describe it. He taunted me."

"Did he ever threaten you, threaten to harm you?"

"No, it wasn't that. He just made me feel worthless. It—it's hard to explain."

"When did you decide to take back your maiden name, Meredith?"

"I decided to do that when I came back to San Francisco. After the divorce."

"How did that make you feel, to have your maiden name again? Did you feel that it was a plus—a victory? Or did it feel like a defeat?"

6

"Well, it—" She bit her lip, shook her head, slightly frowned. "It didn't feel like either, really. I mean, I was born in San Francisco, you know."

He nodded. "Yes, I know you were."

As if he'd admonished her, she looked at him anxiously, then tried to explain. "I mean, it seemed to fit, somehow. This is the only place I ever felt like I—I belonged. And I was Meredith Powell here. In Los Angeles I was Meredith Blake. Someone else. Not me."

To encourage her, he smiled again. This time, though, it was a small, impersonal smile. Then, glancing surreptitiously at the small clock placed to face him on the desk, he allowed the smile to fade. The clock read 11:10; their hour was almost gone. It was time for the hard part.

"We've talked about the men you've been with. And we've agreed, I think, that there's a common thread—a pattern. That's to be expected, of course. We all have our own particular personality patterns. And it's entirely predictable that people with particular patterns of behavior seek out people whose patterns mesh with their own. You'd agree with that, wouldn't you?"

"I—" Uncertainly she nodded. "I guess so. Yes."

"But sometimes," he continued, "these patterns don't mesh properly. Sometimes they clash. And if the clash is bad enough, and the same clashes are repeated over and over, then it's a problem. And the longer it continues, the bigger the problem gets. Is that a true statement, would you say?"

"I—" As if she were deeply resigned to some crushing inevitability, she nodded. "Yes, I—I'd say that's true."

"Good." To encourage her, he nodded gravely. "And would you also say that your present relationship fits this scenario?"

"I—yes," she answered. "Yes, it—it does." She spoke very softly. Her eyes were downcast, her fingers fretful. It was the classic attitude of guilt, of the penitent in the confessional.

"Except," he said, "this relationship you're involved in now is worse than the others."

"Yes . . ."

"In fact, this relationship is a culmination of all the others, wouldn't you say?"

She nodded, murmuring "Yes, I would."

"And, in fact, that's why you're here. You've seen the pattern developing, and you've decided to take action."

"Y-yes."

"The only question is," he prompted, "what kind of action? You've already decided that you want to get out of the relationship. Right?"

"Yes . . ." It was a timid, tentative response that signified hope, not determination.

"You know what you want to do, but you're not sure how to do it. Is that a fair statement?"

"Yes." For the first time she registered animation, a kind of wan conviction. "Oh, yes."

Once more Price glanced at the clock. Seven minutes remained. Should he try for a firm response, a commitment to action? Or should he begin tapering off, bringing her down? But down from what? During the entire interview, they'd hardly connected. He'd done all the talking. Passively, she'd simply agreed. And passivity, in fact, was Meredith Powell's problem.

Therefore, he would change tempo, change timbre, administer a quick, therapeutic, plain-language jolt.

"So why don't you call this guy and tell him to get lost? Tell him you're through playing his sadistic little games." He let one quick, taut beat pass. Then: "Tell him, in the vernacular, to fuck off. As your psychiatrist, I heartily advise you to do it. In fact, I urge you to do it. Immediately."

As he'd calculated, the obscenity had gotten to her, shaken her up. Now, for the first time today, she looked at him full face. Now, in this moment, they were engaged. The next moment, up or down, could be the ball game. Their eye contact held. Would it work, then, this session, score one for the home team? Her eyes were wonderful: a deep, vibrant violet. And the bones of her face were nature's work of art, the ultimate female essence.

For a moment, one single moment, he saw conviction flicker in the violet eyes, saw determination work at the corners of her mouth.

But, as quickly as it came, resolution faded. No, she wouldn't make the call.


11:15 A.M. To himself, Charles grimaced. If there was a pillar in this bustling lobby—an ornate marble pillar—would he be skulking behind it? Perhaps there would be a potted palm beside the pillar, all the clichés pulled to the stops. He would stand behind the potted palm, the fronds parted, plying his petty spy's gameful gambit.

It was a turn-of-the-century melodrama, a nickelodeon plot, beginning with the damsel mincing across the stage. Enter the slick-haired lover, downstage. Ah, she sees him. She flutters. The lover advances. She shrinks away, prettily.

Enter his character, stage left. Ah, he sees them, the damsel and her sleazy swain. Quickly he darts behind the pillar—or the palm. The rinky-tink piano music swells. This, then, is the hero, palm fronds parted before his darkly handsome face.

But there, abruptly, the image faded, the plot fell apart.

Because he wasn't the hero of this tacky drama. His was a bit part. The emperor commanded, the lackey obeyed, a court drama. If the emperor was a dunce, then the barons wore dunce caps.

Accounting for his presence here, at the 450 Sutter Medical Building. Now, at a little after eleven. Skulking. It was the only word: skulking.

Tuesdays at ten-thirty, this must be her regular weekly appointment time, her third successive Tuesday visit to Albert Price, psychiatrist, offices on the eleventh floor.

Three weeks ago, playing another role, the private eye, driving a rental car, every contingency anticipated, he'd parked around the corner from her condo. At ten o'clock, give or take, the garage door had come up. As if he'd done it for years, a pro, he'd followed her. Driving carefully, as she always did, Meredith had gone downtown, driven into the garage beneath the 450 Sutter Building.

Instantly, his first private eye's test, he'd realized that if he also turned into the garage, she might see him. So, never mind the expense, he pulled into a yellow loading zone.

The emperor, after all, would pay.

He'd locked the car and cautiously entered the building's lobby. The building was large, more than twenty stories tall. But the lobby was small, with no place to hide. No place but the adjoining pharmacy, with a show window opening on the lobby. Making a quick decision, he'd gone into the drugstore, concealing himself behind a rack of sunglasses. He hadn't been a moment too soon; almost immediately she'd appeared in the lobby, walked to a waiting elevator with several people already inside. The elevator door had slid closed. Leaving him furious, frustrated.

The only solution, he'd thought bitterly, would have been to disguise himself, enter the same elevator, hope she wouldn't recognize him: the courtier wearing a false beard and wig.

Enter Herbert Dancer, Ltd., private investigators. Their report: Meredith was seeing a psychiatrist. Albert Price. Suite 1107.

The puzzle, then, had been solved; mission accomplished.

But then, predictably, the questions began: Why was she seeing Albert Price? Could sex be the reason, the story of her life? Did they spend an hour screwing, she and Dr. Price?

Or was the liaison innocent, exactly what it seemed?

Yet innocence implied safety, security, harmlessness.

Belying the stark, chilling reality, the utter certainty that if Meredith said too much—to anyone—the emperor could fall.

The emperor, and his principal courtier.

All fall down.

11:10 A.M. Dr. Holland shook his head dolefully. "I hate to be the bearer of bad news, Mr. Hastings. But I'm afraid you need reading glasses. I imagine you knew that when you made the appointment, though, didn't you?"

Resigned, Hastings nodded. "I'm afraid so."

"Otherwise," the doctor said, "your eyes are fine. No sign of glaucoma, no astigmatism. What kind of work do you do?"

"I'm a policeman."

"You are?" Registering mild surprise, the doctor gave him a nonprofessional second look. "Are you—you must be—" Uncertain how to phrase the question, he broke off.

"I'm a lieutenant. I spend about half the time at my desk. The rest of the time I'm out in the field."

"Ah—" the doctor nodded. "Well, you can probably go one of two ways. Either reading glasses that you take off and put on or else bifocals with plain glass on top."

Bifocals . . .

Privately Hastings sighed. Along with arthritis and clogged arteries, bifocals defined the aging process. Football injuries and job-related bruises were part of the game, win some, lose some. But in the aging game, there were no winners.

"You don't have to decide now, of course." The doctor handed over a slip of paper. "That's your prescription. Think about it, then see what an optometrist says." Rising, he extended his hand. "Nice to have met you, Lieutenant. What, ah, part of the police department are you in?"

"I'm in Homicide."

"Is that so?" It was a predictable layman's response, one that required no reply.

11:25 A.M. Hastings pressed the DOWN button and stepped back from the elevator. He'd promised himself that, since he was down-

11

town, he would shop for socks and underwear and two shirts and then have lunch before he returned to the Hall of Justice. As he made sure the ophthalmologist's prescription was safe in an inside pocket, he was aware that, of the three women and one man waiting for an elevator, one of the women was looking at him directly. She was dressed fashionably but not elaborately, expensively but not ostentatiously. Everything was handmade or hand-woven: saddle leather handbag and shoes, a hammered silver-and-turquoise medallion pin that secured a dramatic scarf. Beneath the thick, winter-weight wool skirt and jacket, the line of her body was muted but exciting: full breasted, long legged, narrow waisted. Her thick, tawny-blond hair fell naturally to her shoulders.

Her face was unforgettable: a face that could make a man promise anything.

As their eyes met and held, he saw her lips upcurve in a small, tentative smile of recognition and invitation that could only be meant for him.

Had his trip to the eye doctor suddenly become an adventure?

He knew he was also smiling. But should he speak?

He heard a chime. In his peripheral vision he saw a Lucite bar above one of the elevators glow red. Two of the women and the man were stepping expectantly toward the elevator. But the beautiful blonde wearing the expensive handmade clothing hadn't responded to the elevator's chime. Instead, she came a step closer, just as, unconsciously, he'd moved a step closer to her.

And in that instant, realization dawned: This wasn't the beginning of temptation. This was a memory test.

Because, long ago, he'd known this woman. In another place, another time, long before she'd discovered haute couture, he'd known her.

And a single word confirmed it.

"Frank?"

"That's right . . ." His smile widened. They were standing close enough to touch now. "I'm sorry. I know that—"

"Meredith Powell." She let a beat pass, giving him time. Then: "Kevin's sister. From Thirty-ninth Avenue."

*Meredith Powell . . .*

The images came in a rush: Kevin Powell's sister, the little blond girl who was always around, just a little kid, always so quiet, so shy—always tagging along. When he and Kevin had gone to high school, she'd still been in grammar school, hardly more than nine or ten years old, therefore far beneath their lordly adolescent male notice. When he'd graduated from high school, she'd still been in grammar school, perhaps the sixth grade, all freckles and awkward arms and legs.

But when his mother had died, more than twenty years ago, and she'd gone to the funeral, she'd been a teenager, a breathtaking natural blond beauty.

The same beauty whose shoulders he now held in both hands, drawing her close.

"Meredith. For God's sake."

He sensed her involuntary reluctance as he began to hug her. But the images from long ago were pure, innocent of desire. Therefore, liberated from the conventions of the mating game, he could hug her briefly, kiss her soundly on the cheek, then move her back, for a long look. He held her at arm's length— bifocal length, his little secret.

"How'd you ever *know* me?" As he asked the question, an elevator door opened; another closed. With a hand on her elbow, he moved her away from the elevators.

"I saw you on TV, Frank. Just a month or two ago. I couldn't believe it. There you were, on the eleven o'clock news."

He nodded diffidently. "It's part of the job. I run the Homicide detail with another lieutenant. But he's the inside man. So whenever there's something worth sending a TV crew out for, I'm usually the one on the scene. Listen—" As more people arrived

13

on the eleventh floor and more left, he glanced at his watch. "Listen, it's almost eleven-thirty. How about an early lunch? Have you got time?"

"Well . . ." With the single hesitant word, more images returned. At the funeral, she'd been so painfully shy, so incredibly ill at ease. Even though she was so beautiful, so overpoweringly desirable, she'd seemed constantly poised for flight: a frightened, fragile bird. And now, even after so many years, even though she wore her designer clothes with the assurance of a beautiful woman, he could still hear the old uncertainty in her voice, still see the vulnerability in her eyes. "Well, I'm supposed to—"

"Come on." He put an arm around her shoulders, friend-to-friend, and drew her toward the elevator. "No excuses."


11:40 A.M. As they followed the waitress to a table, Hastings was conscious of the attention they attracted: men and women following them with their eyes, the women assessing Meredith's clothes, the men imagining the body beneath the clothes. And, yes, he was conscious of his own reaction: the dominant male, a little larger than himself, displaying his prize.

"Something to drink?" he asked, after they'd been seated.

"Are you having anything?"

It was the classic AA opening: a chance to matter-of-factly confess. So he shook his head, saying "No. I had to quit. Years ago." As he said it, he remembered her father: a big, burly braggart who drank too much. And in high school, Kevin, too, had made a fool of himself, drinking.

"You mean you—" Disbelieving, she shook her head.

He nodded. "Yeah, that's what I mean. I was as surprised as you are." He smiled. "Do you want the whole story—the Frank Hastings story since Thirty-ninth Avenue?"

She returned the smile. "Of course. Isn't that why we're here?"

"But then it's your turn. Agreed?"

"Yes. Agreed."

But, as she said it, the smile lost conviction. Behind her eyes, a shadow fell. Meredith wasn't eager to take her turn.

"Well," he said, "when I got out of high school, I got a football scholarship to Stanford. And after Stanford I got drafted by the Detroit Lions. But I only played for two seasons before I got my knee screwed up. And if I'd've come back here, to San Francisco, and done something else—anything else—there probably would've been a happy ending. But instead I married an heiress. Her name was Carolyn Ralston, and her father made radiators for General Motors. He was very rich, and Carolyn was very—" He hesitated, searching for the word. "She was very stylish. Every once in a while we'd get our pictures on the society pages. I was a novelty, I guess—a football player who could talk in sentences. And I'd be lying if I said I didn't like it.

"But then I got hurt, and the Lions dropped me. It was no problem, though—at least not for my wife and her father. He set me up with a nice corner office and a nice brunette secretary— and told me I was part of his public relations department. Which meant, I discovered, that I met visiting big shots at the airport and got them settled—and then drank with them. It was one big party, especially if the big shots were football fans. But then—" He shook his head. "But then one day when I asked one of the VIPs how he wanted to amuse himself, he said he wanted a girl. I stalled him, and he didn't like it. And neither did my father-in-law, as it turned out. And that's when the problems started. Because there's a name, you know, for men who get women for other men."

"But you—"

"And then," he cut in, driven by some strange confessional compulsion to tell the whole story to this sister of Kevin Powell, a neighborhood kid he'd never really liked. "And then, surprise, I discovered that I couldn't get through the day without drinking—

a lot." Watching her, he let a last grim beat pass before he finished it: "And then, surprise, I got served with divorce papers. So—" He shrugged. "So I got out of town, came back to San Francisco. A friend of mine got me into the Police Academy. I was the oldest rookie in my class. But I made it. Barely."

"And you quit drinking."

"The line is, I'm a 'recovering alcoholic.' I've been recovering for about thirteen years."

The waitress returned, took their orders, bustled away.

"Do you have children?" Meredith asked the question tentatively, reluctantly—as if she didn't really want to hear the answer.

"Two. They're teenagers now. Great kids." He smiled. "The next time we do this, I'll bring pictures."

"Yes . . ." Dutifully she nodded, wistfully smiled.

"What about you? Kids?"

"No—no kids. I was married. But no kids." Plainly she regretted not having children. And she was in her middle thirties; the biological clock was ticking.

To lighten the mood, signifying that his story was ended, he smiled, spread his hands. "So now I'm a TV personality."

Spontaneously she returned his smile. The effect was electric, triggering an inevitable response, simple sexual arithmetic: one beautiful female body plus one attentive male. But then the smile faded, the eyes came down. Watching her, he appreciatively studied her face and head: thick, lustrous dark-blond hair worn loose, broad forehead, classically patrician nose and chin, a mouth that curved as if the lips were parting to murmur some special endearment. The bones of the cheeks were high, the cheeks slightly hollowed, subtly joining the strong line of the jaw. And, beneath the curve of the eyebrows, her violet eyes were vivid.

"My turn?" she asked.

"Your turn," he answered. "But before you start, tell me about Kevin. I heard he died. An accident."

With her eyes lowered, she nodded. "Yes . . ."

"How'd it happen?"

"He was driving too fast." She let a beat pass. Then, with an obvious effort, she raised her eyes to his. "He was drunk, and he was driving too fast. It was a one-car accident."

He nodded, held her eyes in silence, then asked, "How long ago did it happen?"

"About five years ago."

"Was he married? Any children?"

"No children. He was married once, but it only lasted for a year or two."

"What'd he do? What kind of work?"

"He was a sheet metal worker, in Sacramento. He made good money—when he worked."

"So he was a drinker. That's what you're saying."

"Yes," she answered, "that's what I'm saying."

In memory of Kevin Powell, a kid who probably never had a chance, he let a moment of silence pass. Then: "What about your parents?"

"My mother died—" She paused, to calculate. "It was about fifteen years ago. I'd just started as a flight attendant at United. I was twenty-one."

Twenty-one plus fifteen—Meredith was thirty-six years old. Still so beautiful, so unconsciously sensual.

As she lapsed into another silence, once more lowering her eyes, he tried to recall images of her family. Her mother, he remembered, was a thin, washed-out woman who seldom went out of the house except to shop for groceries. Wearing a faded housedress, trundling a wire shopping cart filled with brown paper bags, head down, she made her dogged trip to the store, her daily burden. Meredith's father was a plumber: a big, beefy, blustering man with a red face and small, baleful eyes—a loud-talking bully, and a drunk. And Kevin, sadly, grew into a pallid imitation of his father. In high school he'd had few friends.

Her mother and brother, dead . . .

There was only one question left.

He waited until the waitress had served their lunch and filled their coffee cups. Then: "And your father?"

She shook her head. As if she were confessing to something shameful, she said, "I don't know where he is, Frank. I lost track of him. My mother waited until I got out of high school, then she divorced him."

He hesitated, then decided to say "There were always rumors that he beat her."

"Every Saturday night, almost." Her voice was hardly more than a whisper. Her eyes were furtive.

He let a moment pass, then said, "He's still alive, then."

"I guess he is, but I don't know. He didn't come to my brother's funeral, and I never heard from him, after that." She shook her head. "In a way, I wish he was dead. At least I'd know. It—it's worse, not knowing." Anxiously she raised her eyes to his. "That must sound terrible."

"It doesn't sound terrible at all, Meredith." He smiled. "It sounds like you're in touch with your feelings. Isn't that the way it's supposed to work—the trendy thing to do?"

She tried to acknowledge his attempt at humor but could summon only a small, sad smile.

"Okay—" He gestured firmly. "Your turn."

She drew a deep breath and began. "I guess it's easier to start at the beginning," she said. "After I graduated from high school, the first thing I wanted to do was get out of the house. My mother and I always got along, but my father—" Jaw set, she grimly shook her head. "His drinking—I just couldn't stand it anymore. So I got a place with three other girls, out near the ocean, and I started nursing school at City College, working my way. But after a year and a half, I realized that I'd never be a nurse. I—I just wasn't tough enough to take it. By that time my folks were divorced. My father was down south somewhere, and my mother had gotten an apartment and was working. We never did own our own home. Maybe you knew that."

He shrugged. "I never kept track. Our parents did, I know—kept track of who owned and who rented. I can remember my folks talking about it. My father was in real estate."

"I don't remember your father very well." She said it apologetically. "But I seem to remember him driving big cars and smoking cigars. And always wearing a tie, very sophisticated."

"Except that he never got those cars paid off." He hesitated. Then, still driven by the urge to share something special with her, he said, "He had a one-man real estate office. One man, and a 'Girl Friday,' as he called her. When I was fourteen, I came home from frosh football practice one day. There was an envelope on the kitchen table. It wasn't sealed, and nothing was written on the outside. So I opened it. My father had gone to Texas with his Girl Friday."

"Oh—gee." It was a spontaneous expression of sympathy, somehow evoking a teenage inability to articulate. "I didn't know, Frank."

He shrugged. Now it was his smile, he knew, that was sad, wistfully forced.

"So your folks were divorced, too," she said.

"No. A couple of years after he left, my dad and his Girl Friday were killed in west Texas, in an auto accident. His estate totaled about six hundred dollars—just enough for my mother to get the house painted, I remember."

"Divorce . . ." The single word said it all: the shame, the defeat, the corrosive loss of hope. Then, confessing, she said, "It happened to me, too. Divorce, I mean. When I left nursing school I worked at the Bank of America for a couple of years, and then I went with United. I flew for a couple of years. And then—" She shook her head regretfully. "Then I met a man named Gary Blake. He had a string of restaurants in Los Angeles. He's a millionaire—a self-made millionaire. That's the way he always described himself, especially when he was drinking—a self-made millionaire. And he was drinking most of the time." With her lunch forgotten, she lapsed into a long, lost silence.

19

"Your father—your brother—your husband—they all drank," he offered.

She nodded. Then, with great effort: "A little while ago—two months ago, I guess—I went to a psychiatrist. That's where I was this morning. I—I never thought I could do it, go to a psychiatrist. It just seemed like something I'd never do. But I—I'm thirty-six years old, and the truth is that the men I get involved with are just as—as crude as my dad. Just as brutal. So I decided that I needed help. Which I do."

"I'm sorry, Meredith. About the men, I mean."

In acknowledgment, she nodded. Then, perhaps driven by the same half-blind compulsion he'd felt to confess, to tell everything to someone who shared deep memories of the past, she said, "We were married seven years, Gary and I. He was older than I was, and he—he dominated me. Completely dominated me. So finally I had to get out. I just had to do it."

"You say he was brutal. Did he hit you? Abuse you?"

"He used me, that's the only way I can describe it. He didn't hit me with his fist. It was words—just words. Gary was smart. Brilliant, I guess. But he's a—a destructive person. When he got drunk, sometimes he—he'd threaten me, push me around. It—mostly it was connected with sex."

Wearily he nodded. This same story was deeply etched in his policeman's lexicon. Sex and violence, his stock-in-trade.

The poets, the songwriters spoke of love.

But his beat was sex, the dark side of love.

Was sex the reality, love the illusion?

"So you got out—" He nodded. "What else could you do? I hope you had a good lawyer."

"I don't think I did have a very good lawyer, as a matter of fact. Either that or Gary got to him. I think that might've been what happened."

"Then you should've gotten another lawyer, Meredith."

"I know—" Resigned, she shook her head. "It always happens that way, it seems."

20

Drawing on countless hours spent in interrogation rooms, he let a beat pass, giving her time. Then, gently, he prompted: "So you moved back to San Francisco. You and I—" To encourage her, he smiled. "We came back with our tails between our legs." She tried to return the smile, unsuccessfully. "Yes . . ."

"And then what? Did you get married again?" His glance strayed to the expensive clothes and the jewelry. Everything suggested that she dressed to please men—or a man.

"No." She spoke softly, with infinite regret. "No. I—I came back here, and I—I started doing what I've done all my life, passing up the nice guys to go with the wrong ones. It—it's never changed." As she spoke, she looked at him quickly, speculatively. Still playing his interrogator's role, he could easily read the look. She was deciding how much more she should tell him—how much she *could* tell him, safely.

Safely? Was that the word?

What was he reading in her face? Fear?

Fear of what? Of whom?

. . . *to go with the wrong ones,* she'd said. Plural. Was it possible—conceivable—that she was a call girl? Was it guilt that he saw, rather than fear?

He must say something, make some response. "Safety in numbers? Is that the plan?" Hearing himself say it, he realized how fatuous he must sound, how silly.

Shaking her head, she tried to smile. "No, that isn't the plan. Maybe it should be the plan, but it isn't."

"One man, then . . ."

Now, still deeply regretful, she nodded. "One man."

"The wrong man."

"Definitely the wrong man."

Once she'd said it, there was nothing left for him to say. She'd said it all, laid it all out for him. She was locked into a bad habit she couldn't break. Enter the psychiatrist.

"I'm sorry to hear it, Meredith. I mean it."

Silently she nodded. He watched her push her plate away,

the food hardly touched. She remained motionless for a moment, eyes downcast, hands helpless in her lap. Finally she said, "I'm sorry, Frank. I—I'm always pretty shaky after I've finished with the shrink. I shouldn't've come to lunch. I knew I shouldn't."

"Are you breaking up with this guy? Is that it?"

She shook her head regretfully. "No, that's not it. I—I wish I could. But I can't."

"One of those can't-live-with-him, can't-live-without-him things? It happens to everyone, sooner or later."

As if she were puzzled, she raised her eyes to his, frowning. "No—no. That's not it either. I mean I—I can't stand to—to have him touch me anymore. But I—I can't get out of it. He—he won't let me go."

"He's jealous, you mean."

"No, not jealous. There—there isn't anyone else. And he knows it."

He frowned. "He's possessive, then."

"Possessive—" As if she were experimenting with the word, she spoke hesitantly, tentatively. Then, bitterly, she repeated, "Possessive. Yes . . ."

"This is really bothering you."

She nodded mutely.

Watching her as she struggled for control of the emotions that tore at the perfection of her face, he let a moment of silence pass before he said quietly, "This guy scares you. You're afraid of him."

Helplessly—mutely—she nodded.

He let another beat pass. Then: "You could leave."

"Run away, you mean."

"Sometimes that's the only answer, Meredith."

"But San Francisco is the only place that means anything to me, Frank. It—it's home. Don't you feel that way? The old neighborhood—sometimes I think that's all I've ever had."

An instant's flash of memory returned. He'd just come back to San Francisco. All his possessions had been checked through on his airline ticket from Detroit: four suitcases and a cardboard box tied with clothesline. He'd stayed at a hotel for the first few nights, while he'd looked for an apartment. One of the addresses had been just three blocks from his childhood home—the home he'd had to sell after his mother died, to pay off the second mortgage. Dreading something he couldn't understand, he'd driven past the house on Thirty-ninth Avenue. Then he'd made a U-turn, returned, stopped in front of the house. And then, inexplicably, he'd begun to cry: deep, wracking sobs. He hadn't cried when his father died, hadn't cried at his mother's funeral. He hadn't cried when he'd left his children in Detroit, only a few days before. But that night he'd cried.

"It means something to me, too, Meredith," he said softly. "It means a lot. More all the time."

Digging in her purse, she found a tissue. She wiped her eyes, snuffled, blew her nose. Her eyes were wet. "I'm sorry. I—I shouldn't've come. I'm sorry."

"Don't apologize. It's a bad habit, Meredith." Gravely smiling, he held her eyes. "For you, it's a bad habit."

She tried to return the smile, finally succeeded. "You're a nice man, Frank. You're considerate. You're tough, I imagine. But you're kind, too. My brother, I remember, used to idolize you. I can't remember him feeling like that about anyone else."

Unable to think of a reply, he nodded.

"I can remember seeing you play football, in high school. I was only ten, but I saw you once. And I can remember the girls on the block. They used to follow you around."

Trying to lighten the mood, he said, "They still do, Meredith. They follow me constantly."

Her smile wistfully widened. Then, hesitantly, she ventured, "Do you—have someone?"

Aware that his reply would only deepen her sadness, he said, "Her name is Ann Haywood. She's a schoolteacher. She's got two sons, teenagers. We've been living together for a little more than a year, all four of us." He hesitated, then decided to say "She looks a little like you, in fact. Blue eyes, same kind of hair, same shape to the face. I'd like you to meet her. Come to dinner."

"Yes . . ." It was really a confession that she'd never do it, never come to dinner. They both knew it.

He let the silence between them lengthen before he said, "If this guy bothers you—" He took a card from his pocket, slid it across the table. "Keep that. Give me a call, if he gives you any trouble. You'd be surprised what a cop knocking on the door can accomplish."

She took the card, thanked him, looked at the card, slid it into her purse. She would probably never call, just as she would probably never come to dinner. She was frightened. Badly frightened, maybe. But she probably wouldn't call. She was the classic victim type, helplessly awaiting her fate. He'd encountered countless women like Meredith Powell—some of them lying in a pool of blood.

"So you won't leave town." Saying it, he put a note of finality in his voice. Finality, and approval, too. She was right: she'd spent enough time running away.

"I guess . . ." She broke off. Then: "I guess I've been less unhappy here than anywhere else. It—it's a wonderful city."

Silently, still watching her, he made no reply. There was something more, he realized—something she wanted to tell him. Something important.

"And there's my doctor, too. I—I can't leave him. At least not now."

"Your psychiatrist, you mean."

She nodded gravely. "He—he's made me see things I could never look at before, things I never thought I'd ever tell anyone." As she spoke, she looked him fully in the face. The mute message was clear. She wanted to tell him—needed to tell him—what she'd told her psychiatrist. He had only to ask. She desperately wanted him to ask.

"What kind of things are you talking about, Meredith?"

She had returned to her previous position, head bowed,

hands listless in her lap. Then, purposefully lifting her chin, speaking with great precision, she said, "It's my father. He—" She broke off, blinked, began slowly shaking her head, signifying an inner defeat of the spirit. Clearly, her confession hung in delicate, desperate balance. But then, in a deliberate rush, she said, "He abused me. I was eleven the first time it happened. And it made me feel so—so guilty, so terribly worthless, so ashamed, that—"

A sudden short, cruel sob choked off the rest of it.

"Jesus, Meredith. I—" Swallowing hard, he reached out to touch her hand. "I'm sorry. I'm terribly sorry."


1:10 P.M. Without being seen, Charles had been able to observe them through the restaurant's plate-glass window. They were sitting at a small table next to the far wall. Each time he'd looked, he'd seen them deep in conversation, their faces solemn, totally engaged. This was no chance encounter, no casual meeting.

It had been a week since the Dancer agency had discovered she was seeing the psychiatrist. Of course the hackneyed, sordid, patient-and-shrink sex scenario had been suspected: the doctor's appointment screening an hour of love.

But now this: another man, another scenario.

So the game would begin again. He was the pursuer, the avenger. His will would prevail. In the animal kingdom, what passed for God? It was the strongest, the deadliest. Therefore, among animals, to kill was to prevail, a natural law. The deadliest was the godliest.

Only in death, then, could the truth be found. Animals killed daily—or died. But man, the highest animal form, had lost touch with death, therefore lost touch with God. It was simple logic.

To kill—to watch the eyes go blank as the muscles ceased to twitch—only that conscious act could complete the cycle.

But first, the cycle must begin.

First cycle, first sequence.

Patience—cold, deadly patience—was the key. In the veld, the lion moved inch by inch, a shadow across the grass.

So days might pass before she must pay. Days or weeks—or only hours, if events fell into focus.

His problem this Tuesday was a reprise of the first problem, two weeks ago: see but don't be seen, the invisible stalker. Therefore, when he'd seen them served their lunch, a guarantee that they would be immobilized for an hour, at least, he'd returned to his car—his rental car. He'd parked the car on Sutter Street, across from the exit leading up from the parking garage beneath the 450 Sutter Building. If they left the restaurant and returned to 450 Sutter, he would follow them. Standing on the sidewalk, shoulders hunched against the cold, fog-laden wind blowing down Bush Street from the ocean, he saw the waitress refilling their coffee cups. The table had already been cleared. Soon their check would come. Then they'd leave the restaurant.

And then . . .

Vividly he could imagine their sordid progression: flesh straining against corrupted flesh in some half-darkened hotel room, guttural background cries of humans in heat.

From his vantage point, he could clearly see the man. In his early forties, without doubt. A big, muscular man, six feet, two hundred pounds. A man who moved economically, confidently. Brown hair, thick, touched at the temples with gray. Regular features: a muscular face, like the body. Calm, calculating eyes. A deliberate man, by his actions, therefore slow to anger. The clothes were Macy's: brown herringbone jacket, dark-brown trousers. Beige shirt, brown striped tie, a banal study in brown. The shirt, though, was button-down oxford cloth, a spurious Ivy League touch, probably a pretension. Yet the big man wore his clothes easily. Some men did, some men didn't.

As he watched, he saw the man reach across the table to touch the woman's hand. Her face was stricken. His face reflected her pain.

Friends?

Lovers?

In minutes, he might know.

**1:35 P.M.** The starter whirred but the engine didn't start. Quickly Charles depressed the accelerator pedal, released it, turned the key again. This time, faltering, the engine caught. Now he must—

Her silver Mercedes appeared: first the hood angling upward, then the car, coming up the parking ramp, with Meredith behind the wheel.

Just the woman, not the man.

Of course, the man's car would be next. In separate cars, they would drive to whatever lair they'd chosen.

Yes, the man was following, driving a small orange station wagon, Japanese made, no longer new.

Quickly Charles put the rented Buick in gear, pulled into the outbound Sutter Street traffic. A white pickup and a black limousine separated him from the Mercedes and the orange station wagon. But the truck and the limo could be a plus. When trailing a suspect, he'd once read, it was good technique to stay back with one or two cars between, protective coloration.

Together, the five of them, they moved toward the next intersection. But slowly. Very, very slowly.

Would the red light catch him? If it happened, he must stop. Downtown, with so much traffic, the police were everywhere.

He accelerated, crowded the limo, went through the intersection on the yellow light. Ahead, with the Mercedes in the right lane, approaching Taylor Street, the station wagon was moving to the left lane. They were side by side now, the Mercedes and the station wagon, both of them stopped at the intersection. He chose the left lane, with one car between him and the station wagon. Traffic was moving again, led through the Taylor Street intersection by the Mercedes and the station wagon. Jones

Street was next. Midway in the block, the man in the station wagon was signaling for a left turn. But the Mercedes, still in the right lane, would be unable to turn left.

Without hesitation, Charles signaled for the left turn. He knew, after all, where to find Meredith Powell.

Heading south on Jones, the man drove steadily in light traffic. A left turn on Golden Gate, a right turn on Sixth Street, and they were across Market Street, once again heading south. This was skid row. Windows were boarded up, sidewalks were littered, derelicts in doorways huddled against the February winds. Beyond Folsom, the station wagon moved into the right lane. Now they were passing through the city's south-of-Market commercial district: wholesalers, printers, warehouses, a few lunch counters and short-order restaurants. Ahead, the station wagon's red taillight began blinking, signaling a right turn. With one car between them, Charles guided the Buick into the right lane, signaled for a turn. As he came to the intersection the traffic light turned yellow; the car ahead was slowing to a stop. With a truck to his left, he was blocked. The station wagon had already made his turn and was traveling west on Harrison, a one-way, six-lane arterial that carried traffic from the Bay Bridge to the southern freeway system. In moments the station wagon would disappear, while he waited helplessly for the light to turn green.

But, instead of accelerating into the traffic stream, the station wagon was slowing, now signaling for a left turn. The driver was waiting for traffic to clear to his left before he moved into the outside lane. Beyond the orange station wagon, the gray concrete bulk of the Hall of Justice merged with the darker gray of the lowering, rain-laden sky. Clear of traffic now, the station wagon turned into a driveway, quickly disappearing.

The traffic light had turned green; the car ahead was moving. Charles turned into Harrison, slowed the Buick, read the sign beside the driveway: HALL OF JUSTICE OFFICIAL VEHICLES ONLY

Maintaining a steady speed, eyes front, he passed the driveway, then began slowing for the intersection just ahead.

A psychiatrist and a policeman . . .

He was aware that his center had gone suddenly hollow. It was an unfamiliar, unpredictable sensation, therefore unpleasant. The name for the sensation was a common one, therefore repugnant, something to be excised.

But first it was necessary to acknowledge that, yes, the name of the sensation was fear.

Cold, raw fear.

4:40 P.M. Seated behind his desk, Hastings watched Canelli frown as he leafed through a sheaf of lab reports, autopsy reports, and interrogation reports.

"Jeez," Canelli muttered, "I know the damn things're here. I even made extra copies, to play safe. And I stapled them together. I remember stapling them, especially." Canelli was a big, good-natured man who almost never registered irritation at anyone but himself. His swarthy moon face was unmarred by either guile or rancor. His brown eyes were round and soft, eternally innocent. Unlike most of his fellow officers, Canelli's feelings were easily visible, therefore easily bruised. Yet, probably because he bruised so easily, Canelli enjoyed a perpetual run of remarkable good luck. Most policemen, in or out of uniform, were easily identifiable; literally, their faces gave them away. Canelli was the exception. If an escaping bank robber took the wrong turn, he would ask Canelli for directions.

"Just tell me what they say," Hastings said finally. "You can find them later."

"Yeah. Well—" Exasperated, Canelli pushed the stack of reports away. "Well, the thing is, Lieutenant—what I wanted to show you, see—is that the goddamn coroner's report and the goddamn lab reports don't agree with each other. And the thing is, the lab report, especially, is so technical that, honest to God, I only get about one word in ten. And the pretrial hearing's tomorrow, for God's sake. Ten o'clock."

29

"Doesn't the DA have duplicate copies?"

Instantly hope dawned. "Hey, I bet he does, Lieutenant. Jeez—" He looked at his watch. "Jeez, I'd better get over there." Anxious now, he began haphazardly gathering up the reports as Hastings handed him a manila folder. Canelli thanked him, rose, and turned to the office door—just as another figure, equally large, appeared framed in the glass of the door. Canelli stepped quickly to the door, opened it, and stood back.

"Hi, Lieutenant Friedman."

Smiling quizzically, Friedman entered the office. "You look a little rattled, Canelli," Friedman observed. "Are the bad guys gaining on us?"

As always, Canelli was unable to decide on a reply to one of Friedman's sallies. He simply ducked his head, shrugged, said something inarticulate, and quickly left the office.

"What I always like about Februaries," Friedman observed as he sank into Hastings's visitor chair, "is the low homicide rate. Have you noticed?" As he spoke, he took a cigar from his vest pocket, unwrapped it, lit it, and—according to tradition—sailed the still-smoking match into Hastings's wastebasket. Also according to tradition, Hastings stared pointedly at the wastebasket as Friedman withdrew a pair of black-rimmed reading glasses from his pocket. "Well?" Friedman asked, waving the glasses. "Are you going to join the club?"

Resigned, Hastings nodded. "Afraid so."

"Are you going to get bifocals?"

"I don't think so."

"You should. It's a pain in the ass, taking them on and off. If you get bifocals, I will, too. The hell with vanity."

"You make it sound like we're kids, for God's sake. 'If you jump off the high board, I will, too.' "

"I observe," Friedman said, "that you're in a sour mood. That's understandable. Nobody enjoys the prospect of his body beginning to run down."

"Who said anything about my body running down?"

Friedman waved the cigar airily. "Okay, forget it. Anything happening?"

"Canelli's apparently lost some stuff he needs for the Forster hearing tomorrow."

"It's my experience," Friedman observed, "that providence protects types like Canelli. And a special providence protects Canelli. That's an established fact."

Not replying, Hastings turned to the window. Rain was spattering against the glass: large, gust-driven raindrops. The heavily overcast sky was almost totally dark. From the west, out over the Pacific, a storm was bearing down on northern California.

"I understand," Friedman was saying, "that you had lunch with a very beautiful lady."

Out of long habit, Hastings declined to give Friedman the satisfaction of asking him how he'd gotten his information. The answer was obvious. An officer had seen him at the restaurant and mentioned it to someone, who mentioned it to someone else, who mentioned it to Friedman. In the police department, there were few secrets.

"You're not talking, eh?" Friedman observed.

Because the conversation with Meredith had been reverberating in his thoughts, Hastings decided to satisfy Friedman's chronic curiosity. As the story unfolded, Friedman's interest plainly quickened. Just as plainly, his outrage mounted.

"I don't know about you," Friedman said finally, "but I've dealt with several women who were abused by their fathers when they were young. Or, usually, their stepfathers. And I can tell you, absolutely, that they're—they're—" Uncharacteristically, Friedman broke off, searching for the phrase. "They're ruined," he finally finished. "They're absolutely ruined. They have this overwhelming sense of guilt. And they're absolutely terrified that people will find out what they've done. They feel—you know—naked. Exposed. Completely vulnerable. But most of all, they hate themselves. So they go through life punishing themselves for what their goddamn degenerate fathers did to them. It's—" Friedman shook his head angrily. "It's one of the most unfair things in the world. Incest—" He sighed heavily. "It's terrible. Just terrible. You always hear that it's a crime against nature, all that biblical stuff. And, God, it's true. They're marked, these women. For life. Christ, I remember interrogating a woman in her fifties, with a totally fucked-up life behind her. And it was all because she was abused. She just couldn't get over it, ever. For fifty years, she was afraid her sister and brother would find out that her father had screwed her."

"What were you interrogating her for?"

"Homicide." Friedman flicked cigar ashes in Hastings's wastebasket. "She killed them, to keep them from ever finding out."

"Killed who?"

"The sister and the brother, of course." Friedman drew deeply on the cigar, sending three workmanlike smoke rings floating gently across the desk. Ritual required that Hastings flap the rings away irritably, just as ritual required that he stare pointedly at his wastebasket after Friedman flicked his cigar ashes in the basket. To Hastings, the motivation behind Friedman's cigar-smoking antics was clear. Friedman was a gadfly, a squadroom Socrates, a psychological tinkerer. Whether he was interrogating murder suspects or supervising subordinates or bantering with friends, Friedman kept them guessing, kept them a little off balance as he constantly probed and poked. Constitutionally, Friedman felt more secure when he had the advantage, however slight. Therefore, knowing that Hastings disliked cigar smoke and disapproved of cigar ashes flipped into his wastebasket, it was Friedman's nature to test Hastings's responses—just as it was Hastings's nature to suffer in silence, secretly hoping the wastebasket would someday catch fire.

"I remember Meredith's father," Hastings mused. "I'm sure he did it, sure he abused her. I can just see him coming home on Saturday nights and knocking his wife around, and then getting into bed with Meredith." Balefully he shook his head. "*Christ!*"

"Well," Friedman said airily, "look at the bright side. Without guys like him, society wouldn't need so many guys like us."

Hastings fixed the other man with a long, hard look.

"Bad joke, huh?"

Hastings nodded grimly. "Bad joke."

"Sorry."

As he nodded grudging acceptance, Hastings tried to think whether he'd ever heard Friedman apologize.


**5:10 P.M.** In response to the blare of the buzzer, he pressed a switch.

"Yes?"

"It's Charles."

"Yes. I'll be down." As he released the switch, he glanced at his watch. Ten minutes past five. Cocktail time.

Play time.

Show-and-tell time.

Was this the beginning of something big, the reason Charles had been gone so long, without contact? Or was it merely the nature of the game they played, master and slave, tag you're it? Games for children. Life-or-death games, transmuted.

All fall down.

Had he ever played the games children played?

Reclining, aware that his body had unconsciously struck a particular pose, as if the camera were rolling, he glanced again at his watch. Time, twelve minutes after five. He would allow eighteen minutes to elapse before he descended, made his entrance. Charles would have time to reflect, in eighteen minutes.

But he must reflect, too, a quid pro quo. Like it or not, he must reflect. The mind was like the heart, always pulsating. If life persisted, then so did consciousness. Even in dreams there was no escape. Because dreams became nightmares.

For as long as he could remember, the nightmares had stalked him, impaled him, left him trembling, pajamas soaking, a scream congealed in his throat, like caked blood.

If she'd bitten through her tongue as she struggled, then she would have choked on her own blood.

*Had* she choked on her own blood? It was important, suddenly, that he know. Yet he couldn't ask. Not directly. Not ever directly. Because then the master would be the slave.

He could only probe. But carefully—cautiously.

Because the nightmares awaited.

Or was it the nightmare, really only one?

Would he ever really know?

Time: twenty-nine minutes after five. Allowing him sixty seconds to rise from the carved baroque chair and let his eyes linger successively on the elements: the bed, the statue, the draperies, the half circle of candles. Yes, everything was in perfect order. And the mirrored wall confirmed it: himself reflecting himself, smaller and smaller, regressing to infinity.


**5:35 P.M.** Of course, Charles had stage-managed the scene. At the bar, one leg elegantly crossed over the other, sipping white wine from a crystal goblet, Charles was seated with his back to the room. But he was facing the back-bar mirror, which revealed everything.

Mirrors, mirrors . . .

For the mirrors, they all played games.

All fall down.

Upon entering the room, he went to the damask sofa. Compelling Charles to turn on the bar stool, finally facing him.

So the game could begin.

"Were you—" He hesitated, selecting the word he wanted. "Were you with her all day?"

Predictably, Charles first sipped the wine, a permissible liberty, subtly calculated. Charles was, of course, transparently expecting instructions to pour a glass of wine, place the glass on the small table beside the sofa. Meaning that the request should be delayed, a question of timing, master and slave.

All fall down.

"From eleven o'clock until about two" came the answer.

"And?" He was satisfied with the inflection: cool but not calculated.

But, even before Charles spoke, he realized that, tilt, something had gone wrong. He could see it in the other man's eyes: that small gleam of pleasure, derived from inflicting even the slightest discomfort.

And, of course, the smallest barbs would come first, their little game, the slave diddling the master.

"She kept the appointment. Same place, same time. But then—" A delicately calculated pause, a small sip of wine. Over the rim of the glass, Charles's dark eyes were utterly still. As always, Charles was impeccably dressed in a dark formal suit, white shirt, gleaming black shoes, conservative tie. "Funereal" was the operative word. The suit, the pale face with its dark, large, lusterless eyes, the dark, curiously heavy head of hair, equally lusterless, the slim, lounge-lizard body that was always so self-consciously posed—this was the image Charles had created, constantly fine-tuned, a creation in search of itself.

" 'But then . . .'?"

"Then she had lunch with a man."

Yes, there it was: the barb, deftly lodged.

But there was more. This, in the lexicon of jazz, was only the intro.

"A man . . ." He nodded. Then: "I'd like some wine now, please. Whatever you're drinking."

Yes, the timing had been optimum, an interruption of Charles's own timing. Which was, after all, the essence of his timing, its ultimate purpose. If the cobra weaved, the mongoose bobbed. Bob and weave, bob and weave.

All fall down.

Accepting the glass, he was able to nod simply. Sipping the wine, he need only wait.

Forcing Charles to continue.

"They ate at Le Central. That has plate-glass windows, you know. So I could see them."

Once more he nodded. He could feel it now. The tension was building palpably. Delicately. Decisively. Deliciously.

"They knew each other," Charles was saying. "It was obvious that they knew each other."

The wineglass was empty, a surprise. Choosing his time, bob and weave, he would ask for a refill.

"They finished lunch about one-thirty," the other man was saying. "I followed him. He's a perfectly ordinary-looking man. He drives a perfectly ordinary car. Except that—" Charles paused, drained his own glass, placed it on the bar. As the light caught the crystal, he realized that his own glass was plain, not crystal. Nothing, it seemed, had been left to chance.

"Except that"—repeated, the words were magnified—"when I followed him, he drove to the Hall of Justice. That's on Bryant Street, near Sixth."

"Yes—" This time, he couldn't calculate his cadence. Therefore, momentarily, he was rendered helpless.

As, inexorably, the words continued: "He drove to the Hall of Justice," Charles repeated. A pause. Then, very softly: "And he drove into the underground parking garage. The sign said 'Official Vehicles Only.' "

"Official vehicles . . . ?"

"The police." The words fell softly, as snowflakes fall, on a grave. "Or maybe the district attorney." A final, definitive pause. Then, speaking more rapidly, technique abandoned now, scorekeeping forgotten, involuntarily lapsing into the vernacular of the streets, his native dialect, after all, the other man was saying "Either she's got something going with this guy, or else she's talking to him because he's a cop. That's the way it seems to me. And if I had to guess, I'd say she was talking to him because he was a cop. I mean, I didn't see any hanky-panky, no kissing, holding hands. Nothing."

"We have to be sure, of course. We can't just assume—"

Suddenly his throat closed. Forcing him to swallow, begin again. "We can't assume the worst, not automatically."

"Except that if she knows about—the other thing, then there could be trouble. The psychiatrist, that was bad enough. People tell things to psychiatrists. But the police—if she's talking to the police—" Charles shook his head.

He realized that his eyes had fallen. This was the critical moment. Lapsing into the vernacular, Charles had revealed weakness, a flaw. Resulting, bob and weave, in this small opening, this fleeting moment of opportunity.

But how to exploit it, translate perception into reality? If he could do it, all fall down, then this was the moment.

And the moment was the motivation.

As, yes, the means materialized: the empty wineglass, on the table beside him. Delicately he grasped the glass, lifted it. His voice, he knew, would not betray him as he said, "I think I'll have a refill, Charles."


10:15 P.M. Meredith took the remote control from the table, touched the power button, and watched the TV anchorman fade away.

For three Tuesdays now it had been the same: this overpowering malaise, this bone-deep weariness of the limbs, this terrible lethargy of the spirit. The meeting with Frank, pure serendipity, a balm, a benign narcotic, had momentarily masked the pain. But, like all narcotics, the effect soon began to dissipate.

On the coffee table beside the remote control and her empty brandy snifter, she saw the card Frank had given her. As if the touch of the card could somehow cure, she picked it up, held it between thumb and forefinger.

*Lieutenant Frank Hastings*
*Homicide Bureau*

Although they'd both been at pains to suppress it, they'd been attracted to each other. She'd felt the attraction, the story of her life. And if she'd felt it, then so had Frank felt it. If she'd learned only one lesson, that was it: the only lesson that was required for someone like her.

He'd said he had someone, a woman with two sons, a schoolteacher.

On Tuesdays, after seeing Dr. Price, it always seemed as if everyone else in the whole world had someone. The animals went two by two into the ark. It was nature's way, nature's universal design. A male and a female coupled, to create new life. And so the world could continue.

Only the human animal could change nature. A quick trip to the drugstore, a visit to the doctor, and the law was repealed. A pill or a piece of rubber, and singles' bar love conquered all.

In another time, another place, she and Frank might have made something happen between them. Even with his commitment to another woman, it was possible that she could have made something happen. She'd done it before, effortlessly. She'd—

Beside the couch, the telephone warbled. The time was ten-thirty, late for him to call. At the thought, the realization that something could have changed, she felt herself wince. The last time he'd called, only a few days ago, she'd been on the phone, talking to Pat Bolton. And for that she'd had to pay.

"Hello . . ."

"Are you in bed?" he asked.

"No."

"Getting ready for bed?"

"Almost, yes. Thinking about it."

"Tell me about it—exactly what you'll do. Be very detailed."

For almost twenty minutes they talked about it, question and answer, master and slave. As the minutes passed, a cumulative weight, these minutes combining with all the other minutes, she felt shame compounding shame, an eternal progression, no way out.

Now, finally sated, his voice changed. She knew that voice-change, knew it could conceal his most calculated queries.

"What'd you do today, Meredith?

She'd had hours to prepare, and the answer came easily. Perhaps she should have been an actress.

"I took the car in for servicing. Then I shopped, had something to eat. I didn't get home until almost three."

"Where'd you eat?"

"There's a new place in Nieman's basement."

"Yes . . ."

From his inflection, she knew he'd been expecting the answer—that answer, or one like it. A lie, not the truth.

Had he followed her, hired someone to follow her? At lunch, glancing out at the street, she'd seen someone who could have been Charles, just a glimpse, a face in the crowd.

She could hear him clear his throat. It was a mannerism that usually preceded the conclusion of a conversation. Therefore, for tonight, she might soon be set free.

"I'll call a little earlier tomorrow," he was saying. "We might be seeing each other tomorrow. I haven't quite decided."

"Yes . . ."


11:05 P.M. He returned the telephone to its cradle and sat motionless for a moment, staring reflectively at a small marble obelisk that shared a shelf with a dried sprig of nightshade. From the floor below, voices were raised: the pleasure seekers.

Should he ask them to leave? Tell them to leave? There were Nero clichés, Titanic clichés: fiddling while Rome burned, arranging the deck chairs. Trivialities, counterpointing cataclysms.

Servicing the car—lunch at Nieman Marcus—all of it an elaborate lie, with malice aforethought.

Liberating him, therefore, from the final restraints, however trivial. If fate was the croupier, then she was the mark. Sit long enough at the table, and everyone lost.

As he walked down the hallway and began mounting the stairs to the chamber, he was aware that, yes, calm was returning, a balm, a triumph of the will. Was that the title of an old movie? A German classic, pre–World War II?

The balm of calm . . .

It was a nonsense phrase, one of hundreds—thousands—random words and phrases, signifying nothing, yet entangled in his thoughts. All his life, records with needles stuck, words had echoed and reechoed. When he'd been small, they'd taken him into the judge's chambers. He could remember the large leather armchair they'd given him. The chair had been brass studded, with wings. He'd felt lost in the chair, surrounded by shelves of law books. A nonsense phrase had gone round and round: *soft maybe bunting.* He'd never known what it meant.

The balm of calm . . .

This phrase, at least, rhymed.

He fitted his key to the lock, entered the chamber, closed the door, secured it. Here, soft lights always glowed, controlled by the console placed beside the chair. Delicately his fingers caressed the console, lowered the lights, switched on the tape: *Danse Macabre.* Earlier in the day he'd loaded the VCR, allowing him now simply to touch a switch.

Tonight there was more than simple erotic indulgence. The cassette would run about twenty minutes, exploring the intricacies of Saturday night's encounter. During that time he would make his decision. When the ending approached, he with his fingers at her throat, the decision would be inevitable—one step beyond, the last step, the final step.


11:20 P.M. As he brushed his teeth, Hastings surveyed the bathroom, still perfumed from Ann's shower, still steamy. A single sweat sock was draped over the open clothes hamper. Behind the toilet he saw a single sneaker. The sock and the sneaker were Bill's, the razor beside the basin was Dan's. At age seventeen, Dan was shaving regularly—once a week, primarily the upper lip.

When he and Ann had decided to live together, most of their misgivings had centered on her sons. Ann's concern had been that the two boys would be reluctant to accept a "dominant male," as she'd once expressed it. Hastings's concern had been mostly a matter of geography. Ann's bottom-floor Victorian flat was huge, with three sizable bedrooms. But there was only a bath and a half. Thus the sock and the sneaker and the razor. As she always did, Ann refused to pick up after the boys. If the sock and the sneaker and the razor were still there at breakfast time, Ann would lay down the law. As always, Hastings would remain silent. But his expression, a concerned frown, would put him firmly on Ann's side.

He rinsed the toothbrush, rinsed his mouth, placed the toothpaste in the cabinet and the toothbrush in the rack, and switched off the light.


11:55 P.M. Hastings settled himself more comfortably in the bed, sighed, glanced at the clock. The time was almost twelve. When he'd first come to bed, sliding beneath the covers, turning toward Ann, kissing her, the pattern of their caress had acknowledged that, tonight, by mutual consent, it was too late to make love. The conclusion was companionable, and after he'd returned to his side of the bed they'd begun to talk of the day's events. Ann had described the ongoing sexual adventures of Eva Jane West, her good friend and fellow teacher at Lick Elementary. Then, after Ann had playfully commiserated with him in his "midlife bifocal slump," he'd described his meeting with Meredith Powell, at 450 Sutter. Once having started the story, he realized, too late, that he had a choice: either tell Ann he'd invited Meredith to lunch or else lie about it. A change of subject hadn't worked; Meredith's story had aroused Ann's sympathy, and she asked for

41

more details. When Hastings had finally mentioned the lunch, he'd sensed that his timing was wrong, out of its natural spontaneous sequence. But, to his fine-tuned interrogator's ear, Ann's response rang true, unclouded by pique, as she said: "We should have her to dinner, Frank. It sounds like she's in trouble."

In the bedroom darkness he smiled. "Maybe we should have her with Eva Jane. We could make it a counseling session."

"Secretly," she answered starchily, "Eva Jane enjoys her problems. This is something else. This is incest. For a woman, there's nothing worse. Rape is bad enough. But incest—" Lying on her back, Ann shook her head. "She never had a chance. That's the hell of it."

"I know . . ." He yawned, settled more comfortably.

"But you *don't* know. I don't mean you. I mean *men.*" In her voice he could clearly hear the beginning of a polemic. "A man simply can't know the effect on a woman when she's raped. They experience sex differently."

"How true." Feeling his way, he spoke humorously.

"Men externalize, women internalize. Men conquer, women submit, that's the folklore. But if women don't submit with love, then they're violated. And a girl's who's raped, she's never the same. And if it's her father—" Outraged, she let it go unfinished.

"Hmmm . . ."

"You're going to sleep."

"It's a possibility."

"Oh—" She dug her elbow sharply into his ribs.

Reluctantly he roused himself. "I feel very, very sorry for Meredith Powell. I think I have some idea what happened to her—what her father did to her. But you have to remember that I've never believed in taking the office home with me. It makes things worse, not better."

"She's your friend, though. She's—" Ann hesitated, searching for the phrase. "She's part of your past."

"You're right. Altogether, I maybe said a hundred words to

42

Meredith Powell as long as I knew her. I never liked her father, and I wasn't crazy about her brother, either. But, still, you're right. The old neighborhood—childhood—" He sighed, lapsed into silence.

"You said you think she's in danger."

"I didn't say 'danger.' I said 'trouble.' "

Another silence followed. Then he felt her move closer, felt her fingers lightly brush his cheek.

"Okay," she said, "close your eyes. But you've got to promise we'll have her to dinner."

"Mmmm. . . ."

"Promise?"

"Promise."

# WEDNESDAY
# FEBRUARY 14

8:15 A.M. All night, sometimes asleep, sometimes wakeful, he had seen the images flicker and flare. His mother had worn a black witch's hat, his aunt stood in the docket with blood-gushing stumps instead of hands, arms resting on the courtroom's wooden railing. The images of the railing constantly reappeared; its thick wooden spokes were the bars of a cage. The cage, too, reappeared; from outside, sometimes, he saw himself imprisoned. The women's faces flickered and flared, some of them flesh, some of them pigment, all of them goblin faces within, models' faces without, smooth porcelain masks.

But there were no eyes, nothing but empty sockets.

Only she had eyes, his first duchess, a literary allusion. Her eyes were wide open forever, risen from the dead.

He was lying on his back, staring at the ceiling. It was Wednesday, February 14.

The day she must die.

St. Valentine's Day. He smiled. Yes, Valentine's Day.


10:30 A.M. Naked, Charles stood before the mirror. In his blue period, Picasso had done three paintings that had always reminded him of himself: pale, slim youths with long legs, a spare torso, a narrow, deftly rendered head. It was an altogether pleasingly proportioned male body, no muscles bunched, no self-consciously struck poses.

Last night, in the vernacular, he'd scored. She'd come to the party dressed in a white nylon jumpsuit, with a neck-to-crotch zipper, a large brass ring attached. As the party progressed, the zipper dropped lower, exposing more and more of her breasts. When he arrived, she'd already been high: a raw, lusty twenty-year-old, beautifully built, literally a refugee from a Fresno farm, milk fed, come to San Francisco for the action. All she needed was a change of jumpsuit, spare underpants, a diaphragm, and a loud laugh. Last night had been her first time out at a party where anything was available, the farm girl's fantasy. Her sheer animal energy had quickly become the party's focus. All evening, each in their own way, touching and feeling, taunting, patronizing, they'd all used her, fresh new meat. In another year, two parties a week, she'd be drugged out, used up.

All night, shrilly, senselessly, she'd caromed from man to man—woman to woman. But he knew he'd take her home—her place, not his place, never his place. She'd tumbled onto the sofa. He'd drawn down the zipper. He'd done it slowly, a celebration of sensation, a ceremony within a ceremony. Then he'd roused her, the first necessity. And then he'd begun: quick, deft, decisive manipulations. At first she'd been insensate. Then, roused, she'd begun her resistance, the first imperative. He'd—

From the bedroom, the telephone was ringing.

Yes—at ten-thirty, the timing was predictable. Utterly predictable.


10:33 A.M. He replaced the telephone in its cradle and sat silently for a moment, eyes downcast, staring at the telephone.

In less than a minute, one short, cryptic conversation, the commitment had been made, the decision taken. Already he was conscious of a quickening, a tightening.

So much of life, someone had written, was anticipation. Sex

45

began in the imagination. A woman's body, naked, was never as erotic as that same body imagined beneath the clothing. An orgasm was always incomplete; only the next orgasm promised perfection—and the next—and the next. Drugs promised visions that never materialized: sketches in black and white, colors left to harden on the palette. The pleasure principle would always promise more than it delivered. It was simple logic.

Leaving pain, the eternal constant.

Pain never promised more than it delivered; the equation always balanced out.

But pain, like pleasure, was transitory. The sharper the pain, the quicker it ended.

Leaving only death.

Sometimes he wrote it out: those five magic letters. He'd first done it, first dared to do it, when he was sixteen. Realizing that the inscription would be magical, his subconscious had guided him. He'd just learned that Carmody had been expelled. Hardly aware of his own movements, he'd gone to his room and locked the door. He'd gone to his desk and sat down. The time had been one o'clock; he'd been due at his American Government class. He'd been aware that reality was shifting; somehow he existed apart from himself. He could visualize himself as he sat at the desk, head slightly bowed, staring at nothing. The scene seemed to glow, everything incandescent. No, not everything. Just himself, the outline of his body.

And as he sat there, existing in a different dimension, he allowed himself to remember the scene. Carmody had made the arrangements. Carmody had found the woman and rented the room. Cleverly, Carmody had gone to the best hotel in town, saying that his parents were coming for an end-of-the-semester visit. And Carmody had gotten the liquor, too: Dewar's Scotch, the whiskey his father drank.

They'd paid her fifty dollars. Almost forty years ago, it was a princely sum, for which she'd promised to do them both. "Satisfaction guaranteed," she said, drinking from the bottle. Then, at Carmody's request, she'd turned out the lights. He'd gone first, an artless, ineffectual stab, over before it began. Carmody, the experienced one, had taken longer, doubtless done it better. The whiskey bottle had remained on the bedside table. He could remember the sound she made, greedily swallowing the whiskey. Today whores used heroin, two-hundred-dollar-a-day habits. Forty years ago—thirty-seven years ago, actually—a bottle of liquor had sufficed.

When the bottle was drained, she'd announced that she was going. He could remember the careless sound of her voice, casually contemptuous. Drunkenly Carmody had argued with her. She'd promised to stay with them, do them again, Carmody said. She said something obscene. Carmody pushed her; she slapped him. Instantly the three of them were fighting, the half-naked woman wearing black panties and a black bra. She'd fought like a man, viciously, fists closed, head down, cursing them. He'd struck out at her, felt his fist sink into the soft, yielding flesh of her breast. He'd struck her again. She began to scream. Carmody was on the floor, both hands clutching his crotch. "Stop her," he'd gasped, his voice hoarse, rattling in his throat. "Shut her up."

He'd thrown himself on her, fingers locked at her throat. As they struggled, her body wild against his, he'd come to climax. Then consciousness had faded. He'd heard Carmody's voice only faintly: "You'll kill her. For God's sake, let go. You'll kill her."

Sitting at his schoolboy's desk, thirty-seven years ago, he'd recalled the scene in reverse, beginning with Carmody's voice, ending when the whore had knocked on the hotel room door. Then, fixing the episode forever, a permanent part of his consciousness, he began again, first to last. He'd remained motionless at the desk for more than an hour, oblivious to the passage of time.

No, not quite oblivious. And not quite motionless, either.

Because, unconsciously, he'd written the word DEATH on a slip of paper. The word had been spelled out in capital letters, the letters unevenly spaced.

Just as now, unconsciously, he'd printed DEATH on the scratch pad beside the telephone. In capital letters. Unevenly spaced.

**10:45 A.M.** "A croissant, please. And coffee. French roast, please."

Behind the glass showcase, the clerk remained motionless for a moment, simply staring at her. His round, muscular arms were spread wide on the counter. He was in his early twenties. Dark complexion. Black, insolent eyes. A go-to-hell mouth. Thick black hair, medium long, custom cut. Arabic, perhaps, or Italian, or Mexican. His expression was indolent: the Latin stud, strutting his stuff, making his macho moves. Meredith had seen this same face in a dozen countries, on countless piazzas. And, yes, her response had always been the same: involuntary sexual attraction, tempered by bitter experience.

"A croissant, did you say?"

"Yes. And French roast."

He wore a plain white T-shirt that showed off his weight-lifter's torso. Without looking, she knew he would be wearing weathered blue jeans, tight at the crotch and buttocks. Flexing a bulging bicep, he gestured. "Sit down. I'll bring it over."

"That's all right. I'll wait."

"No—come on—" He started a slow, sensual smile, gestured to the table. The dominant male, asserting himself. "Sit down."

Was it dominance? Or narcissism? Unless she went to bed with him, she'd never know.

"Thank you—" Meredith went to an oak table beside the plate-glass window. The small Italian-style café served only pastries and sandwiches and closed in late afternoon. Most of the patrons were local and differed according to the time of day. In the mornings young mothers with their babies came in, usually for a quick, often-harassed cup of coffee on their way to a nearby park or playground. Because the neighborhood was Russian Hill, and the prices were therefore expensive, almost all of the café's patrons spoke with the accents of the privileged: voices refined in good eastern colleges, voices that were accustomed to dealing with inferiors. She'd been coming here regularly for more than a year. During that time, growing one year older, her envy of the mothers and their babies had grown acute, a self-inflicted wound that never healed.

Today, because of the dark sullen clouds and the light rain that had begun to fall, there was only one other customer in the café, an older man with a lean, aristocratic face. His eyes were a clear, vivid blue: eyes in constant motion, unclouded by age or defeat. He wore a small white military-style mustache, carefully clipped. This was a face, young or old, that a woman would never forget.

She was aware that the waiter—was that the word?—was making his approach. Standing very close to her, his thigh within an inch of her arm, he placed the croissant and coffee on the table. Now he stepped back and stood looking down at her.

"Anything else?" He spoke softly, his voice an insistent caress.

Some women were defined by their careers, or their clothes, or their husbands, or their children. Her life was defined by men like this hot-eyed youth with his bulging biceps and bulging private parts and his thighs big beneath his jeans.

"No, thank you." As she said it, she deliberately turned her gaze to the window. The café was on Hyde Street, a block beneath the crest of Russian Hill. A cable car was approaching from the south, rattling and clanging. Because the weather was bad, only a handful of tourists clung to the outside stairs.

"If you want anything else, you'll be sure and tell me, won't you?"

Some women, she knew, would respond curtly, sending him on his way. Others would insult him with a withering look. She chose merely to break off a corner of the croissant and begin nibbling as she watched the cable car pass. And, a reprieve, two young matrons came in, both of them dressed in trendy foul-weather gear. When the women moved expectantly to the glass display case, the waiter had no choice but to resume his post.

Yesterday at this time she'd been at 450 Sutter, with Dr. Price. How much was she risking, seeing him? Was the risk worth the reward?

She'd told him about her father on her second visit. She hadn't intended to tell him. She hadn't done it under a deep trance; she hadn't even been lying on the psychiatrist's couch, that tired cliché. She'd simply been talking, telling Price how it felt when she'd realized that she had to get out of her marriage. Why? Price had asked. What was it about Gary that she found objectionable?

"Objectionable," she'd said, snorting derisively. Then, hardly aware that she was doing it, she'd told him about Gary—about the endless ways he abused her, sometimes without ever touching her. It had all come out in a blind rush, a torrent of words with their own momentum—words and phrases she hadn't realized she even possessed, a revelation. As she talked, she'd begun to cry; softly at first, then hopelessly, without pride: deep, wracking sobs. For a time Dr. Price had sat silently, his face expressionless. Then, calmly, he'd taken a box of tissues from a drawer and handed the box to her. He'd waited for her to blow her nose and wipe her eyes. Then, still calmly, he'd said that her father and her husband were similar personalities: men who got off abusing people.

Something in the way he said it, so dispassionately, so matter-of-factly, had made her tell him. And in seconds—in the time it took to say a half-dozen words—she'd told him about her father.

And then yesterday, again without forethought, in a single blind, blundering rush of words, she'd told Frank.

In her whole life, until yesterday, she'd hardly spoken to

Frank. If she hadn't happened to see him on TV a month or two ago, she would never have recognized him when they'd met at 450 Sutter. Yet, an hour later, she'd told him about her father. Why?

Why had she kept the secret for so long, then told two men, one a doctor, one a detective, both of them relative strangers?

Carrying paper bags filled with pastries and coffee in Styrofoam cups, the two trendy young matrons were leaving the café, laughing as they walked. The lean, self-possessed gray-haired man had put on a pair of half-glasses and was reading the *New York Times* as he sipped his coffee. Behind the counter, the young Latin's dark eyes had hardly left her.

The scene was a miniature of her life, one of those experimental one-act plays, people in pantomime on a surreal stage, each actor representing a part of her life: the hot-eyed stud with his tight pants, the two self-assured women who spoke a language that excluded her, the intriguing man of substance who politely ignored her.

But then the scene changes. Light fades into shadow, overcome by the night. Two figures emerge: evil figures, monsters of menace. One of them bulks in the backlit frame of her bedroom door. He advances on her as she desperately pretends sleep, her only defense. The small bed creaks with his huge weight. If the bed should break, everyone would know—her mother, and everyone else.

The other figure sits enthroned in a carved wooden chair. A console rests on an inlaid table beside the thronelike chair. His hand rests on the console. With the touch of a fingertip he controls the lights, the draperies, the camera. With a word he controls her.

One word: death.


1:15 P.M. He watched Charles stride to the huge plate-glass window that looked out on the Golden Gate. Today the bridge was obscured by the dark, leaden clouds. He watched Charles's movements appreciatively: the rhythm of the long legs, the angle of the arms. Usually Charles moved deliberately, in constant self-constraint. But now agitation had introduced an appealing complexity. Had Charles ever dabbled in homosexuality?

With his back turned, Charles stood at the window. Was he brooding? Inwardly raving?

Inwardly quaking?

They'd been here for almost an hour, talking about it. Before Charles came, he'd taken mescaline, for perspective. Mescaline, and a single glass of white wine, a judiciously conceived prescription. It calmed him, gave him height, balance, detachment. As if he'd been a third party to the negotiations, not a partner in the planning, he'd seen himself from beyond himself. And yet, small miracle, he'd seemed to see Charles from within, privy to the other man's innermost thoughts. Then other images had intruded: slab-sided monsters, gargoyles with centaur bodies. Sometimes their voices came from far away, delicate as wind chimes. Sometimes the blare was so blatant that words were lost, leaving only sounds: trapped beasts, enraged. They were—

Words from Charles:

". . . want to know," Charles was saying, "is whether you told her about the other thing. *Did* you tell her?" Charles was facing him now. As always, Charles wore a dark formal suit.

*The other thing . . .*

Originally it had been *the thing*. Singular. But now, with the decision made, the thing was the other thing. Meaning that the new thing would be called simply *the thing*.

Two things, after tonight. No longer one thing. Simple addition, one thing plus one thing. Two things now.

Could he have computed it without the mescaline? Could . . . ?

Charles was speaking again. "I want to know whether you told her."

His own voice was indistinct, hardly more than an echo, answering. But what had he answered? The words were blurred.

"So you *did* tell her." Advancing on him, the slim, elegant figure took on bulk as it came closer. Was it time to mention money?

More words, mumbled. Bumble mumble, a childhood phrase.

Ah, the memories. Mumbling. Bumbling.

They were close now, close enough to touch. The other man's figure was changing, now larger, now smaller. Only the eyes remained the same, those dark, dead eyes.

"I knew you told her. I *knew* it."

More words, answering. His voice. His words. Deflecting. Protesting. Then: "Tonight. It'll happen tonight. It'll be the same. Just the same."

Yes . . .

But had he actually said it, actually pronounced the word?

Or was it another echo from childhood?

Mumble bumble.


3:30 P.M. Meredith pulled the parka's collar up, dug her chin into a woolen scarf, and lengthened her stride. The raw February wind blew in gusts up from the west slopes of Russian Hill, funneling between the apartment buildings and town houses. Even though the rain threatened to return, she felt better for having gotten out of the flat, free from the temptations of daytime TV. Except that if she was honest with herself, she would admit that the clock had freed her, not willpower. At three o'clock, the soaps were finished; children's programming had begun.

She was approaching the corner of Hyde and Union. It was here that she made her decision. She could walk down the Union Street hill to Polk Street, where she could shop, then have coffee.

No, have coffee and then shop, so that she wouldn't have to juggle parcels and sacks in the coffeeshop.

Or she could walk straight ahead, passing by the small playground at Hyde and Broadway.

She decided to let the traffic light make the decision for her, and followed the green light across the intersection, south on Hyde Street.

The playground was just ahead. It was a small urban playground. No grass, no real trees. Only concrete and redwood chips, only swings and a slide and a teeter-totter and a complicated jungle gym and a round sandbox with a concrete rim. From the morning's rain, the sand was dark and wet. Except for a man and a small child, the playground was deserted. In the cold, raw, sunless weather, the child, a boy, was bundled up so thoroughly that his arms extended out from his sides, like the Michelin tire man. A brightly tasseled stocking cap was pulled down low across the boy's eyes. His nose and ears were pink. The father wore hiking boots, jeans, and a down jacket. He was a tall man, slightly stooped, about thirty-five. A recognizable San Francisco type: medium-long dark hair, a full mustache, rimmed glasses that made a statement: consciously not aviator-trendy, therefore emblems of intellectual independence. His face was seamed, probably beyond his years. The effect was Lincolnesque. Craggy. Heathcliff, on the moors. On closer examination his jacket, too, made a with-it statement: L. L. Bean, or Abercrombie's, or Eddie Bauer. Playing the guess-what-he-does game, she picked a high school teacher, or perhaps a playwright, just breaking in. Or he could be an artist. Or else a house husband, yet another yuppie spin-off.

Or he could be a widower. Or divorced.

She entered the playground and sat on a bench at a right angle to the bench occupied by the man with the intriguing face. If she regarded his child with interest, the man would probably speak to her. It was built in, an absolute certainty. And if she encouraged him, mentioned that she often walked this way on weekday afternoons, anything could happen. They could fall in love, live together, even get married. The little boy would love her. She would be redeemed.

In another life—another time—it could all happen.

But in this life—her life—there were two choices. She could walk away—or she could die.

Even a flirtation, he'd told her, would be "serious." An affair meant certain death.

He'd said it like that, in those exact words. But his manner, his voice, had been mild, merely a mocking monotone.

They'd been in bed when he said it. Sated, she'd been half asleep, dozing. He'd been rambling on. She'd learned to expect it, his habit of talking after sex: long, complicated monologues. Sometimes she listened, sometimes she didn't. Sometimes, while he talked, she thought about her things. Different things. Expensive things.

In those first days, first weeks, those first months—they spent two days a week, at least, shopping. Sometimes they shopped for household items—sometimes for a car. Or an apartment. Or jewelry. Or paintings. Or books. Or clothes. And when they weren't shopping, they were making plans to shop.

Another child, a girl, came into the playground. The girl, too, was bundled up. She was blond and wore Mickey Mouse ears. Her mother sat on the same bench with the man, with perhaps five feet separating them.

In earlier years, in her teens, she used to lie in bed during the night and imagine what her life would be like. She would, of course, marry. It was inconceivable that she wouldn't marry. Because she had no experience beyond San Francisco and the Sunset District, she'd always imagined that she would live there—in a house similar to her parents' house but better. Her husband would work in an office. What kind of an office was unclear, but the distinction was important. Her father worked with his hands—his dirty, callused, brutal hands. So her husband would work in an office, with clean hands.

And, of course, they would have children. Two children, first a boy, for her husband, then a girl, for her.

For a moment she focused her attention on the two small children, both of them playing on the jungle gym, beginning to pay attention to each other. But, as if they were tethered, her thoughts turned back on themselves, remembering how it had started.

It began, really, with her clothes. He'd come to her old apartment one morning, unannounced. As if he were an appraiser, he'd gone from room to room, closet to closet. He'd hardly spoken, but his conclusions were clear. The next day they'd gone shopping for clothes. Because he was paying, she couldn't object to his choices. He consulted with hairstylists and beauticians. When she moved to the condo, she left everything behind: her furniture, her old clothes, her prints, most of her books, even her cosmetics. He had the condo decorated. The Mercedes was a birthday present. The whole process—her transformation from herself to someone she hardly recognized, even in the mirror— took less than three months.

As the externals of her life changed, so did her erotic life. But it had been a slow, insidious change, almost as if the ideas were hers, not his. He never demanded, he merely suggested. She'd once read a long article on brainwashing. The expert practitioner, the article said, didn't raise his voice, didn't bully, didn't harass. The expert worked slowly, subtly, all according to a meticulously calculated plan, one brick carefully placed on another brick until the wall was completed, and there was no escape.

And that's how it happened to her. She hadn't realized the wall was completed until she was trapped.

She'd met him at one of his parties. He'd hardly seemed to notice her, and she'd felt ill at ease, talking to him. But a week later he'd called. And a week after that they'd gone out to dinner. She'd felt uncomfortable, never quite sure she was saying the right thing.

So she'd been surprised when he'd called again, and again.

Their first dates were always the same. He'd pick her up outside her apartment building and take her to an expensive restaurant. Then he'd take her home, drop her at the apartment house door. He didn't suggest that she ask him up, and she hadn't offered. Secretly she'd felt he was laughing at her.

Then he'd called to ask her to one of his parties—a fête, he'd called it. He'd told her to come by cab, and to bring a nightgown and toiletries and a change of clothing, since she'd be staying overnight.

She'd wished that she'd had someone she could confide in, someone to ask for advice. But there'd been no one, really. Until the last moment, with her finger poised to touch-tone the phone for a cab, she hadn't been able to decide whether to go to the party. Except that, really, she'd known she would go.

During that party, her second at his house, he'd hardly paid her more attention than he had at the first party. He'd simply sat enthroned, watching his guests perform. Finally, in the wee hours, she went up to him, told him she was tired—and a little drunk—and she wanted to go home.

"But you're staying," he'd said. Adding condescendingly, "Don't you remember?" Then he'd taken her to her room, and given her a key, and said good night. And then he'd kissed her, the first time he'd done it, the first time his flesh had touched her flesh.

She'd locked her door, and lain in the bed, and thought about the kiss. And in that moment, it had begun. In her head, it had begun.

From the first, she'd had her suspicions. The word was "misanthrope," dimly remembered from high school, a man who hates everyone.

Then she'd learned the other word: "misogynist," a man who hates women.

There were other words, too. Sadism. Sadomasochism.

It had begun subtly, sensuously. He'd been patient. Persistent, yes, but always patient. And perceptive, too. Diabolically perceptive. Sometimes it seemed that he could sense her moods and her wishes before she was aware of them.

"You're my work of art," he'd once whispered.

But Pygmalion's Galatea had been created out of love.

She'd been created out of hate.

At first, he hardly touched her. Sometimes he would only look at her, as if she were a model and he was a painter, experimenting with poses. When he touched her, arranging the poses, it was only with his fingertips, so lightly that she began to crave more. When they finally made love, it was as if they were experimenting with one more pose.

And, yes, the first time they'd done it, she'd wanted more. Everything had been planned to make her want more. She knew that now. Too late, she'd learned.

At first it had been exciting: a world she'd only imagined, only read about. Money, she learned, made a difference. She'd been raised to worry about money; there was never quite enough. But for him, people like him, money was meant for self-gratification, for the acquisition of possessions.

Possessions like her.

Across the playground, the little boy and the little girl were at the swings. The woman and the man were pushing their children. Gentle, measured pushes calculated to excite but not to frighten.

Gary had once said he wanted children. Or, rather, a child. But by that time she'd realized that their marriage would never work. It had taken her years to get out of the marriage—long, agonizing, destructive years. Desolate years.

Yet those years—seven years with a cruel, self-centered, sadistic husband—had been merely preparation for the last two years. Merely a warmup.

It started about three months after they'd first made love: actual, physical, male-and-female love. It started with props. "Enhancements," he called them. Just as he'd done in the beginning, he'd made the change slowly, subtly. He'd made it seem as if they both wanted something new, not just him. Slowly the props had become more elaborate, more important.

And finally there'd been the camera.

And the camera had done it. Completed the circle, closed off all escape. All along, it had been the camera. For him, the camera was what it was all about—the camera, the videotapes. He didn't get off playing sex games. He got off watching himself.

It was then that she began to draw back. Immediately he'd sensed what she was thinking. It was eerie, how he could do it. They'd been lying in bed. They hadn't spoken for some time. Then he said, "You can't do it, you know. I won't let you leave."

And then, speaking quietly, with perfect self-control, he told her about Tina Betts. "My last duchess," he'd said, ironically mocking. "She tried to leave me . . ."

He'd hesitated, for dramatic effect. Then, still speaking very softly: "And she died."

Now the man in the down jacket and the woman were extricating their children from the swings. The children returned to the jungle gym and began climbing. The little girl was agile, adventurous. The boy was more cautious. The woman and the man were returning to their bench. They were walking together, smiling, quietly talking. As she watched them, the two young parents and the two little children, she felt raindrops on her face.

*My last duchess . . .*

It was, she knew, the title of a poem, one she might have read in high school.

*And she died . . .*

Tina Betts had died.

"I wanted to tell you," he'd said, "so that we'd be bound together. You understand that, don't you?" A pause. Then: "You can't leave me now. Because I can't let you leave. Do you see?"


4:15 P.M. Charles watched the clerk complete the rent-a-car form and present it to him. She was a young Chicano with a bad

59

complexion and stubby, ugly hands. In another decade, some said, Chicanos would total a third of California's population. People like her, this dull, inferior creature with the thick accent, could tip the electoral balance.

He initialed the agreement, signed it, retrieved his credit card and driver's license.

It was a risk, to rent a car. But it was an acceptable risk. Actually, on balance, he was minimizing the risk, not magnifying it. This was planning, not execution.

As the clerk passed him the key, she smiled. "It's a white Tempo," she said, simpering. "Enjoy."

She was flirting with him, incredible but true. An overweight, pimply-faced Chicano with grotesquely arranged hair, actually flirting with him.


**5:15 P.M.** Charles turned the Tempo right, then left. Through the rain-streaked windshield, the headlights revealed a rutted two-lane graveled road that paralleled John F. Kennedy Drive, Golden Gate Park's main thoroughfare. It was a service road that ran along the southern perimeter of the park's polo field and riding stables. Thick, head-high brush grew on either side of the road. Because of the rain and the low-lying clouds, the sky was almost completely dark.

As dark as it would be later, when he came this way again.

Slowing the car until it was hardly moving, he switched off the headlights—as he would do later. He'd already selected the place, just around the next turn in the road, easily identifiable by the angle of the stables, just ahead.

Next time he would traverse the entire length of the narrow gravel track without lights—just as he would later. And when he'd done that, he would be prepared. All the variables would have been anticipated.

Only the variable of the police remained.

At five o'clock in the evening, in a midwinter rainstorm, the police probably wouldn't question a driver traversing this road without lights. They might keep him under surveillance, but they wouldn't take the time to question him. This, after all, was the commute hour. And the rush hour—the dinner hour—wasn't the time for dark deeds.

But as the night lengthened, the park emptied. Except for the main drive, there were no streetlights. Shadows changed substance; familiar landmarks disappeared. The man-made parkland became a jungle. In the darkness, animal sounds began. Predators emerged and began to prowl—animal predators and human predators.

And the police, too, began to prowl. Spotlights were turned on couples entwined in parked cars. Empty cars were investigated, their license plates were computer-checked. A car running without lights on a back road would likewise be checked, possibly stopped.

But the only alternative was one of the park's paved roads, where hiding places were far from the curbside. Carrying his telltale burden across open country, he would be exposed, could be impaled in the cold white glare of a spotlight's shaft. He would be—

Ahead, two shapes emerged in the windshield. Startled, he reached for the headlight switch. It was a man—a tramp, walking beside a rain-bedraggled dog, both of them turned to face the oncoming car. In outrage, the man's mouth was open, his voice fading as the car's speed increased:

"—the fuck you think you're—"

And the dog, aroused, began to bark.

6:10 P.M. Meredith shook out her hair, toweled off her face, and looked at her wristwatch that lay beside the washbasin. In twenty minutes the network news would begin. There was time, then, to complete the daily ritual. Standing in front of the bathroom's steam-misted full-length mirror, she would towel herself, scent herself, comb out her hair while it was still damp. She would wrap herself in the thick white terry-cloth robe. She would then go to the kitchen, select a stemmed glass from the Lucite rack beneath the cabinet, and pour a glass of cold Chenin Blanc. With five minutes to spare, she would settle herself in front of the TV.

Of all the daily rituals that had become her life during the past two years, this was her favorite: Sitting on the sofa, luxuriating in the terry cloth's caress on bare flesh while she sipped the wine, feet tucked up, she could contemplate another day that was more than half finished. If he didn't call, dinner preparations and a TV movie would get her through until eleven o'clock, when she could go to bed.

Facing the mirror, she toweled her torso, then her arms, then each leg. That morning the scales had revealed two extra pounds. Tonight, then, she would prepare a salad. Two glasses of wine would be her limit.

Unless he called.

She strapped on her watch, pinned up her hair, and wrapped the tawny bundle in the towel. With her arms raised, elevating the breasts, she looked at her reflection in the mirror, another daily ritual, every woman's fate, she'd always imagined. If a man suffered to pay the bills, then this was the woman's penance: this daily confrontation. She allowed her arms to fall and turned to the right, in profile. Yes, the silhouette was acceptable. Still acceptable, offering the promise of a few more years, the end of a long free ride.

She opened the bathroom door, took the terry-cloth robe from the wardrobe closet, wrapped it around herself. Years ago, she'd seen a vintage movie from the thirties, the title long forgotten, along with the plot. All that remained was the image of Norma Shearer, elegant in a thick white terry-cloth robe, her hair towel-turbaned.

She'd been married to Gary when she saw the movie. One of Gary's restaurants was in Hollywood and attracted a scattering of patrons from the fringes of the movie industry: assistants to assistants, bit players, a few stunt men. It had always amused her to see them coming on to each other, posing, preening, showing the profile, dropping names.

In the kitchen, as she poured the Chenin Blanc, she glanced at her watch. Almost six-thirty. She could—

Close beside her, the phone rang.

She placed the glass of wine on the counter. As she turned to face the phone, she felt the numbness begin, the retreat into a waking oblivion that shriveled the soul.

Because it must be he, calling. Who else could it be?


7:30 P.M. With the time coming closer, preparations must be finalized. Psychic preparations, not physical preparations. The physical arrangements were complete. Since yesterday, when fate had taken a hand in the sequence of events, the chamber had been readied. The camera had been loaded, its function checked. The lighting had been optimized. After considerable thought, he'd decided on the music: Rachmaninoff's *Isle of the Dead*. Then he'd gone to the gallery and carefully selected complementary pieces: a collage by Walsh, a painting by Dubinsky, premier Mayan artifacts he'd been saving for something special. Then he'd summoned Charles, to finalize the time frame.

After Charles was gone he'd switched on *Isle of the Dead*, timing the entire symphony. When the French horn began to play in the second movement, he decided, the ceremony would begin. At the crescendo ending the second movement, he would give her to Charles.

During the time between now and then, he must prepare himself. As meticulously as the priest rehearsed the rituals of his sect, or the conductor scored a symphony, or the actor immersed himself in his greatest part, so must he bring himself to full self-realization.

When—how—had it happened, his emergence, his realization that whatever he conceived he could command? It had begun, certainly, in the dark, secret rooms where women tended him.

Faceless women who existed only in shadow.

His mother existed only in light: flickers and flashes and flares. The other women were obscured. Permanently obscured.

The women stayed, but his mother left and returned, then left again. One of the women taught him to touch her—and then she touched him, his reward.

Other images followed: girls, boys, whispering, touching softly, touching harshly, sensations that soared, sensations that consumed, promises never fulfilled, penalties never paid.

The only constant was the whore, his fingers locked around her throat.

Sex, then, was the secret. But sex transcended. The price was high, the terms specific. Money was part of it, but entitlement was what remained: Certain superior beings were destined to pierce the veil, step through to the other side, take what inferiors could only covet.

There were many who sought to self-destruct. With him or without him, they would have killed themselves. Drugs, cars, the streets—there were countless ways, all of them leaving him merely a spectator, denied his own fulfillment.

And then had come Tina Betts.

And then, one of life's little coincidences, Charles had appeared. And the unity had been completed.

And so Tina Betts had become his last duchess.

The price—the penalty—had been Charles. Without Charles, he could never have done it. And without him, Charles would never have done it.

"Could" and "would," two sides of the same fateful coin. Words that could bind, deeds that would kill.

9:30 P.M. About to touch the radio's ON switch, she drew back her hand. Music could soothe, sometimes anesthetize, make the mind a merciful blank. But this trip must be made in silence, in full awareness.

Because this trip could begin her liberation.

Time had doubtless begun the process. Only yesterday, it seemed, she'd been thirty. Only tomorrow, she'd be forty. Time was running out: ever more sand in the bottom of the hourglass. But then she'd found Albert Price. She'd taken the first step, unaided. And then, one of life's benevolent accidents, she'd met Frank Hastings, a face from the past—and more.

It had been three hours since tonight's call had come.

As she'd done for almost two years, she'd begun the process of the unthinkable that had become the predictable. She'd scented herself and anointed herself with oil, a phrase from the Bible, one she'd never forgotten, because of its poetry, its imagery. Carefully she'd made up her face, mindful, she knew, of the camera, an involuntary response, everyone a star, wishfully thinking. Because her hair would be disarrayed, she'd done it loosely. For her underclothing, a sheer lace bra and matching lace panties, on command. Like the underclothing, the dress was chosen for its sexual utility: unloosen a belt, release two snaps, and it fell free.

Sometimes, as she dressed for him, it seemed as if she was really wearing two tassels and a rhinestone G-string.

But other times she saw no difference between the dress she wore and the black cocktail dress, tasteful single strand of pearls—real pearls—and the impeccable coiffeur and smile that many women parlayed into seven-figure marriages, even including children, part of the package deal.

She was driving south on Van Ness. Ahead, at the Broadway intersection, traffic was stopped; a police car's signal lights were flashing, alternating red and blue.

Fate had taken a hand, then, delaying her arrival. She would, of course, mention the traffic problem. He'd told her to be there by ten o'clock, a direct order.

Now traffic was moving; the lights on the police cars were no longer flashing. Reluctantly she put the Mercedes in gear.

When she searched for answers, asked herself why she did it, was doing it, had she factored in the Mercedes? And the condo? And the clothes? And had she admitted that, yes, the games they played excited her?

She'd heard about snuff films and the games. She'd heard that, once aroused, the edge of oblivion could make her orgasm explode. He'd offered to show her. And she'd accepted—just as she'd accepted the car, and the condo, and the clothes. He enticed, she went along. What pervert could ask for more—for a better return on his investment?

But the first time she felt his fingers at her throat, the first time the edges of her consciousness began to blacken, she knew she'd gone too far. Finally she'd gone too far.

It was then that he'd told her about Tina Betts. That very night, as they lay in bed, afterward.

And it was then, months ago, that she'd first thought about a psychiatrist. Some women drank. Some took drugs to ease the pain. She'd decided to try psychiatry.

The next day, at random, mostly because his office was at 450 Sutter, a prestige address, she'd called Dr. Price.

And tonight, after she'd finished dressing, she'd taken Frank's card from her purse. She'd gone to her desk. She'd selected a sheet of thick, blue notepaper and a matching envelope. Like the desk, and the tooled leather blotter, and the other accessories, the notepaper had been chosen for her, all a part of the grand design. She'd addressed the envelope to Lieutenant Frank Hastings, at the Hall of Justice. After some thought—with the time going fast—she'd decided to begin by thanking him for lunch. Then she'd said she'd like to buy him lunch, what about next Tuesday, same time, same place? She knew he was busy, she said. But there was something, she went on, that she had to talk to him about. Something very important.

At lunch she'd tell Frank everything. Even though she was ashamed, she would tell him everything. He would tell her what she must do. A sealed letter telling everything could be put in a safe-deposit box, to be opened in the event of her death.

Suddenly it seemed a favorable omen, this sequence of events. If she hadn't gone to Dr. Price, she wouldn't have met Frank. It was a miraculous coincidence. She had helped herself, and would now be helped by others. In *Reader's Digest*, long ago, she'd read about upward spirals: people who ascended, people who descended. Both spirals, the article had said, had their own momentum.

She turned the last corner and brought the Mercedes to a stop in front of his house. The time was exactly ten o'clock. As she set the alarm and locked the Mercedes, she let her fingers linger on the roofline above the door. She would miss this car.

**10:45 P.M.** Charles realized that, yes, the tension of the last half hour had become palpable. It was important, he knew, to acknowledge the tension, recognize it for what it was. He was afraid. This time he was afraid. The first time there'd been no fear. Instead, two years ago, there'd been a kind of schoolboy bravado: dare and double dare. Then her eyes had rolled up, and her whole body had begun to twitch.

They'd done it.

They'd agreed to do it. They'd planned to do it. But until that last moment it had been theory, not fact. It had been the perfect synthesis: the carnal and the aesthetic and the theoretical, the Tina Betts unity. But when her eyes had rolled up and she'd begun to twitch, and her urine had soaked the bed, the unity had shattered. They'd been scared. Just plain scared. Terrified.

Then he hadn't known what the ending would be.

Now, tonight, he knew.

Two years ago, before the fact, he hadn't been able to define why he did it. Was it pure aesthetics? Was it ambition? Greed? Then, an actor without a script, he hadn't known.

Now, tonight, he knew.

He stood guard at the head of the staircase. Resting on the intricately carved newel post, his hand was slightly trembling. Was it fear? Anticipation?

Two years ago there'd been no time for anticipation, therefore no time for fear. *Thus doth conscience make cowards of us all.* It was a line from Shakespeare. Except that conscience really meant thought, reflection, worry. The teacher had been careful to point that out. Miss Crawford, the eleventh-grade English teacher. He'd been one of her favorites. She'd sensed his special talents. "They'll hear from you, Charles," she'd once said. "You may be famous someday."


**10:50 P.M.** Eyes closed, she felt his fingers touch her breast, at first so lightly, so delicately. Now she felt her body beginning its response. It was an autonomic response, a term she'd learned in nursing school, so long ago. Her body, then, would go along with the game, just this one last time. Leaving her free to let her eyes close, let her thoughts run free. Sometimes she was a child again, laughing as she opened presents. Christmas presents, usually. Especially the Christmas she got a two-wheeler. The memory of that Christmas morning with the bike beside the tree was magical.

But now, tonight, the images failed her, turned back on her: phantasms, fugitive from nightmares. In bed—a narrow bed in a small, dark room—she'd awakened at the click of the doorknob. Two clicks, really: two tiny sounds, nothing more.

But after he'd first done it, come into her room the first time, and drawn back the covers, and come into her bed, those two clicks had seared her consciousness. At first there'd been the clicks, followed by the squeak of the hinges as the door opened— followed by the sound of his footsteps on the bare floor of her room. Then came the odor of his breath: harsh, stale liquor. Always the odor of liquor. Then came the touch of his hand on the bedclothing, drawing back the covers.

He'd never been able to change the sound of the doorknob clicking. But, after the first time, he'd oiled the hinges so they wouldn't squeak.

She bought a skeleton key at Taylor's Hardware, but the key hadn't worked. Neither had another. Or another. Using her allowance money, she'd gone downtown to another hardware store. She'd bought a set of three skeleton keys, with instructions. One of them worked.

Three nights later the rattle of the lock had awakened her. One rattle, then another rattle. Instantly she'd realized the danger: Her mother would hear the angry rattling. Her mother would *know*.

So she'd gotten out of bed and unlocked the door.

Two small metallic clicks, when she was eleven years old.

Transformed, now, into the almost inaudible whir of the video camera.


11:15 P.M. As he placed his hands on her shoulders he saw her eyes close. It was an aberration, utterly out of phase, an impermissible liberty. She knew the importance of precise replication. She was aware that her eyes must remain open until her knees touched the floor. Therefore, discipline was mandatory. But the flays were beyond his reach—and time was passing. His contract with Charles was self-limiting, inherently irreversible.

Slowly, therefore, he exerted pressure, forcing her to her knees beside the bed. The floor was oaken; the small Persian rug marked the camera's field. Her knees were touching the rug, centered. Thus the circle was closed.

Unless she opened her eyes.

At the thought, he felt the first flicker of fear, the first telltale tremor. It was expected, already factored in, therefore discounted. His breath was coming quicker. That, too, had been anticipated, combining arousal and apprehension. The word, after all, cause and effect, was "murder."

Her breathing, too, had quickened. This was the sign, the signal. As he moved his body closer, his flesh upon hers, precisely as he'd instructed her, his last command, he was aware that his hands were moving. Without conscious volition, his hands were moving in unison, moving from the firm flesh of her shoulders to the softer, more yielding flesh of her throat.

Without volition, therefore without guilt.


11:18 P.M. She felt his hands move slowly from her shoulders to her throat. His touch was delicate, incredibly knowing, a master's touch: artist's fingers, probing, shaping, exploring. Sometimes he whispered: strange, fragmented phrases. Sometimes he was silent, as he was tonight. She realized that her body was arching, moving closer to his. His fingers caressed the back of her neck, under the hair. His thumbs rested against her throat, one thumb on either side. The music was swelling; the crescendo was approaching. Rachmaninoff had become her fate. Where the music went, she must follow. Until death—*The Isle of the Dead*. Had he intended it to be a joke, one of his little jokes? She would never know.

Never know . . .

Was this room—this chamber—soundproofed? She'd never thought to ask. Had she ever heard a sound from outside? She couldn't remember.

In the mailbox at the corner of her block the letter to Frank awaited collection, her salvation.

At her throat, the pressure was increasing. The music was swelling. Her eyes came open. His eyes were wild: stranger's eyes, a madman's eyes. Struggling to rise, she struck at him, felt fingernails sink into flesh. But the music was fading; her legs were failing. With consciousness caught in her throat, bursting, clogging, the center was falling away, a confusion of lights dancing against darkness. Her arms were growing heavy; her legs had gone slack. Only memories remained. Random images: the patent-leather dancing shoes she'd loved, the pink-colored conch shell Grandma Ferguson kept on her coffee table—

—and, forever, the skeleton key, turning in the lock.

11:22 P.M. Sensitized so acutely to the sound, Charles heard the lock snap, heard the doorknob turn. With his eyes on the door, he saw it begin to open. Containing the plastic dropcloth, the roll of tape, the rubber gloves, and the revolver, the airline bag had been placed close beside him, ready to his hand.

As the door of the chamber opened to its full width and the familiar figure materialized in the darkened hallway, Charles drew a deep breath and picked up the airline bag. The bag was heavy. Unreasonably heavy, considering its contents.

11:25 P.M. Charles could feel the shift: substance gone, sensation both consumed and consuming, each running wild, a manic kaleidoscope, time and space locked together, convulsed, the essence of it all.

In the chamber's dim light she was pale and still, the ultimate aesthetic verity, everything and nothing, the second resolution, his first and final statement: death serving art. From this moment of liberation would flow fame incarnate. His name would be repeated: *Charles, Charles, Charles.*

She had been arranged in the classic pose, principal to the composition. The plastic sheeting had been spread beside the bed, on the far side. Her purse was there, too, and her clothing, everything in readiness, checklist complete. There were, after all, temporal necessities. Even a sculpture required filaments.

As he bent over her, he heard the camera's soft whir.

*Charles. Charles. Charles.*

11:40 P.M. According to plan, so carefully calculated, Charles had first taken her keys from her purse. Leaving her in the chamber, he'd gone downstairs, gotten her car, driven it into the garage, closed the garage door. They'd wrapped her in the plastic, carried her down to the garage, laid her on the floor beside the car. The light inside the garage was dim, so that her face beneath the plastic was only suggested, not defined. With great difficulty, he'd removed the bulb from the trunk's interior light. So that now, effortlessly, he could lift his plastic-wrapped burden, balance it on his right hip, lever it into the trunk. The only light came from small, high windows set into the garage door. Beneath the plastic, her face would be invisible.

12:10 A.M. This was the spot, earlier in the day, that he'd encountered the tramp and the dog, two derelicts. And just beyond, around the next curve, was the place he'd chosen: a thick, higher-than-head-height tangle of undergrowth and low-growing shrubs and trees.

With headlights switched off, the Mercedes was moving slowly ahead, lurching on the uneven, rutted road. The night was heavily overcast, without starlight or moonlight. The rain had stopped, but the cold, raw wind was—

*The rain.*

*Mud.*

The instant he got out of the car, the instant his feet touched the ground, mud would cling to his shoes: thick, incriminating mud. At the police lab, scientists could match the mud on his shoes to this particular soil.

Ahead, he saw the spot, the low-growing tangle only dimly defined against the geometric shapes of the stables.

He could continue, drive past, then switch on the headlights when he reached the park's main drive. He could drive out to the ocean. He could turn left, drive down the coast. Between Pacifica and Half Moon Bay he remembered small, unsupervised beaches where surfers gathered, where couples with picnic baskets clambered down steep footpaths from the narrow, winding two-lane road to the beaches below. There were small turnouts beside the road. He could park in one of the turnouts, check the angle of the cliffside. A moment to stop the car, lights out, brake set, engine switched off. Carefully, calmly, he would—

No.

A passing motorist's headlights could impale him, a lone clifftop figure against the night sky. If they couldn't identify him, they would certainly remember the car.

He braked, switched off the engine, took the keys from the ignition, swung open the door. Shoes could be cleaned. Shoes could be thrown away.

He was at the trunk, fitting the key into the trunk lock. The rubber gloves—surgical gloves—were causing difficulty. But now, suddenly, the trunk deck flew up. In the stillness, the *thunk* of the deck against its stop was thunderous. His heart was hammering, blood pounding in his ears. From the close-by underbrush came the sharp, sudden sound of scurrying: an animal, frightened, running away. Was its heart hammering, too?

# THURSDAY
# FEBRUARY 15

**8:15 A.M.** As consciousness came clear and sleep faded, Granville Foster realized that he'd been dreaming of Miss Ames, his fourth-grade teacher. At certain times, in certain places, he dreamed of Miss Ames. She was a small, fat, excitable woman who had once cried in class. The day report cards came out, just before summer vacation, she'd asked him to stay after class. She looked sad, he remembered; her mouth had been puckered and her eyes misted. She told him that he would be repeating the fourth grade. She was sorry. She'd wanted to tell his mother first, but their telephone had been disconnected, and there hadn't been time to write a note.

He'd repeated the sixth grade, too. By that time, most of the boys in his class and some of the girls were calling him "dummy." On the school bus, during those long, terrible rides, he wanted to sit on the backseat, so no one would notice him. Instead, the driver made him sit on the floor beside him. He would be protected, the driver said. Mr. Pass was the driver, with tattooed arms and a missing finger. But everyone could see him at the front of the bus, and make faces at him. And at home, if he went out of the house, boys followed him, hooting and hollering. Day after day, he'd had to fight them—or run. One day three of them had cornered him in a vacant lot. There was a FOR SALE sign lying in the dirt: a square piece of metal attached to a long wooden stake. Crying so hard he could hardly see, he'd picked up the sign. Then, eyes closed, he began blindly swinging it. He'd felt something solid, heard a cry. When he'd opened his eyes, there was blood on the sign.

When he'd gotten home, Ezzard Wise was waiting for him. In the tiny foothill town of Potter's Bend, there were three policemen. Ezzard Wise was the biggest—and the meanest. While Officer Wise talked, Granville's mother had cried. What could she do? she'd wailed. On welfare, no husband, four children—him and three other children, all smaller, all smarter.

All "normal."

It was his last clear memory of childhood. He never really knew how it had happened, that he'd lived in other houses, with other families. All he could ever clearly remember was his dog Chum running beside the car when they'd driven him away, only the third time he'd ever been in a car.

But his mother had written to him, and twice she'd come to see him. Both times she'd brought cookies. And she'd sent him birthday presents, too—presents, and a birthday cake.

At the thought of the cookies and the cake, Granville realized that his stomach had begun to growl. Had the thought of food made his stomach growl? Or had he been hungry first? Sometimes he thought about it, what made him hungry.

Beside him, Chum was stirring.

Every dog he ever had he named Chum, after his first dog. It was still so sad, to think of Chum, the first Chum, running beside the car, tongue hanging out so far, while they were driving him away in the car.

But that Chum was small. This Chum was big.

Beneath the plastic sheeting, a dropcloth, really, that he'd taken from a construction site, Chum was getting to his feet. Careful to drain the water away from them, Granville pulled the plastic sheeting aside. Adjusting his cap, from army surplus, he looked up into the sky. Even though the sky was gray, all gray, with no sun, he knew that the time must be about eight in the morning. Or nine. Maybe nine. Once he'd had a watch, but he couldn't remember what happened to it.

He got out of the sleeping bag, stretched, and moved away several yards, toward the riding stable. Because it had been raining yesterday, food would be scarce in the trash containers along the park's main drive. And if he didn't go with Chum, getting to the containers before the garbage truck, then Chum would go off himself, looking for food. And if that happened, then Chum could disappear. Forever disappear.

Granville was unbuttoning his overcoat and beginning to unbutton his pants, looking both ways up and down the narrow dirt road, when he realized that Chum had found something in a tangle of underbrush. He could always tell when Chum found something special, the way Chum's head and shoulders were close to the ground, with his rump high and his tail carried low, not wagging, cautious.

With his pants half unbuttoned, Granville moved to come up behind Chum. Once Chum had found a snake and had stood like that, head and tail low. Snakes made Granville's heart hammer and his throat go dry. Even small snakes scared him. So he'd learned to stay behind Chum, who was burrowing a little farther into the underbrush now. With his feet planted close behind Chum's rear paws, Granville leaned cautiously forward, using both hands to part the branches.

He saw two bare legs, very white against the moist black dirt and the brown leaves. And then he saw the rest of her: a woman, blond, lying with her head jammed into the fork of a small, stunted tree. The dirt smudged her face; the dead leaves were tangled in her hair.

As he quickly straightened, letting the branches come together, he put a hand on Chum's collar. With his face turned away, avoiding the sight of small patches of white flesh visible through the branches and the foliage, Granville realized that, yes, his heart was hammering. If the still white body had been a snake, alive, he couldn't feel worse, couldn't suddenly feel any more hollow inside, empty, violently trembling, almost sick.

But, still, he knew what he must do.

After he pulled Chum away, and then tied the dog to a tree, taking no chances, he must put his things in his pack, with the plastic sheeting outside, because it was wet. Then they'd go down to the main drive, just down the slope, and check the cans, because of the garbage trucks. And then, right on his way, they'd go by the boathouse, which would just be opening and sometimes had leftover food.

And then he'd go around Stow Lake until he came to the culvert where Tim Welch slept when the weather was bad. It had rained last night, so Tim was probably there, in the culvert.

And if Tim was there, he'd tell Tim about the dead blond lady in the underbrush, about fifty yards from where he'd slept last night, maybe only twenty yards. He was never sure about distance, or feet, or yards.

He would tell Tim about the lady, and he'd do what Tim told him to do. Because Tim read books, and knew languages, and spoke like teachers spoke. The good teachers. Miss Ames, and the other good teachers. Even though they'd kept him back.

10:05 A.M. Canelli braked the cruiser to a stop, took the microphone from its hook, keyed the microphone, and called Central Dispatch.

"This is Inspectors Fifty-three," he said, "responding to that nine ten in Golden Gate Park. Have you got the information?"

"Negative. Nine ten, you say?" It was a woman's voice, clear and concise, a voice Canelli didn't recognize. Yesterday, over coffee, he'd heard that a new dispatcher, female, still in her twenties, looked like a hot number. With five or six dispatchers on duty, and considering that he was talking to a strange female, it was odds on that she was the hot new number.

He lowered his voice, for a more masculine projection. "That's affirmative."

"When was that reported, do you know?" Yes, there was a certain lilt to the voice, a certain nonprofessional warmth. Had she heard of him?

"About an hour ago, I think. What I want to know is—"

"Stand by, please."

Canelli released the TRANSMIT button and sighed. If she was new on the job, then she was learning early the arrogant little one-up tricks of the dispatcher's trade.

"Inspectors Fifty-three?" It was a male voice: Joe Fields.

"Fifty-three."

"Go ahead."

"That nine ten in Golden Gate Park. Is that south of the polo field?"

"That's affirmative. About three hundred feet from the riding stables. Two units are on the scene. What's your position?"

"I'm on JFK, the main drive. Near the duck pond."

"You want to hold your position? I'll have one of the units swing by for you."

"Well, I can—"

"Just hold your position, Inspector." Fields was elaborately condescending, score another one-up point for Dispatch. "I'll have someone come for you."


10:20 A.M. About to take another step, Canelli stopped short, his right foot an inch above the muddy earth of the narrow dirt road. Angry with himself, he drew back, shook his head, sharply sucked at his teeth. The body was lying a few feet away in a large clump of brambles. The thicket was entirely surrounded by muddy ground that would take perfect impressions. Already he could have compromised vital evidence. Sometimes it seemed to Canelli that he would never quite get it right.

Two black-and-white units were at the scene. They were about fifty feet apart, equidistant from the crime scene. Underbrush grew thick on either side of the narrow dirt track, so the two black-and-whites made a natural barricade against the curious. And, yes, even though the weather was gray and cold, and the area was far from the park user's beaten track, there were already gawkers, doubtless attracted by the two patrol cars.

Taking another step backward, Canelli beckoned Jerry Kennealy to walk with him to his unmarked car. Kennealy and Canelli had gone through the academy together, five years ago. Canelli had graduated twenty-first out of forty-seven; Kennealy had graduated third. Sometimes Canelli suspected that Kennealy, a spit-and-polish man who was still in uniform, might be jealous of Canelli's promotion to the Inspector's Bureau and then to Homicide. Since Canelli himself had been puzzled by the promotions, he could sympathize with Kennealy's discomfort.

At his cruiser, Canelli took out his spiral-bound notebook. Then he began a search for his ballpoint pen.

"Here—" Kennealy said, clicking a pen and offering it to Canelli. Kennealy's expression was long-suffering.

"Thanks, Jerry. Listen, can I borrow this? I seem to've—"

"Keep it," Kennealy answered shortly. "I've got more."

"Well, Jeez—" Canelli looked at the pen. "Thanks."

"Don't mention it. Please."

"Okay—" Canelli placed his open notebook on the hood of his car, dated a page, noted the time. He frowned momentarily, as if something important had slipped his mind. Finally he shrugged, then said, "So what's it look like?"

"Have you called a lieutenant yet?"

"No. I wanted to talk to you first—you guys, on the scene. Anything?"

"Not much." With his squared-off chin, Kennealy indicated the scene of the homicide. "I gather it was phoned in anonymously about nine-thirty—an hour ago. Dispatch said they couldn't keep the informant on the line. We got here in the area maybe five minutes after we got the call. But it took us awhile to locate the victim. Fifteen minutes, maybe."

With the pen poised, Canelli asked, "Who was the dispatcher?"

"Susan Wallace. She's that new one."

"The sexy one?"

Kennealy lifted his chin. His clear blue eyes were remote as he said, "I haven't seen her."

"If she's the new one, then that's her—the sexy one."

Lips pursed, Kennealy chose not to respond. Even though the weather was cold and raw, Kennealy wasn't wearing a jacket. His uniform shirt, Canelli noticed, was pressed to knife creases.

"So you were first on the scene," Canelli said.

Standing at parade rest, Kennealy nodded. "Right."

"Okay—" Canelli wrote in the notebook. "So what happened when you got here?"

"Well—" Kennealy pointed to his right, down a slope in the opposite direction from the body. "We came in there, from the main drive. It's a loop, you know. A one-way loop. Both ends stop at the main drive. It took us three times, driving real slow, before we spotted the body. As soon as we saw it, we pulled back, put in the call. Christ, this is the second body this year in the park. And it's only February."

"Has anyone come forward? Any witnesses?" As he spoke, Canelli looked at the half-dozen onlookers. Had one of them discovered the body and made the anonymous call?

"Nobody."

Canelli nodded thoughtfully, then said, "Okay, I'll call for a lieutenant. How about if your guys talk to the gawkers, see what they say?"

"Shall I get addresses?"

Canelli considered. It was Lieutenant Friedman's theory that onlookers were more cooperative if they weren't asked for their addresses. Lieutenant Hastings wasn't so sure.

"Maybe just get the names, not their addresses—not unless they've got something." Canelli looked at the other man anxiously. "Okay?"

Kennealy shrugged. "Whatever you say." Abruptly he turned away. Sensing Kennealy's irritated impatience, Canelli sighed. Then he opened the door of his cruiser, switched on the radio, spoke into the microphone. Moments later he was talking to Lieutenant Friedman. Because it was radio, not the telephone, Canelli spoke cryptically, verifying that, yes, there was a nude body, female, no suspects, no opportunity to determine the probable cause of death because of the terrain.

"Okay," Friedman said, "I'll make the calls. Lieutenant Hastings is in the field. I'll see if I can find him. Otherwise, I'll come myself. Have you got enough personnel on the scene?"

"So far, no problem, Lieutenant. It's real—you know—woodsy, here. Limited access, except for this little dirt road. There're four of us. So I'd say no problem."

"Okay. I'll turn out the troops."


**12:40 P.M.** As Hastings locked the door of his cruiser and turned toward the line of cars crowded into the dirt track, he felt the first rain from a storm system that had turned the western sky a dark, leaden gray. According to the twelve o'clock news, rain would be heavy during the afternoon and evening, with possible clearing later. Tomorrow would be unsettled, the announcer had said, with more rain due the following day. In Marin and Sonoma counties, flood watches had been posted.

Walking past the coroner's van and the crime lab's van, he saw a vintage Porsche, fire-engine red. Deputy coroner Al Fink was on the scene. As Hastings raised the hood of his parka, he saw Canelli, who was turned away. Canelli was wearing a short red poplin windbreaker, a black-and-orange Giants baseball cap, shapeless corduroy slacks, and mud-caked running shoes. If past performance was any guide, Canelli had neglected to bring a raincoat. If the rain worsened, Canelli would get soaked.

As Hastings drew closer, a uniformed patrolman nodded and straightened his stance, acknowledging the presence of a superior officer. Seeing the patrolman's reaction, Canelli turned.

"Oh, hi, Lieutenant. Just get here?" His smile was cheerful.

"That's right." Hastings nodded to the patrolman, whose name he'd forgotten. As Hastings stood still, surveying the scene, Canelli came to stand beside him. It was part of an established routine, a protocol. Since death in other than ordinary circumstances was the category, code nine ten, the men from Homicide were in charge. Therefore, it was accepted that when Hastings arrived on the scene, he would be briefed by his subordinate from Homicide. During their conversation, no one would interrupt them, with the possible exception of the deputy coroner, whose rank equaled the officer in charge.

"So what's it look like?" Hastings spoke quietly, deferring to the dominion of death that touched them all.

"Well," Canelli said heavily, "the plain truth is, we haven't made a whole hell of a lot of progress, Lieutenant. Partly it's the layout. We can't see much the way she's lying without we screw up evidence. And we can't move her until everything's set. I guess you know how the squeal came in."

"Anonymous."

Canelli nodded. "Right. About three hours ago, give or take. The lab guys've been here for about an hour."

"How'd they handle it?" Asking the question, Hastings looked beyond Canelli, studying the crime scene. Clear plastic sheeting covered perhaps twenty-five feet of the road, ending at the yellow tapes strung across the road. A large piece of white-painted plywood stenciled SFPD had been placed on the sheeting opposite the body. Looking inquiringly at Hastings, Al Fink stood on the plywood, his black satchel beside him. Hastings's nod signified greeting but granted no permission to proceed. First Canelli must answer the question.

"They took maybe a hundred pictures, flash and Polaroid, all angles, the usual sequence on a deal like this. Then they took maybe eight square feet of plaster castings, all keyed and everything. They took up the castings about fifteen minutes ago. So then—" Canelli sighed heavily. "So then, after it was all signed off, and everything, I went out on the plywood, and pushed back the branches, and took a look. She's absolutely nude, not a stitch. It seems like she was strangled, that's pretty clear. I'd say she was maybe thirty, well built—very well built, matter of fact. She looks to be—you know, well nourished and everything. Blonde. A real blonde, if you know what I mean." Canelli ventured a smile.

"Nothing at the scene? Weapons? Anything?"

Regretfully Canelli shook his head. "As far as I can see, Lieutenant, there isn't a goddamn thing except twigs and dead leaves and a couple of candy wrappers on the ground. And I looked, too. I really looked. But as far as I can see, all we've got is a good-looking naked lady stuffed in a bunch of bushes. Except for some broken branches, that's it." Canelli shrugged apologetically.

"So she was dumped, probably."

"That's what I'd say. Someone could've driven up, dumped her out, taken off. There're tire tracks, probably, in the dirt. And footprints, too, probably. Except that the first unit on the scene drove past three times before they saw her. And then they had to walk to where the perpetrator did, probably, to get a look at her. So I don't know how lucky we'll get on the physical evidence." Canelli sighed again. "It's the same old story. Nobody starts worrying about evidence until it's too late."

"Okay—" Hastings looked once more at Fink, this time nodding encouragement. "I'll take a look, then we'll get her out of there, so Fink can make his examination. Right?"

Canelli nodded agreement. "Right."

Walking carefully over the plastic sheeting to the plywood, Hastings looked at the dirt beneath the plastic as he walked. Yes, the moist dirt had taken the imprints of tires and shoes.

"Hello, Frank."

"Hello, Al." As the two men shook hands, Fink gingerly stepped off the plywood.

"Been here long?" Hastings asked.

"Twenty minutes, maybe. I can't work on her in those bushes."

"I know—" Conscious of a bone-deep reluctance that never eased, the worst part of the job, Hastings turned toward the tangle of brambles that concealed all but a patchwork of white flesh: arms, legs, and torso. Using both hands, he drew back two large branches. She lay on her side, feet toward the road. Her face was jammed against the base of a small, low-growing tree. Her hair was dark blond and covered most of her face. A scattering of dead leaves and debris was sprinkled across the body, as if the earth were already claiming her. Because she'd been dead for hours, the bodily fluids had settled, flattening the body at the bottom, another claim of nature upon the flesh of the dead. Yet, even though the muscles no longer functioned, the lines of the body were still exciting. As Canelli had said, a good-looking naked lady. And, yes, she'd probably been strangled. Through a parting of the hair, bruises on her throat were clearly visible. Her mouth was open wide, as if she were still gasping for breath.

Hastings released the branches, stepped to the edge of the plywood, and parted a different set of branches for a better look at her face. Yes, beneath the sheer spread of blond hair he could see the curve of her cheek and forehead.

About to release the branches and step back, he hesitated. To look into the victim's dead eyes, forever stilled, was the worst chore of all. Yet, unaccountably, he was shifting his grip on one of the branches, for a fresh grip. If he arched his body forward and to the left, he could see—

Meredith's face.

Her eyes empty, her tongue bulging.

A face made grotesque in death, an obscenity.

But Meredith's face, once so beautiful. Even as a little girl, Kevin's little sister, always so beautiful.

Lurching, he stepped quickly forward, regaining his balance—saving himself from crashing through the thick-growing branches to lie beside Meredith.


**12:45 P.M.** Granville took a fresh grip on the rope that he'd hooked around Chum's neck, to hold Chum back. Whenever anything unusual happened, even joggers going by, Chum wanted to investigate, join right in. Chum was like that, always so friendly, ready for anything. Sometimes Granville tried to remember how his life had been before he'd found Chum, just a tiny little puppy, soft and furry, that someone had let go in the park so long ago.

When he'd told Tim Welch about the dead, naked lady, Tim had warned him not to go too close to whoever came to look at the dead lady. Tim hadn't told him why, he'd just told him what to do. And he knew, without being told, that if he let Chum go down among all the cars and the men with faces so serious, and the yellow streamers, then when he called Chum, they would follow Chum, and they'd find him.

Had he ever seen someone dead before?

Animals, yes. The park was filled with animals. Wild animals. And animals killed each other. Sometimes he heard them cry, at night. Horrible cries. They were death cries, Tim Welch had said. The last sounds they ever made. So sad. So terrible, when it happened.


**12:47 P.M.** Mouth open, eyes wide, voice awed, Canelli said, "She was a *friend* of yours, Lieutenant? A *friend?*"

"I grew up with her. Christ—" Hastings shook his head. "Christ, I saw her two days ago. We had lunch together."

"Oh, Jeez—" Deeply shocked, Canelli spread his hands

wide, palms up. It was a gesture of helpless compassion. "Jeez, this is terrible, Lieutenant. Just terrible."

Without replying, Hastings turned back to face the murder scene. Fink was gesturing to the two coroner's assistants, standing by with a stretcher. Both men wore identical hooded dark-blue foul-weather gear, departmental issue, and their apathetic resentment was apparent in their stance. Their job was unpleasant enough, their body language projected, without the added inconvenience of the rain, now worsening.

Standard procedure, Hastings knew, would be followed. The coroner's men would bring the body out of the brush. If rigor permitted, they would straighten her out, so that she lay on her side, on the stretcher. Fink would make his preliminary examination. To try to establish the time of death, it was essential that Fink take her temperature. Because it was the body of a woman who had been beautiful, remarks would be made. It was routine that remarks would be made.

Turning away, he spoke to Canelli: "Tell them to keep their goddamn mouths shut. Do you understand?"

"Yessir," Canelli answered. "I understand."


2:00 P.M. A glance at Friedman's face as he entered Hastings's office and sank into the visitor's chair told Hastings that Friedman had heard the news.

"This Golden Gate Park thing—" Friedman gestured: an uncharacteristically tentative lifting of his thick hand. "Is she the one you were telling me about, day before yesterday? The one that was abused when she was a child?"

"That's right." As he spoke, Hastings stared at the file folder lying on his desk. He'd just printed "Meredith Powell" on the folder's tab. Technically, it could be the wrong name, since she'd been married. So he might not even know her legal name.

By now her body would be in the morgue, on a stainless-steel table. Because Fink knew of her connection with Hastings, and because Fink knew that time could be crucial in a homicide investigation, he would give the autopsy top priority. Already Fink could be at work—slicing her up the middle, probably opening her throat, certainly taking off the top of her skull to check for substance abuse.

"Maybe you shouldn't take it," Friedman said, speaking quietly. "Maybe you should let me have the case. Give yourself a break."

"No—" Hastings shook his head. "No, it's okay."

"Stubborn, eh?"

Hastings shrugged. Friedman let a final beat pass, then spoke briskly. "Okay. So what've we got? Anything?"

"Nothing. I've got her phone number, but that's about it. It's unlisted, so the phone company is calling back, with the address. I don't even know her married name. She told me, but I can't remember. I've tried, but I can't."

"You knew she was in trouble."

"She was in a relationship with a guy who scared her. She wanted to get out of it. She said he—"

His phone rang, the intercom line.

"Yes?"

"I've got the address for you, Lieutenant." It was Culligan, the newest man in Homicide. "It's Twenty-one Fifty-two Hyde Street."

"Right—" He wrote down the address. "What about a car?"

"They're still checking."

"Consumer's credit?"

"Not yet."

"She lived in Los Angeles until a couple of years ago. See what you can find down there. She was married, though, for most of that time. So the name'll be different."

"I'll see what they say. It'd sure help, though, if we had a driver's license, or canceled checks."

"I should have something for you, once I see where she lived." He broke the connection.

"I talked to Canelli," Friedman said. "It sounds like she was dumped out there."

"No question."

"Golden Gate Park—" Friedman shook his head reflectively. "The biggest, the most natural park in the world, they say. I love the place. When my kid was growing up, we used to spend part of almost every weekend there. But, Christ, the place is a goddamn jungle after dark. Bodies half eaten by animals. Bodies cut up and stuffed in trash cans. Asian refugees trapping dogs to take home and eat. It's enough to make you—"

"Listen, I don't need the background. Okay?"

Friedman shrugged diffidently. But from Friedman, Hastings realized, a shrug was the equivalent of an apology. "Yeah. Okay," he said. "So what'd you want me to do?"

"I meant to get the numbers on the black-and-white that"— he broke off, swallowed—"that discovered the body. I want the lab to take the tire prints, for elimination." As he spoke, Hastings rose to his feet and reached for his jacket.

"Right." Also rising, Friedman watched the other man prepare to leave for the field. They stood facing each other tentatively. For this moment, this situation, they had no precedent. No words were available to them, no stock phrases. Finally Friedman shrugged again, spread his hands again.

"I guess it's a lottery," Friedman said quietly. "It's just a goddamn lottery."

"Life, you mean."

Friedman nodded gravely. "That's exactly what I mean."


3:15 P.M. The crest of the Hyde Street hill was a tourist attraction second only to Fisherman's Wharf. Cable cars, each one designated a historical landmark, labored up a series of lesser hills from Market Street before descending the long Hyde Street hill that ended at the southern shore of San Francisco Bay. From the crest, the view of the Golden Gate Bridge was unobstructed. But today the bridge was invisible, obscured by the angry, wind-whipped fog blowing in from the ocean. In the cable cars, only a few hardy passengers in down jackets and stocking caps braved the cold of the outside steps.

After locking the driver's door of his Honda, Hastings turned to face 2152 Hyde Street. Atop Nob Hill, offering some of the world's most magnificent urban views, this block of Hyde Street real estate was as expensive as any in San Francisco. And 2152, across the street, was typical of Nob Hill architecture: a brick and frame and stucco building that was divided into either apartments or flats, probably condominiums. The building was about fifty years old, Hastings judged, doubtless as sound as the rock of Nob Hill itself. Probable value: at least two million dollars.

Could Meredith have lived in this building?

Did the man she feared live there?

As he walked across the street, Hastings realized that he could be making a mistake—one of those mistakes that police-men only make once. Meredith had been frightened. She'd been in a relationship she'd wanted to get out of but couldn't. It was possible that Meredith had been killed by her lover. And her lover could reside at 2152 Hyde Street, just across the street.

It was also possible, therefore, that Hastings, without back-up, might be about to ring an odds-on murder suspect's doorbell. It was a rookie's mistake. A dumb rookie's mistake.

Requiring, therefore, that he stop. Look. Listen.

Standing in the building's entryway, he looked at the polished brass nameplates, each with its own buzzer. There were three names: "C. L. Persse," on the first floor, "W. & A. Cowperth-waite," on the second floor—and "M. Powell," on the third floor.

Three Nob Hill flats, each with a a world-class view of the bay. To rent, maybe three thousand dollars a month. If they were condos, the price for each unit might be almost a million dollars.

What had she done to make it from Thirty-ninth Avenue to the top of Nob Hill? How many nights had it taken, on her back?

He turned to the glass door and looked into the foyer. There was a narrow marble table with a bowl of flowers, and two gilded metal chairs placed at either end of the table. He saw three matching doors, one of them with a small round window, an elevator door. Another door would lead to the garage, and another to an interior staircase. The wall paneling, the carpeting, everything translated into money. Lots of money.

He tried to twist the polished brass doorknob, unsuccessfully. He pressed the illuminated bell button beside "M. Powell." He waited, tried again. Then, leaning closer to a perforated brass speaker disc, he pressed the Cowperthwaites' button. The Cowperthwaites weren't answering. Were they both working, bringing home enough money each month to make the rent? Were they at a museum, lunching at an upscale restaurant? He tried "Persse," also unsuccessfully. There was no service door; the trash doubtless came out through the garage, which would require an electronic opener to operate from the outside.

The regulations governing the situation were clear: call the DA, who would call a judge, who would issue a search warrant. Then call a locksmith. Elapsed time, probably eighteen hours. Minimum.

Or he could return to his car, call Communications, tell them to contact a cooperative locksmith, who, in consideration of a triple fee, would arrive within an hour. Meanwhile, he would sit in his car and watch the door of 2152 Hyde Street.


4:00 P.M. "When you get it open," Hastings said to the locksmith, "I want you to keep the door latched." He spoke softly, cautiously. "Do you understand what I mean? I want you to keep it closed. Then I want you to leave. Get in the elevator, and go downstairs, and get in your truck and leave. Understand?"

The locksmith was a lady: young, well built, quick-moving, self-assured. She looked at him with dark, lively eyes.

"Is this—you know—cops and robbers? The real thing?" Her voice, too, was low.

"It's called being smart."

"Gotcha." She turned her attention to the lock and began working. Moments later, with a small flourish, she turned the knob, carefully tested the closure, and nodded.

"Piece of cake," she said.

He tested the latch for himself, then stepped back, jacket unbuttoned, hand on the butt of his service revolver. "Okay," he whispered, moving his head toward the elevator. "Thanks. Go. Tell your boss to send the bill to my attention." As he spoke, he looked up and down the silent, elegantly furnished hallway.

"I *am* the boss."

"Congratulations."

"Thanks, Lieutenant." She handed over several cards. "Hang on to those, will you?"

"I will. Incidentally, next time you're on a police job, bring rubber gloves, okay?"

"Right." Jauntily she closed her toolbox, hefted it, and strode to the elevator, which still stood open. Her blue jeans were tight enough to capture a pleasing, provocative play of buttocks and thighs. Somehow the spectacle was a wistful one. Ten years ago he might have made a move on her.

Slowly, carefully, he pushed the door open. Inside, he saw a hallway. He stepped quickly inside, closed the door, shot the bolt. Then, revolver in hand, he went through the apartment, opening every door, even looking under the bed. Satisfied, he holstered the revolver and reentered the short interior hallway. If the flat gave evidence that she'd shared it with a man, he would take a quick look and then leave. In the ghetto, entering without a warrant wasn't a problem. But the rich, he'd learned, called their lawyers.

The short hallway led to a large living room that spanned the full width of the building, probably twenty-five feet. A floor-to-ceiling window dominated the far wall.

Meredith's living room . . .

He stood still in the doorway, trying for a feel of the place. It was an off-white room: off-white walls, off-white woodwork, off-white wool carpeting, wall to wall. The furniture was simple: two long, low, squared-off sofas upholstered in nubby, natural wool, two matching chairs, a large round coffee table with an inch-thick glass top set on a simple criss-crossed brass frame. A basketball-size rock crystal was placed in the center of the table. Magazines were arranged in a studied fan on the table: a fashion magazine and three others, all glossy. Built beside a fireplace that obviously wasn't used, high walnut shelves dominated the wall opposite the view window. Stereo equipment, an expensive TV, a VCR, and a large collection of records and tapes took up most of the shelves. The books were either hardback popular novels or large, expensive art books. The novels looked as if they might have been read; the art books didn't. Like most San Francisco real estate, the house was built on a narrow twenty-five-foot lot, attached on two sides. The huge window, facing west, was the only source of light in the living room. The north and south walls, floor to ceiling, were hung with a breathtaking collection of modern paintings, most of them abstract. Primitive wood and stone statues were arranged on a low dais that had been placed in front of the window. A higher dais held a five-foot sculpture: pieces of black-scaled metal, rough-welded into what could have been the abstract of a huge praying mantis.

Could this be Meredith Powell's living room? Had the girl from Thirty-ninth Avenue, the daughter of a beer-bellied plumber, chosen this sculpture, these paintings? Where were the odd bits of clutter that revealed so much: the scattered newspapers, the coffee mug, used ashtrays, a half-done crossword puzzle, worn paperbacks, a well-thumbed TV guide? Where was the evidence that she'd really lived here?

Three rosewood drawers were built into the bookshelves. Gingerly he opened each drawer in turn. One of the drawers was empty, a second contained tape cleaning equipment, the third contained a miscellaneous collection of pencils, paid bills, a few coupons, a wristwatch that didn't work, a necklace with a broken clasp—and, finally, a TV guide. Perhaps, then, this flat had really been home for Meredith. Perhaps she was one of those people who passed through life without leaving deep footprints.

Like the living room, the dining room was furnished with sterile, high-styled tables and chairs that seemed calculated to show off the paintings and outsize collages that covered the walls. Two French doors opened on a miniature Japanese garden that had been planted in part of a large airshaft.

The kitchen was a marvel of upscale cabinetry and high-tech equipment, all of it set off with natural wood cabinets and burnished copper and brass utensils. The kitchen, too, looked out on the airshaft, really a central court. In the sink, a coffee mug, a wineglass, an earthenware dish, and a plate were filled with cloudy water.

He stepped to the refrigerator, opened one of the two doors. Refrigerators, he'd discovered, could be revealing; he'd once found a severed hand in a meat tray. But there were no surprises in Meredith's refrigerator: two bottles of white wine, an opened carton of milk, some leftovers, all neatly stored and covered.

Like the kitchen, the bathroom was high tech. Unlike most homicide victims, Meredith had been neat and clean. He looked in the shower. She'd left her flowered shower cap on the shower head. He looked in the medicine cabinet. One of the shelves held bottles and vials of prescription drugs. The labels meant nothing. But, sum-totaled, the collection seemed about average, suggesting that she'd been in good health. The contents of other bathroom cabinets were also predictable: towels, soaps, perfumes, Tampax, toilet paper, several boxes of Kleenex. When he'd first gotten out of the academy, years ago, he'd felt guilty prying among a victim's personal effects. That feeling of guilt had slowly dissipated—until now.

A small mirrored dressing room adjoined the bathroom and revealed nothing of particular interest. A large hall closet contained several coats, a vacuum cleaner and cleaning equipment, suitcases, boxes, a long yellow rain parka, two pairs of expensive boots.

So it was in the last room, Meredith's bedroom, that he must find what he needed: names, addresses, check stubs, pictures, diaries, ticket stubs, a safe-deposit key, mementos from childhood—all the bits and pieces that, fitted together, might tell him who murdered Meredith Powell.

The east wall of the bedroom was glass, overlooking a deck and a garden beyond. There was a king-size bed, two small armchairs, a vanity table and chair, two small bedside bureaus with crystal lamps, two low chests of drawers and a desk. Except for the door, the west wall was one large wardrobe closet, its sliding doors mirrored. All of the furniture appeared to be either genuine antique or expensive reproductions: fine woods intricately carved, some naturally burnished, some painted and glazed. To furnish this one room, Hastings knew, had cost more than most families spent furnishing their entire home.

Because the overcast sky was darkening, he flipped a switch beside the door that lit an overhead crystal candelabra. When he slid open one door of a wardrobe, a light came on inside. Predictably, there were racks of expensive clothes and shoes. Drawers held blouses, underwear, stockings, handbags, accessories. One of the two high shelves was stacked with fancy boxes. He would remember those boxes, if it became necessary to return. One of them, probably a small box in the back, could be a detective's treasure trove.

As he'd done in the living room, Hastings stood still for a moment, absorbing the feel of the room that, more than the others, should tell him something. Had Meredith been happy here? Sad? When she'd made love in this bed, had she cried out in ecstasy? Had the man she feared so much stood right here? He surveyed the paintings, which were softer, more pastel than her other paintings. Still, he was somehow unable to match the art to the woman. He walked to the small glass-topped vanity table. Beneath the glass he saw a cluster of a half-dozen faded snapshots. The light from the chandelier was too dim to make out the faces. He switched on one of the bedside lamps—and felt himself suddenly go hollow at his center. There it was: a picture of Meredith and Kevin, she about ten years old, he about sixteen, both of them squinting into the sun. The picture had been taken in the driveway of their home; he could recognize the house in the background. The picture was clear enough to reveal that, yes, the paint on the garage door was peeling. Another picture showed a smiling Meredith, all grown up, in her stewardess uniform. Legs crossed in a shy, self-conscious cheesecake pose, she was sitting on a low stone wall with palm trees in the background.

There was a picture of Meredith in a cap and gown, Meredith posing with someone who could have been Willie Nelson—

—and Meredith, a child, with her mother and father. Except for their clothes, both of them dressed up, her parents were just as he remembered them: the timid, mousy mother, the big, bluff father boldly smiling full face into the camera, his fedora pushed jauntily back on his head. One of his hands rested on Meredith's shoulder.

Aware that he'd been standing very still, aware of the pull he felt confronting the picture, he let one final beat pass. Then he began systematically going through the drawers of both the vanity and the small writing desk. The two top drawers of the desk yielded what he'd been hoping to find: a collection of check stubs, a bank statement, an address book, a few bills, a leather-bound notebook with a gold Cross pen attached, a key ring with more than a dozen keys, probably spares. Sorting through the keys, he saw a safe-deposit key. He took a plastic evidence bag from an inside pocket, filled the bag with everything but the keys, and went to the flat's door. Yes, one of the keys fitted. Satisfied, he locked the door and went to the interior stairs.

**4:20 P.M.** Hastings pressed the doorbell button for the third time, listened at the door of the second-floor flat, then slipped his card with its handwritten "Call me, please" message between the door and the frame. Later he would send someone back to interrogate the Cowperthwaites. He took the stairs to the first floor. On the second press of the "C. L. Persse" button, the door came quickly open to reveal a teenage boy, tall, slim, blond, clear blue eyes, improbably handsome. Here was the prototypical California golden boy: plainly overprivileged, completely at ease inside his khakis, his scuffed white running shoes, and his pale-blue sweater that was probably cashmere.

But, overprivileged or not, the youth's eyes widened as he looked at the gold inspector's shield held in the palm of Hastings's hand.

"I'm Lieutenant Frank Hastings. I need some information."

"Ah—" He looked at the badge, swallowed, finally met Hastings's gaze. "A lieutenant? Really?"

Hastings nodded. "Really. If you've got a few minutes—" He advanced a half step, looking past the subject. "It's about Meredith Powell, on the third floor. It won't take long."

"Oh. Well. Sure." Hastily the boy stepped back, gestured. "Sure. Come on in."

The flat's living-room area was identical to Meredith's, but the feeling of the room was dramatically different. This room was home to a family—people who left tracks, people who made messes. As they sat facing each other across a cluttered coffee table, Hastings put the evidence bag on the floor beneath the table, then took out his notebook and ballpoint pen.

"What's your name, please?"

"It's Lee. Leland, really. Leland Persse."

"Age?"

"Sixteen."

"How long have you lived here, Lee?"

"It's been—let's see. Three years. We moved here when I started the ninth grade."

"You and your parents live here."

"Right."

"This flat must have two bedrooms, then."

Persse nodded. "Right. The other two have one bedroom. Our rear bedroom makes a deck for the people upstairs."

"Where're your parents now?"

"They're both at work, should be home in maybe an hour."

"I smell something cooking." Hastings smiled.

Nervously Leland Persse returned the smile, which quickly faded. "I cook dinner most nights. That's the deal."

"What're you having? I'm just curious."

"It's stew, really. Stew and salad." The smile returned. "I put some red wine in it, though, and call it ragout."

Hastings nodded appreciatively, then allowed his own smile to fade. Time for business.

"Did—" He caught himself. "Do you know Meredith Powell, on the third floor?"

"Well—" With the single word, caution clouded the vivid blue eyes, momentarily tugged at the easygoing, all-American musculature of the face.

Caution?

Why?

"Well—" Lee Persse swallowed. "Well, I don't *know* her, exactly. I mean, we—we've talked a few times, like that."

Eyeing Persse thoughtfully, Hastings allowed a long moment of silence to pass. Because silence, he'd discovered—a hard, watchful silence—could often reveal more than a dozen questions.

But Persse's momentary facial spasm, origin unknown, passed as suddenly as it had come. Requiring, therefore, more probing.

"How long has she lived here, would you say?"

"Oh—" Persse calculated. "Maybe two years."

"You say you talked to her?"

Persse shrugged. "A few times. Six, seven times, maybe."

Hastings nodded, decided to let another moment of silence pass. Then: "I've just come from her flat, Lee. Have you ever been up there? In her flat?"

"No—" The denial came quickly. A single beat too quickly. "No, I've never seen her place, never been inside, up there."

"You talked—where—in the hallway? The lobby?"

Again the shrug, a disclaimer. "Yeah, the lobby. And out in front, sometimes."

"What kind of a neighbor is she, would you say?"

Persse frowned. "How do you mean?"

"Did she give wild parties, cause any trouble? Were there lots of people coming and going in her place, would you say?"

The youth shook his head decisively. "No—no. She's real quiet. You'd never know she's up there. Just—you know—comes and goes, minds her own business."

"Did—does she keep regular hours?"

The puzzled frown returned. "I'm not—"

"Does she come and go at regular times? As if she were going to a job, for instance?"

Persse shook his head. "No, I don't think she works. I'd be surprised if she works. She's—" He shrugged: a teenager, searching for the phrase. "She's too—too classy, for that. Too elegant. You know?"

"Yes—" Spontaneously regretful, Hastings sighed. Lee Persse had summed it up: Meredith had been too classy, too elegant, for her own good.

"What about visitors?"

Persse shook his head. "I can't ever remember that she had a visitor, not that I saw, anyhow."

"When was the last time you talked to her?"

"Oh—a week ago, maybe. Something like that."

"When was the last time you saw her, whether or not you talked to her?"

"Well—" Another moment of calculation. "Well, just seeing her, not talking, like you said, that would've been last night."

"Last night?" Hastings felt his heartbeat quicken. It was a rookie's reaction, a random flash from the past: other interrogations, in other rooms. "When, last night?"

"Oh, maybe nine o'clock, like that. Maybe a little later, but not much."

"What were the circumstances?" As he spoke, he jotted down 9 P.M., 9:30, *Leland Persse.*

"She was just coming out of the garage."

"Driving, you mean?"

Persse nodded. "Right."

"What kind of a car does she drive?"

"It's a Mercedes Three-eighty SL." Persse sighed gently: the male teenager, infatuated with cars. "It's silver. Beautiful."

Writing in the notebook, Hastings felt the rookie's rush return. In San Francisco, there were probably less than a hundred 380 SL owners.

"Can you tell me anything about her?" Hastings asked. "How was she dressed last night?"

"It was too dark to tell. I could just see her head."

"Was she alone?"

"Right. Alone."

"Did you speak to her? Wave to her?"

"No. I was in a car, with a couple of friends. We were going down to Tower Records, and we were just taking off. But—" A thoughtful pause. Then: "But there *was* something that happened last night."

99

"What was that?" Asking the question, Hastings was conscious of a small, significant visceral shift.

"Well, after we went down to Tower and got a couple of CDs, we went to this girl's house—Christine Hejanian—to play them. They've got a big room over their garage that's all wired for sound and everything. And a couple of other people came by, and everything, until it was kind of a party. So I didn't get home until about one o'clock. That's when he dropped me off—Jack Thiede, he was driving, had his mother's car. So anyhow—" Persse paused, for breath. "Anyhow, we were parked across the street and down a few houses, talking. I was sitting in the front seat. And I saw her Mercedes come up the hill and turn into the garage. And I remember thinking that it was strange, how it happened. I mean, usually, whenever anyone goes into the garage, he punches the electronic door opener when he's maybe fifty feet away, you know. The door opens, and whoever it is drives inside, no waiting. But last night she pulled into the driveway, and she just sat there, nothing happening. I guess she was having trouble with her opener, or something. Or maybe there was someone else in the car, and they were talking. But anyhow, finally the door came up, and she drove inside."

"Are you sure she was driving? Did you recognize her?"

"No. I couldn't see into the car. But I wondered, like I said, whether she had someone with her."

"Why do you say that?"

"Well, there's a door that goes from the garage into the building, right?"

"I'll take your word for it."

"Yeah. Well, there is. Which is what she did. Went into the foyer and took the elevator up, I guess. But then, maybe a minute or two later, the garage door came up again. And a guy came out."

"A guy?"

Persse nodded.

"Did you get a look at him? A good look?"

"No. He turned left and walked down Hyde, toward Filbert. We were parked at the corner of Greenwich. There's a fireplug there, and we were just—"

"Let's get back to this man. Describe him as much as you can. Was he young? Old? Fat? Skinny?"

"Well, he was slim. Maybe a hundred sixty, something like that. And he moved like he was young. But that's about all I could tell. See, we were parked at the corner, and it was real dark, and—"

"How was he dressed?"

"Oh—" Persse shrugged. "A jacket and pants, like that. He was bareheaded. I remember that, because it was raining, and I remember thinking he'd get wet if he walked far without a hat."

"Was his hair dark or light?"

"Dark."

"What time was this, that you saw him?"

"Probably about twelve-thirty, maybe one o'clock."

"That's late," Hastings said. "For someone in school, that's late."

"Yeah—well—" Persse shrugged. "It doesn't happen very often."

"How're your grades? Pretty good?"

"B average," Persse answered promptly. "I'm going to Yale."

Hastings nodded, pocketed the notebook and pen, and rose. "Okay, Lee, thanks a lot. You'll be here, I assume, if we need to talk to you again."

Instantly Persse's face tightened. Another shadow crossed behind his clear blue eyes.

Signifying what? Revealing what?

"Wh—" Persse licked at his lips. "What's it all about, anyhow? I mean, that sounds pretty heavy, when you tell me to, you know, don't leave town, or anything."

With both of them on their feet, facing each other, Hastings let a long, silent beat pass as he stared at Lee Persse. Then, speaking very quietly, Hastings said, "What it's all about is that Meredith Powell died last night. Someone killed her."

"Oh, no." As if to deny it, push back the truth, Persse raised his hands, palms forward. "Oh, God. No."

**4:45 P.M.** Aware that he was holding his breath, Hastings opened the door and stepped into the half-light of the garage—

—and saw it, parked along the far wall: a silver Mercedes roadster. Probable value: forty, fifty thousand dollars.

A condo in one of the city's most expensive neighborhoods, original paintings and sculpture, a fifty-thousand-dollar car. No marriage license, no visible means of support. She'd been thirty-six. She'd gone from a rented house in the Sunset District to a condo on Nob Hill—and then to a thicket in Golden Gate Park, finally to a drawer in the morgue, in thirty-six years. Born naked into the world, died naked, tossed beside the roadside.

He walked to the car, used a handkerchief to try the driver's door. It swung open; the interior lights came on. He leaned inside, looked at the floor in front. Except for a sprinkling of debris, there was nothing. Carefully he pushed the driver's seat forward. Nothing, on the floor, or the backseat, or the package shelf. He returned the seat to its upright position and saw the electronic wand that controlled the garage door. After a moment's thought, he noted the position of the OPEN button, then folded the wand in his handkerchief. He swung the car door shut, went to the trunk, and found the key on Meredith's ring that opened it. Even in the dim light he could see traces of dirt on the carpeting of the trunk, and dead leaves. He closed the trunk, went to the garage door, and pressed the OPEN button, through the handkerchief. He would find the nearest phone and call Friedman. He would then return to the garage and wait with the car until the lab crew arrived. He would supervise the removal of the car to the lab. He would sign the police seal and see that it was posted on Meredith's door. He would see that the door was padlocked.

Then he would go home. If Ann hadn't started dinner, he would offer to take her out. Just Ann, not her two sons. Over dinner, he would tell Ann about Meredith—about the way Meredith had lived, and about the way she'd died.


**9:15 P.M.** Tonight he would remain aloof, allowing his mind to expand through time and space, counterpointing the babble of the rabble below.

Yes, the babble of the rabble . . .

Had it just occurred to him, this glitzy phrase, this garish little rhyme? Where did the words come from? Where had they gone? Everyone on earth, it was said, had breathed an atom of Julius Caesar's dying breath. Did words likewise live on? Was Caesar's death rattle still extant, somewhere in the void?

No.

Caesar's last exhalation was measurable. Theoretically measurable. Words, though, were lost. Yet soldiers marched and died because of words. Cities burned.

Dead in the dust, dead in the morgue.

Rabble. Babble. Dabble.

Even through the closed door he could hear them at play, the rabble, babbling. Gregory was doing the music, Cynthia the choreography. Food and drink, courtesy of the house. Cocaine courtesy of the culture, catch as catch can.

Decor, courtesy of Charles.

Continuity, courtesy of Charles.

And, last night, resolution courtesy of Charles, that pallid young man who was consumed from within: giant worms, feeding on corruptible flesh. The more Charles consumed, the longer the worms grew, the more insatiable. Just as Charles, babble and rabble, was insatiable.

Sitting in the intricately carved chair, one hand on each of the lion's heads that adorned the arms, he allowed his eyes to close. It was necessary, now, to release his thoughts, let them go free. He must follow where the tendrils of the mind burrowed.

The smaller the tendril, the more dangerous. Because tiny roots found tiny fissures. Then, when roots expanded, the structure could collapse.

Seeking, penetrating, expanding, finally exploding.

Thoughts destroyed. Swords pierced armor. Flesh rotted. Worms wriggled in eye sockets.

Rabble.

Babble.

Dabble.

# FRIDAY
# FEBRUARY 16

**9:20 A.M.** Friedman dropped a file folder on Hastings's desk and sank into the visitor's chair. He unwrapped his first cigar of the day, lit it, and sailed the smoking match into the paper-filled wastebasket, his customary morning sally.

"How's it going?" Friedman asked. "Anything?"

Hastings described Meredith Powell's apartment and detailed his conversation with Lee Persse. Listening, Friedman reclined at his ease, his heavily lidded eyes half closed, his broad, swarthy face expressionless. When Hastings finished, Friedman pointed to a large manila envelope, marked "M. Powell, #N 11659 A, Personal Effects."

"Anything there?" Friedman asked.

"An address book and a checkbook and some keys. The check stubs go back almost a year."

"Ah, check stubs—" Friedman nodded, elaborately sagacious. "Give me a checkbook, and I'll tell you what the subject eats for breakfast—and what he uses for hemorrhoids, too."

"Well—" Hastings pushed the envelope across the desk. "Be my guest. I didn't find a hell of a lot. We'll know more, of course, when we get a warrant to look at the bank records. She wrote checks for about two thousand dollars a month. And there were regular deposits of four thousand a month. Plus four deposits during the year for odd amounts."

As Hastings spoke, Friedman clamped the cigar in his teeth and opened the envelope, spilling out the contents. Squinting, head tilted against the smoke, Friedman found the check record and quickly scanned the entries. "Her expenditures—" Friedman tapped the checkbook with a thick forefinger. "They're for odds and ends. Visa and American Express, mostly. Where's the rent payments, and the mortgage payments, and the car payments, and the insurance?"

"Maybe she owned the condo and the car."

Friedman took the cigar from his mouth, raised his eyes, and studied the other man for a long, thoughtful moment before he said quietly, "Come on, Frank. From everything you tell me— every inference we can make—she was a sensational-looking woman, and some guy was paying her bills." Still eyeing Hastings steadily, Friedman let an uncompromising moment of silence pass. Then he pointed to the file folder he'd brought. "I've made a list of things that I've got in the works. When we get the answers, I figure we'll have a better handle on this thing." He flipped open the folder, consulted a list, and recited: "Who owns the building she lived in? If she rented, who'd she rent from? If she owned a condo, who'd she buy it from? Who's the car registered to—and who paid for it? From what you say, her art collection was worth a bundle. I know a guy who's plugged into the local art scene. Maybe he can identify the artists, or the galleries the paintings came from."

"As long as you're checking—" Hastings reached across the desk for the address book. He opened it, riffled the pages to "P," and pointed to an entry that read simply "Dad (818) 824-4076." "As far as I know, her only living relative was her father. That's a Los Angeles number. I tried it last night, but it's been reassigned. Her father's name was—is—John Powell. Can you check him out?" Hastings spoke crisply, the professional plying his trade. Then, quietly, he added, "Someone should be told. About her death, I mean. So arrangements can be made."

"No problem."

"Tell him I'll meet him at the airport, find him a place to stay."

"Right." Friedman made a note. Then, pointing to the address book, he asked, "What's that look like? Anything?"

Aware that he felt as if he were breaking faith with Meredith, Hastings admitted, "There isn't much. Most of the entries are just single words and phone numbers. Like 'Plumber' and a phone number. Or 'Marge' and a number."

Friedman had put the checkbook aside and was riffling the address book. He sighed, shook his head, closed the address book. He drew reflectively on the cigar before he said, "It's always sad, going through a victim's effects. I mean, usually—" He shrugged, shook his head, sighed again. "Usually there're a few names in the address book, and a few bucks in the bank, and maybe a few snapshots, and that's about it. You tag everything, and write a report, and you ship the body off to the morgue, and that's all there is. The end."

Dropping his eyes, Hastings made no reply. Finally Friedman levered his two hundred and forty pounds out of the chair and picked up his folder and the manila envelope. "I'll get started on this," he said. "I already told the lab to have preliminary reports by early this afternoon. I'll assign Meyers to start checking the numbers in the address book. I'll handle her father, though, try to run him down."

"Yes—" Hastings nodded.

"What about her apartment?" Friedman asked. "Is the lab on that?"

Hastings nodded again. "They're there now. Canelli's with them."

"Canelli called in. I told him to be here about two o'clock. How's that sound, for a meeting?"

"That sounds fine," Hastings answered, his voice dull. Ann had brought home work last night, and her two sons, as usual, had turned dinner at home into a high-volume discussion of sports and rock music. So it hadn't been until they were in bed that he'd been able to tell Ann about Meredith—about how she'd lived, and how she'd died. As he told the story, Ann had touched him gently, with compassion. Feeling the caress, he realized that she was hearing more than just the story of Meredith Powell. They'd talked until almost two o'clock, exchanging childhood stories. Then, gravely, they'd made love. And this morning, they'd—

"—about you?" Friedman was saying. "What're you going to do?"

"When I saw her at Four-fifty Sutter," Hastings said, "she'd just seen a shrink. There're two stubs in her checkbook for checks made out to Dr. Price. And there's a psychiatrist named Price at Four-fifty Sutter, on the same floor with my eye doctor."

"Good." Friedman nodded approvingly. "I talked to the media people yesterday, but there wasn't anything on the TV that I know of, and nothing on the radio. It made the *Sentinel* this morning, on page five. Do you want me to keep after the TV guys? Yesterday there wasn't the Nob Hill angle, the big-money angle—the beautiful lady with her exotic car. If you want to do it, if you think we could show a profit, we could probably get some ink on this. What'd you say—should we trade a couple of crazies confessing for the chance of finding a witness or two?"

Hastings considered, finally nodded. "Sure. Let's do it. Give them the block on Hyde Street. Not the address, just the block. Maybe someone else saw that guy driving her car into the garage and then leaving."

"Right." Friedman waved airily, his accustomed parting gesture. But then, at the door, he turned. "It'll work out. I have an intuition."

"Good."


11:30 A.M. "You understand," Miss Perkins said, "that Dr. Price can only give you a few minutes. He's fitting you in." A thin, fretful woman with anxious eyes and a petulant mouth, Miss Perkins spoke primly, properly.

Hastings nodded. "I understand."

Miss Perkins nodded in return, eyeing the detective covertly as he leafed through a copy of *Sunset*. When she'd pressed him for the reason he wanted to see the doctor, he'd told her only that it was police business involving a patient. When she'd asked for the patient's name, he declined to answer, giving no explanation. Plainly, Miss Perkins concluded, this big, uncommunicative man was accustomed to behaving as if he spoke for the totality of police authority. It was a mentality that was universal among policemen, Miss Perkins suspected, bred in the bone. Or, more accurately, conferred upon graduation from the police academy, the same invitation to arrogance that doctors got, graduating from medical school.

Yet, to be fair, the policeman could be excused for his natural inclination to remain aloof. Like soldiers and fliers and others who shared high-risk professions, *Lancet* had said in a recent article, policemen faced the constant risk of violent death, a factor that both unified them and also estranged them from the general populace. On some beats, Miss Perkins had read, it was war: a remorseless war that never ended. Result: Statistically, only dentists had a higher suicide rate than policemen. At least, according to *Lancet*.

**11:45 A.M.** *"Murdered?"* As he said it, Price's face puckered disapprovingly, as if Hastings had committed an unforgivable faux pas. The psychiatrist was a small, spare man, almost totally bald, with a narrow, pinched face, a permanently pursed mouth, and small, skeptical eyes. He was dressed in an expensively cut three-piece suit, a stiff white collar, a paisley printed red silk tie, and matching breast pocket handkerchief. "When?"

"It happened sometime Wednesday night. She was discovered yesterday morning, in Golden Gate Park. We're still waiting for the autopsy results, but it seems pretty obvious that she was strangled. And then—" Suddenly, inexplicably, his throat closed. "Then her body was dumped in the park."

"That's—" Price's tongue tip circled the tightly compressed oval of his lips. Seated in a black leather swivel chair behind an elegant walnut and rosewood desk, Price spread both hands on the polished wooden surface, as if to brace himself. Plainly Price was unwilling—or unable—to continue without first mastering his emotions. "That's incredible." Now he frowned. "Wednesday night, did you say?"

Watching the other man, Hastings nodded. "That's right."

Now Price let his impersonal eyes lose focus as he allowed a long moment of calculating silence to pass. Then, decisively refocusing his eyes on the man across the desk, Price spoke crisply, coldly. "So what is it that I can do for you, Lieutenant?"

"You probably knew more about Meredith Powell—more about her life, and her problems—than anyone else."

"Oh?" It was a cautious response. He let a moment of impersonal silence pass. Then: "Why do you say that?"

"Because I knew her, too. We grew up together."

"You did?" In spite of himself, Price spoke spontaneously, visibly surprised. "Really?"

Allowing a slow, deliberate beat to pass, matching his interrogation-room expertise against Price's bag of psychiatric tricks, Hastings held the other man's eyes with his.

"I had lunch with her on Tuesday, Mr. Price." The substitution of "Mister" for "Doctor" was carefully calculated.

The vexed frown returned, concealing the other man's surprise, perhaps his discomfort. "You had lunch?"

"Right."

Once again letting his eyes lose focus, Price sat silently, still with his hands placed flat on the desk, still very erect in the expensive black leather chair. Finally, after what could have been a reluctant decision, he said, "I saw her on Tuesday." Another pause. Then, warily, Price asked, "Did she tell you?"

"Yes, sir, she did. That's why I'm here."

The frosty frown returned. The eyes narrowed, then steadied. "I'm afraid I don't follow you, Lieutenant."

"I think," Hastings said, "that Meredith was involved with a man who frightened her. And in this business, when a woman's killed like Meredith was killed, we look for her husband, or her lover. That's why I'm here. I'm looking for a name."

"Well, in that case, Lieutenant, I'm afraid you're wasting your time." As he spoke, Price drew back a gleaming white cuff, consulted a gleaming gold watch.

"Did Meredith tell you about the affair she was having?"

"Meredith told me a lot of things," Price answered curtly. "All of them confidential. Now if you'll excuse me, Lieutenant, there's a patient waiting."

Making no move to rise, Hastings said, "I can understand why you wouldn't want to divulge information about someone who's still living. But Meredith Powell's dead. And I intend to do everything I can to find out who killed her."

"Does that include causing me to screw up my entire patient schedule, Lieutenant?"

"No, sir, it doesn't. I'll gladly come back. Just tell me when."

"I'll call you."

"When?"

"Today. This afternoon."

Hastings rose, placed his card squarely in the center of the impressive desk. "If I don't hear from you, you'll be hearing from me."

Price's only response was a precisely measured inclination of his bald head.


**2:10 P.M.** Hastings pushed open the door marked HOMICIDE and entered the squadroom. He glanced across the room, and through the glass partition saw Friedman talking on the phone in his own office. Seated at one of the squadroom desks, Canelli smiled and lifted his hand, a characteristically tentative wave of greeting. In response, Hastings inclined his head in the direction of his office, at the opposite end of the hallway from Friedman's. Canelli nodded and began pawing through the papers that littered his desk. As Hastings entered the hallway he caught Friedman's eye. Friedman nodded, held up two fingers. Hastings entered his own office, hung up his tan gabardine raincoat, then turned to his desk and his "in" basket. Sorting through the interrogation reports and surveillance reports, he found a personal letter: a blue envelope, addressed in longhand to him. The handwriting was small, slightly uneven. The return address was 2152 Hyde Street.

She'd written him a letter.

Meredith had written him a letter. The postmark was yesterday—the day her body had been discovered.

As he held the letter flat on his desk and slit it open, the image of his grandmother in her coffin returned, followed by the image of her collection of Dresden figurines. His mother had inherited the collection. She'd arranged the figurines on the top of her dresser. The first time he'd taken one of the small figurines in his hand, he'd felt as if his grandmother was touching him from beyond the grave.

Mindful of possible fingerprints, he carefully withdrew a single sheet of matching blue stationery. He opened the folded sheet, edged in white.

*Dear Frank,*

*It was wonderful to have lunch with you yesterday, a wonderful surprise.*

*Could we do it again, Frank? Could we have lunch again next Tuesday, same place, same time?*

*I told you so much about myself, more than I'd intended to tell, really. I know it was probably boring for you, considering your work.*

*But now, Frank, I'd like to tell you more. Because I'm
scared, Frank. I'm very scared. And you're the only person I
feel that I can tell about it.*
    *Please call me, Frank. I don't have an answering ma-
chine, so if I don't hear from you, then I'll call you.*
                                                Sincerely,
                                                Meredith

    The handwriting had an unformed, uneven, uncertain qual-
ity—just as Meredith had been unformed and uncertain.
    He read it again—and again. Then he slipped the envelope
and the opened letter into a clear plastic evidence bag. He sealed
the bag, dated the seal, and signed it.
    *I'm very scared.*
    She should have called him. If she'd called him, she might
still be alive. He could have helped. If she'd given him a name,
he could have helped her. A knock on a door, a flash of the
badge, the threat of close surveillance, and she might still be
alive.
    Raising his eyes, he saw Friedman coming down the hallway
from his office. Canelli was coming from the squadroom. They
entered his office, took seats, placed matching manila folders on
Hastings's desk as he handed the letter in its plastic bag to
Friedman. While Friedman read, Hastings looked at the two
men. Physically, they were almost a match. Both weighed at least
two hundred thirty, not all of it muscle. Their features were
remarkably similar: dark eyes, faces broad and swarthy. Their hair
was thick, Canelli's dark, Friedman's graying. Both men needed
haircuts.
    But the men behind the faces were utterly different. Canelli
was the squadroom innocent; Friedman was Homicide's gadfly,
the chessmaster, the eternal devil's advocate. Canelli's eyes were
perpetually anxious, in constant search of approval. Friedman's
eyes were inscrutable. Canelli's emotions were always visible;
Friedman's were deeply buried.

In sympathy, Friedman silently shook his head, handed the note to Canelli. "Police work is bad enough," Friedman said quietly, "without prepackaged guilt."

As Canelli read the letter, his brow furrowed. When he finished, he looked at Hastings, spoke with deep feeling. "Jeez, Lieutenant—" Canelli waved the evidence bag helplessly. "Jeez, that's terrible. It came just a day too late, I guess."

Hastings made no response, but Friedman turned to Canelli, his favorite satirical target. "Canelli," he said, "you've done it again."

"Done what, Lieutenant?"

"You've stated the obvious."

"Oh. Well—" Canelli broke off, frowned, began struggling to frame a reply.

"So what've we got?" Hastings spoke brusquely, his habitual first line of defense. "How about the lab and the coroner?" He pointed to Friedman's folder.

"Well," Friedman said, putting on a pair of heavy black-rimmed reading glasses and opening the folder. "There isn't exactly a plethora. But there's something, at least. And, for sure, everyone's rushed this thing through." He riffled the reports, finally found the one he sought. "She died of asphyxia. She was strangled, probably with bare hands." As he spoke, he unconsciously lapsed into departmental officialese, concisely reciting: "From body temperature, not the contents of the stomach, they figure she'd been dead for at least eight hours, maybe more like ten, before she was discovered."

Hearing "contents of the stomach," a standard phrase, Hastings couldn't shut out the image of Meredith on the coroner's stainless-steel table, her stomach opened by a scalpel that could cause no pain.

"There weren't any other traumas to the body," Friedman continued, "except for the bruises at her throat. There was, ah—" A momentary pause. Then, carefully objective, he said, "There was semen present." As he said it, he kept his gaze resolutely focused on the report. "The coroner figures she probably died soon after the, ah, semen entered her body. We'll send the sample to the FBI, and try for a DNA profile. That'll take awhile, though." He cleared his throat, riffled more pages. "That's about all the coroner's autopsy shows. Their report from the scene—" He adjusted his glasses. "They don't think she was killed where she was found, which pretty much makes it unanimous. As for the lab reports, there's a little more, since yesterday. In fact, they turned up a couple of surprises." More papers were shuffled, more notes were consulted. Watching the other man, drawing on the years they'd worked together, Hastings suspected that, yes, Friedman was building the suspense, his favorite game.

"The lab found," Friedman said, "that tire marks at the scene match the tire marks of her car."

Excited, playing his straight man's role, Canelli sat up straighter. "No kidding?"

Plainly pleased with the on-cue reaction, Friedman gravely nodded. "No kidding, Canelli. Plus they found traces of both feces and urine in the trunk. Indicating, it seems to me—" Once more, Friedman took refuge in objective officialese. "It seems to me that she was wrapped in something, probably, and she was carried in the trunk of her car to the park, where she was dumped. I say that because, if she wasn't wrapped in something, there would've been more waste matter present in the trunk."

"So if we find the guy," Canelli said eagerly, "and he left prints in the car, and seeing that we can put the car at the scene, and if the guy's blood type fits the semen, and if the feces and urine are a match with the victim's blood type, then we're home free."

"Very good, Canelli." Elaborately Friedman nodded encouragement. "Very good indeed."

"And her clothes and effects were probably dumped some-where," Canelli continued, "maybe along with whatever it was she was wrapped in when she was put in the trunk."

"I think you've got it, Canelli. I really think you've got it."

Friedman's voice was gently ironic. Leaving Canelli, as always, unsure of Friedman's true meaning.

"What about the rest of it?" Hastings asked, speaking to Friedman.

"I got a current address for her father from the Social Security people. And a phone number, too." Friedman looked at Hastings. "Do you want me to contact him?"

"No. I'll do it."

"Right." Friedman wrote on a sheet of notepaper and passed it across the desk. "I made a fake phone call and got the feeling that the phone was in the hallway, not in John Powell's apartment. You might want to keep that in mind."

"I will. Anything else? Printouts?"

"Not much yet," Friedman answered. "I've got a request in to get her bank records and hopefully gain access to her safe-deposit box. I've got Ferguson working on the ownership of her apartment, or condo, or whatever it is. He should have something pretty soon. I checked out the car, which was registered to her. Consolidated Casualty carries the insurance, according to the paper in the glove compartment, and I'm trying to find out whether the policy was in her name. So far, I've got zero. I checked her out in Los Angeles." Once more Friedman adjusted his reading glasses, consulted his notes. "Apparently she was a perfectly respectable citizen. Nothing but parking tickets, good credit, all that stuff. However, ten years ago, approximately, she married Gary Blake, who had—has, I guess—a string of restaurants and bars, a real high roller, a real swinger." Friedman consulted his notes. "He's had three drunk driving convictions, and he's been sued a total of five times. There was an assault charge, too, that was dropped. And a paternity suit, also dropped."

Canelli shook his head sympathetically. "It sure sounds like she picked a shitheel."

Again, Friedman studied Canelli for a long, quizzical moment before he finally nodded, mock-sagaciously. "Yes, Canelli," he said, "I guess you could say that."

Canelli nodded tentatively, then smiled tentatively.

"What about you, Canelli?" Hastings asked. "Anything?"

"Oh. Yeah." Always uncomfortable in the company of both his commanding officers, Canelli sat up straighter. First he frowned, then shrugged, then spread his hands, palms up. "Well, there were three of us, out at Golden Gate Park. We stayed there all day, asking around. Except for a couple of places where some homeless were holed up, we didn't come up with anything. If we got more TV coverage and more in the newspapers, I bet that'd help. I mean—you know—if anyone saw anything, they were probably neckers, something like that. So the only way we'd know, probably, was if they—you know—came forward. But, just in case, I left Phil Toll out there till midnight last night. But he's in court this morning. So I haven't heard anything. Except that I think I'd've heard from him. You know—a message, or something—if he'd turned up anything. So—" Canelli spread his hands again. "So I didn't get much."

"Someone, though, phoned us," Hastings said. "Whoever found her phoned. Anonymously. Him, we want to interrogate."

"Yeah, well, I'll sure keep at it, Lieutenant."

"What about her residence? Anything? More witnesses?"

"Well," Canelli said, "I tried there last night. I took Asher with me, and we talked to everyone in the building, including that kid you talked to, Lieutenant." He consulted his notes. "Lee Persse. And everyone seemed to agree, pretty much. She was quiet, kept pretty much to herself. They all agreed she came and went pretty much at random, so she probably didn't work. I asked about visitors, naturally, and a couple of them agreed that, a few times, a middle-age guy in an expensive car came to visit. But then, of course, nobody could agree on what the guy really looked like, or what kind of a car he drove, or anything. You know—" Canelli shook his head, heaved a dolorous sigh. "You know, the usual. I'll keep trying, of course. But so far I don't know whether the guy was fat or skinny, or bald, or whatever. Just middle age, whatever that means."

"So Lee Persse's statement is all we've got that a young, dark-haired guy left the garage after she drove in on Wednesday night."

"Afraid so, Lieutenant." Canelli spoke regretfully, apologetically.

Friedman turned to Hastings. "This kid—Lee Persse—did he see how many people were in her car?"

"No. I don't even think he was sure she was driving."

"I think that's right," Canelli offered. "I took Lee Persse down to the street and had him show me where he was parked. That was about nine o'clock last night. I had two kids, in fact— Lee Persse and Jack Thiede, who was there Wednesday, with Persse. We sat in my car, the three of us, just like they did Wednesday night. Persse was sitting in the passenger's seat, in front. And the other kid—Thiede—he was driving, Wednesday, so he sat in the driver's seat. I sat in back, like the third kid did. So then I had Asher drive toward us and turn into the driveway, like she did Wednesday, going into the garage. Asher has a Honda, which is about the same height as her Mercedes, so the angles were just about the same. And it was nine o'clock—dark, like it was Wednesday, but not raining. But anyhow—" Canelli drew a breath. "Anyhow, all we could make out was that there was someone driving, that was it. I mean, if it was raining, she'd sure have her windows up, which Asher had. And with the windows up, if there'd been a passenger, we couldn't've seen him. So—" He spread his hands. "So it was all pretty much a zero, I guess you'd say."

"How long was it," Friedman asked, "between the time she entered the garage and the time this guy came out?" He looked at Hastings.

"The impression I got from Persse," Hastings said, "was that it was just a little while, maybe two minutes." He looked at Canelli, who nodded.

"Because I'm wondering," Friedman mused, "whether she might've been strangled inside the garage. Maybe it was—you know—a sex thing. They entered the garage together, in her car. They started to fool around, whatever. She denied him, and he lost control. God knows, it's a standard scenario, especially if they were drinking."

"Or maybe he was waiting for her inside the garage," Canelli offered. "Maybe it was robbery, which would account for her missing effects."

"Or he could've been outside," Hastings speculated. "He could've gone in with the car, when the garage door went up. He could've been on the far side of her car, so Persse wouldn't've seen him going in. He killed her, and took her purse, and left."

Slowly, with the elaborate, long-suffering forbearance of a schoolmaster dealing with recalcitrant students, Friedman shook his head. "No, no, it wasn't robbery. You've got it all wrong. Sex, maybe. But not robbery."

Annoyed, Hastings said, "Robbery *and* sex, then. *That's* a standard scenario, too."

"If it happened within two minutes after she entered the garage," Friedman countered, "then it sure couldn't've been sex. Christ, sex takes time."

"Not for a rapist."

"And strangulation takes time, too," Friedman pressed.

Canelli was nodding, saying speculatively "That's true."

"Then there's the whole question of what happened next, after the murderer left," Friedman said. "If we assume that she was murdered inside the garage, by either a rapist or a thief, or both, and if we assume that he took off, like Persse says, and if we assume that she was put in the trunk of her car and taken to the park, then the question is, why would the murderer come back after leaving on foot? It doesn't make sense."

Canelli nodded again. "That's true, Lieutenant. I was thinking about that myself."

In the short silence that followed, the three men speculated. Finally Friedman said, "One problem here is that all we've got is this kid, Persse. We're violating the first rule, if we buy his story without confirmation. Christ, he could've killed her himself. He could've seen her coming in her car, and he could've accosted her inside the garage. I gather he's a good-looking kid. Let's say he'd been drinking, which'd be easy enough to check, probably. Let's say they had something going, Persse and the victim." Friedman threw Hastings a quick glance, acknowledging the other man's sensibilities. But the force of his words was undiluted as Friedman continued: "It's another standard scenario, the teenage stud and the sexy older woman. It's almost a cliché, in fact." He let a beat pass while the other two men considered the possibilities. Then Friedman briskly concluded: "Or he made a move on her, and she wasn't having any. There was a struggle. Next thing, the kid is staring down at her body, wondering what happened. She's dead. He panics. He gets something to wrap her in, drives to the park in her car, and gets rid of the body, which he's stripped. He gets rid of her clothes and purse, maybe in a dumpster. He drives her car home, goes to bed, sleeps it off." He shrugged. "Everything fits."

Hastings shook his head doubtfully. "I got the feeling she was completely intimidated by someone—terrified of him. I just don't see Persse like that."

"She could've had both things going at once," Friedman said. "The way it's beginning to look, the picture I'm getting, some rich guy was—" He hesitated, to choose the least offensive phrase. "He was paying her bills. But he didn't come around much, meaning that she had time on her hands. And right downstairs was this beautiful kid with his smooth, supple body. It's a natural."

"Well," Hastings said, "all we need is a few hairs from his head. If his DNA matches the semen, then we've got something."

He paused, looked at Canelli with questioning eyes. Then: "Come to think of it, though, when I talked to Persse about her, I thought I got a buzz from him. How about you?"

Canelli nodded promptly. "I was just thinking the same thing, Lieutenant. I really was. Except—" Plainly perplexed by a new thought, Canelli frowned. "Except that, if Persse did it, then his buddies are lying, too."

In the silence that followed, they considered the possibilities. Finally Friedman said, "If we keep Persse in mind, which I think we should, we've got to remember that we've got a minor child with rich parents. And rich parents have expensive lawyers." As he spoke, he glanced at his watch, began gathering up his papers. "So why don't you two return to the field, or whatever, while I see what's on the computers. I'm also going to put the arm on the media. What we need now is for people to come forward and tell us what they saw in Golden Gate Park, and also in the twenty-one hundred block of Hyde Street, Wednesday night."

"We'll get some crazies," Canelli said.

"I'd rather have crazies than nothing," Friedman said. "And that's what we've got now. Nothing."

3:40 P.M. As he heard the phone begin to ring, Hastings pulled a notepad closer, and clicked his ballpoint pen.

"Blake Enterprises," a woman's voice said. "This is Charlotte."

"Yes. This is Lieutenant Frank Hastings, with the San Francisco police department. May I speak to Mr. Blake, please?"

A brief pause. Then, abruptly, the voice said, "Someone's already called from your department."

"I know. Lieutenant Friedman called. This is something else."

"Just a moment." The line clicked dead, followed by a long silence. Finally: "Yes. This is Gary Blake." It was a brusque, abrasive voice—a cop hater's voice. "Who's this?"

"This is Lieutenant Frank Hastings, Mr. Blake. I'd like to talk to you about your ex-wife—about her murder."

"I've already talked to someone. And I'm in a meeting. There's nothing I can add to what I said. Nothing at all. You'll have to talk to the other lieutenant. Friedman."

"I've talked to Friedman. I've got two questions that'll take maybe sixty seconds to answer. Now, you can either answer them, or else I'll call up the LAPD and have them send someone to talk to you at your office. That'll take a lot longer than sixty seconds. But it's your choice."

"A tough guy, huh?"

"I'm afraid it goes with the territory, Mr. Blake. It's a tough job."

"Hold on a minute." Once more, abruptly, the line went dead. Then: "All right. Sixty seconds. Go."

"You and Meredith were divorced several years ago."

"Right."

"I want to know how much she got as her end of the divorce settlement."

"That's not public information."

"I can get it, though. It'll take more work—more calls, lawyers and judges, down there. But I can get what I need. Believe it."

"Oh, I believe it, all right. I certainly do believe it."

"Well?"

A short silence. Then: "It came to about a hundred fifty thousand."

"How long ago?"

"Two years. Maybe three. I'm trying to block it out, not remember it."

"Okay. Second question. Someone's got to make burial arrangements. As nearly as I can determine, it's either you or her father. There isn't anyone else."

"Call her father. You want her buried, call her father. Anything else?"

"Nothing else that's official. Would you like to hear what I'm thinking? Unofficially thinking?"

"Oh, sure. I can't wait."

"I'm thinking that you have an attitude problem."

"You're right. I don't like cops. Your sixty seconds are up, Lieutenant." The line clicked dead.

**3:45 P.M.** Someone picked up the phone before it had finished its first ring.

"Yeah?"

"I'd like to speak to John Powell, please."

"Powell. Hold on." As if it had been hit, the phone transmitted a jarring clatter. Then Hastings heard voices raised in the background, one of them calling "Anyone seen Johnny?" A full minute passed, and another minute. Finally: "Hello?"

"Is this John Powell?"

"Yeah. Who's this?"

"This is Frank Hastings calling, Mr. Powell. I'm sure you don't—"

"Who?"

"Frank Hastings. I—we knew each other a long time ago, in San Francisco. Kevin and I went to school together. And I knew—"

"Kevin? You knew Kevin?" The question was blurred, asked in a roughened, fragmented voice. Was it alcohol? Age? Both?

"We went to high school together, Mr. Powell. But that's not why I'm—"

"Kevin's dead. He died a long time ago. Years."

"I know that. I found that out from Meredith, Mr. Powell. I saw her Tuesday—three days ago. And she told me about Kevin. And her mother, too. Meredith told me her mother died."

"You saw Meredith? Three days ago?"

"Yes, I did. I'm a police officer, in San Francisco. And Meredith and I just happened to meet, by accident. We had lunch together and talked about old times, the old neighborhood. So now I'm—"

"What'd you say your name was again?"

"Hastings. Frank Hastings. My dad was in real estate. He—"

"Oh, yeah. Good-looking guy. Always drove big cars and wore a tie. I remember him."

"That's right. He—"

"I remember you, too. Big kid, looked like your father. Didn't you play football?"

"Yes. I—"

"Yeah, you made all-state, I remember. I used to follow football. Always thought I should've played. I'm big enough, you know. I was a big kid, too. Bigger'n you."

"Well, to tell you the truth, Mr. Powell, I'm not so sure I'd do it again. A long time after the newspaper clippings turn yellow, you've still got the sore knees."

"Hmmm. Yeah, I see what you mean."

Hastings let a beat pass. Then: "I'm afraid I've got some bad news for you, Mr. Powell. I—"

"Bad news? What'd you mean?"

"Well, it—it's about Meredith."

"Meredith?"

"Yes, sir. Meredith. She—Wednesday night, we think it was—there was a—a crime committed. And Meredith—"

"A crime? What kind of a crime?"

"Well, it—it was a homicide, Mr. Powell. And Meredith— well—she was the victim."

"Homicide." A pause. "Th-that's murder. Homicide is murder."

"Yes, sir." He drew a deep, regretful breath. "It's murder. She was murdered Wednesday night. She—her body wasn't found until yesterday. And after that, it took us awhile to locate you. So we couldn't—"

"Meredith was *murdered*?"

"Yes, sir, she was."

"B-but how? W-why?"

"We don't know, Mr. Powell. Not yet. But we're working on it, believe me. We're doing everything we can."

"Murdered . . ." A silence. In the background, Hastings could hear voices raised. Finally Powell muttered, "Someone wants to use the goddamn phone."

"Would you like to get to another phone and call me back? Collect?"

"No," Powell answered. "No, that's all right. I'll—I'll just have to think about it, think about what happened. It-it'll take time, that's all."

"I know that's true, Mr. Powell. And I'll do anything I can, to help."

"Yeah. Well, thanks. Frank, isn't it?"

"Yes, sir. Frank Hastings."

"Yeah, I remember. Didn't Kevin break his arm one time, and a couple of you kids brought him home? Wasn't that you?"

The instant's image returned: Kevin, sobbing, huddled in the wagon, holding his left wrist with his right hand, three of them propelling the wagon—yes, a little red wagon—up the Judah Street hill, two of them pushing, one of them pulling, taking turns. They couldn't have been more than ten years old, any of them.

"Yes, sir," he answered, speaking softly. "Yes, that was me."

"Yeah . . ." The other man's voice trailed off into a bleak silence.

"Listen, Mr. Powell, I know this is a bad time. It's always a bad time when something like this happens. But the thing is, you're Meredith's next of kin. And there're—" He cleared his throat. "There're arrangements to be made."

"Arrangements?"

"Funeral arrangements, Mr. Powell. Burial arrangements."

"Yeah, but—" A short, bemused silence. "Yeah, but I—I haven't seen her for years, I don't know how many years. It's— we—" The voice died, then came back. "She lived here, you

125

know, in Los Angeles. She lived here when she was married. And we never saw each other, all that time. So I—I don't see why—I don't see how—" Once more the voice faded, died, remained silent.

And in the silence, Hastings's silent self flared: *She didn't want to see you because you raped her, you degenerate son of a bitch.*

"If it's the money," he said, his official self, "that won't be a problem. She's got assets, I'm sure. And I can get you flown up here as a material witness—and put up at a hotel. It won't cost you a thing."

"A material witness? What's that?"

"It's just a technicality. But there're papers that the next of kin has to sign. Otherwise, they'll put her in a county grave, like she was a transient. And we don't want that. Do we?"

"Well, no. But—"

"What I want you to do, Mr. Powell, is get ready to come up here. Tomorrow. I want you here tomorrow. Right?"

"Y-yes, I suppose I could—"

"I'll get you an airline reservation, and I'll meet you at the airport. I'll take you to the hotel, on the city and county of San Francisco. I'll also make arrangements with a funeral home. So all you'll have to do is get on a plane and get up here. That's all."

"But I—I don't—"

"Do it, Mr. Powell. Just do it. I'm going to have someone make the arrangements. Then he'll call you. I don't want her buried as a ward of the county. Do you understand? Do you hear what I'm telling you?"

"Well, sure. Yeah. I—" The other man's voice caught, strangled by a sudden sob. In the silence, Hastings's silent self flared again: *You cry now, you bastard. What'd you do twenty-five years ago, after you raped her? Did you cry then?*

Now Powell's voice was muffled, tear-gurgled: "She was always so pretty. Even when she was little, she was pretty."

"She was pretty when she died, Mr. Powell. Very pretty when she died."


4:10 P.M. For the fourth time in the last ten minutes, Hastings's telephone warbled.

"Lieutenant Hastings."

"This is Walters, Lieutenant. Reception. Downstairs."

"Yes."

"There's a TV crew here. They say Lieutenant Friedman called them, and that they should ask for you. They've got a deadline, they say."

"Okay. Tell them I'll be right down."


4:14 P.M. Standing beside their KGBA van, each of them was dressed in the separate uniforms of their trades: the cameraman in jeans and a down jacket, the coordinator in khakis and a down jacket, the anchorperson in stylish boots, a calf-length tweed coat, and a long colorful scarf that trailed in the cold, raw wind. The anchorperson was Terry Tricomi. She was less than five feet, a smart, vivacious woman with dark, lively eyes and a clear, crisp, straightforward voice.

"Hello, Lieutenant." Smiling, she extended a small, muscular hand.

He smiled down at her. "How about 'Frank'?"

"How about 'Terry'?"

"It's a deal." Still holding her hand, he slightly increased the pressure, smiling into her eyes. When thoughts of wayward sexual adventures beckoned, these eyes were sometimes a feature of his fantasy—her eyes, her vital, exciting body.

The coordinator stepped forward. "Okay, you two. Time. We've got a three-minute slot on the six o'clock news, maybe four minutes. So let's concentrate on doing something riveting, how about it?"

They laughed together, took back their hands, turned together to face the coordinator, introduced as Bill Sigler.

"What we were thinking," Sigler said, "is that we'd go over to the entrance to the morgue." He gestured across the large Hall of Justice parking lot. "We'd do about a minute on this woman— Meredith Powell, right?" He looked at Hastings for confirmation.

Hastings nodded. "Right."

Turning now to the cameraman and to Terry Tricomi, using his hands, Sigler spoke swiftly: the tightly wound professional, doing his job. "We'll start with how she died. We'll come in close on the morgue sign while Terry does a voiceover, laying it all out. That'll be one minute. Then we'll go to the two of you—" He gestured to Hastings and Terry Tricomi. "It'll be a straight interview, nothing fancy, no cutaways. Then I think we'll go back to the sign for maybe a fifteen-second tag, voiceover. Something about life and death in the city, never mind whether you're rich or poor, something like that. Right?" He looked at each of them, then turned toward the entrance to the morgue. As Sigler and the cameraman began walking ahead, Hastings fell into step with the woman.

"Lieutenant Friedman called in about half of his markers on this one," she said, "but he didn't say why. Do you know why?"

"She was a friend of mine," Hastings answered. "I grew up with her."

"Ah—" Quickly, spontaneously compassionate, she turned toward him. "I'm sorry."

He nodded.

"Do you want to get into that?" she asked. "Your friendship?"

"No, I don't. Not at all. But we want to pull out all the other stops. Beautiful woman, beautiful Nob Hill condo, top-of-the-line Mercedes. Brutal murder. No real witnesses. Mostly it's the witnesses we need. That's why Friedman called you."

As they talked about it, making their plans while they walked side by side across the parking lot, Hastings was once more aware of her closeness, of her body, sometimes brushing his.

4:40 P.M. Hastings lifted the phone from its cradle, at the same time drawing a notepad close.

"This is Albert Price, Lieutenant."

For a moment the name failed to register. Then he remembered: Meredith's psychiatrist.

"Yes, Dr. Price. Thanks for calling."

Ignoring the pleasantry, Price said, "I'm between patients and don't have much time, I'm afraid. But I wanted you to know that I've been thinking about Meredith Powell. According to my notes, she has only one living relative. Her father. There's no—ah—current husband, no children. Is that correct?"

"Yes, sir, that's correct."

"And her father's pretty much a derelict, a burned-out case."

"That's my understanding."

"The reason I want to confirm all this," Price said, "is that I didn't want to reveal anything that would do damage to Meredith Powell's reputation in the eyes of her family. That's always our first consideration. Ethically—and also, let's face it, legally—we have to be aware of the damage we can do. We don't want lawyers, or lawsuits. Which is why we always try to tape our sessions. Do you follow?"

"Yes. Certainly."

"However," Price continued, his speech pompously lapsing into a professorial singsong, "however, from all I gather, her relationship with her father had deteriorated. Is that your understanding?"

Deteriorated . . .

*Yes, definitely deteriorated,* his silent self responded. *Beginning twenty-five years ago, Doctor. Or didn't you know?*

129

"Yes, sir, that's my understanding."

"I gather that time is of the essence."

"Time is always of the essence in a murder investigation, Doctor. The more time goes by, the deeper the murderer crawls into his hole."

"Ah—" A dry, mirthless chuckle. "Very good." Then the academic again: "I have patients until six, and I have notes to make after that. But there's a bar—Cassiday's—on Sutter Street near Powell. Are you familiar with it?"

"I'll find it."

"Shall we say six-thirty, at Cassiday's?"

"That'll be fine."


6:15 P.M. On the TV screen the anonymous figures performed against a soundtrack of meaningless muddle, the medium's sop to the masses, society's great leveler, the local TV news: anchorpersons with blow-dried hair reciting the day's cacophony of the cosmic and the trivial, ludicrously intermingled: yes, there'd been a drug raid, yes, there'd been a sell-off in the stock market, yes, the city had decided to build a domed baseball stadium, and, yes, a light plane had crashed.

And, yes, in Brighton, England, an eighteen-year-old music student had proclaimed himself the messiah.

Thus the day's passage was recorded, with no knock on the door, no policemen mouthing stock policeman's phrases, asking their proscribed policeman's questions.

The first time, Tina's turn, policemen had come. Those moments had been magic: life focused by death, banalities concealing the ecstasy of mortal danger roiling within.

That morning, in the *Sentinel*, page five, at the top of the page, there'd been a story about Meredith. The police had asked for witnesses and given a phone number to call. He'd clipped the story. Then he'd burned the newspaper in the fireplace. If anyone found the newspaper, the cutout could be incriminating. The penalty: death.

He'd taken the clipping to the chamber. He'd locked the door and reread the clipping. As he'd read, he'd felt the rush: forbidden fruit, so sweet to the palate. Then, yes, he'd played the videotape, the ultimate manifestation, himself supreme.

Yet the tape could kill him.

Therefore, the tape was both the focus and the fulcrum, knuckles rapping on the door, red lights flashing, onlookers gawking. The tape could—

On the TV screen, the camera was close-focused on a sign: CITY AND COUNTY OF SAN FRANCISCO MORGUE.

He touched the remote control, brought up the sound as the camera shifted to the head and shoulders of a young, dark-haired woman dressed in a tweed coat, a colorful scarf thrown around her neck. She held a microphone. Her voice was somber.

"Yesterday morning," she was saying, "the body of a woman was found in Golden Gate Park. She'd been murdered, probably late Wednesday night or very early Thursday—yesterday. The nude body had been thrown in some bushes on the south side of the park's riding stables. There was no identification.

"With me," she continued, "is Lieutenant Frank Hastings, who is co-commander of San Francisco's Homicide Bureau." As she spoke, the camera drew back to reveal her standing beside a big, dark-haired man. He wore a tweed sports jacket, a button-down shirt, striped tie. His clothes were faintly inspired by Brooks Brothers, but doubtless bought off the rack at Macy's. His dark eyes were calm and self-possessed; the mouth complemented the eyes. It was a conventionally proportioned face, squared off, a serious, civil servant's face. As the camera held on the two of them, the reporter spoke to the policeman.

"You're looking for cooperation on the crime, Lieutenant—cooperation from the public. Isn't that so?"

Like his face, the lieutenant's voice was serious, his speech measured. "That's correct. As you've said, she was found Thursday morning—yesterday morning—in Golden Gate Park. We think she was killed elsewhere and taken to the area behind the riding stables—the south side of the stables, as you said. There's a dirt road that leads to the area. We think she was left there about midnight, maybe an hour or two later. We were able to identify her as Meredith Powell. Age, thirty-six. Residence, Hyde Street, between Greenwich and Filbert."

The woman moved the wand microphone beneath her own face to ask, "Do you want to give us her address, Lieutenant?"

"Not at this time. However, I would like to say that we have reason to believe that someone—a man—drove her car from Golden Gate Park to her apartment house. And we'd like to talk to that man."

"That would be what time, Lieutenant?"

"Between midnight and one A.M., we think. Wednesday night."

"So someone drove her car from Golden Gate Park to her apartment. And that was done after she was murdered. Is that correct?"

"We're not sure about the sequence of events. That's one of the questions we'd like to ask this individual."

"Would you care to describe him?"

The policeman shook his head. "Not at this time."

"But you do have a description. Is that correct?"

He nodded. "That's correct."

With the words—the two words, two quiet-spoken detonations—the camera shifted to the woman, who said, "Is there a special number, Lieutenant, that people can call?"

"No. The Homicide Bureau is enough. That's in the Hall of Justice."

"The Homicide Bureau—" As the woman repeated the words, the camera began moving, closing on her face. "If there's anyone out there who can help Lieutenant Hastings and the men in Homicide find the person who murdered Meredith Powell on Wednesday night, we join with the police department in asking you to help, to come forward. In eight out of the past ten years, the annual homicide rate in San Francisco has risen. We can't reverse the trend unless you help." A long, terminal pause as the woman looked solemnly into the camera. Then, the sign-off: "This is Terry Tricomi, KGBA news."

It was important, he knew, that he chronicle his reactions: the physician, taking his own pulse.

*But you do have a description.*

It was, after all, a part of the calculus, a calculated risk, calculus and calculated, the same root. Laws were made for the masses, but a snare laid for a jackal could entangle a lion.

*That's correct,* the policeman had answered.

The woman had asked whether the police had a description of the man. The policeman had nodded, then mouthed the phrase: *That's correct.* Echoing now. Reechoing.

When they'd come to the door to ask about Tina, he'd been in control: the lord of the manor, receiving his serfs. Yes, he'd known Tina. No, he couldn't help them with their investigation. Yes, he'd call them if he thought of anything.

After he'd closed the door he went to a window and watched them walk to their car. They were detectives, like the man in the TV news. For several minutes they'd sat in their car, talking, occasionally glancing at the house. Watching them, he'd begun to tremble uncontrollably.

Just as now he was beginning to tremble: a terrible, tremulous quaking, his body unhinged.


**6:20 P.M.** "This is Terry Tricomi," the woman was saying, looking squarely at the camera. "KGBA news."

The small portable television set was on a low bench: a weathered wooden driftwood plank resting on two fieldstone pedestals. Except for the bench, a leather sling chair, an easel, and a high wooden stool, the stark white room with its lofty ceiling and its roughly plastered walls was bare. The room was illuminated by overhead track lighting: contemporary black fixtures contrasting with the rough white texture of the walls and ceiling. A rectangle of black canvas rested on the easel.

Dressed in a long, roughly woven peasant caftan, barefoot, Charles stood leaning against the wall, his eyes fixed on the TV screen as a studio announcer began describing a train derailment in Nevada. He stepped to the TV, switched it off.

*But you do have a description,* the woman had said.

*That's correct* had come the answer.

Two words, spoken by the same man he'd seen on Tuesday lunching with Meredith Powell.

Standing beside the bench, Charles held out both arms, fingers widespread. They were steady. Superhumanly, triumphantly steady. Just as he, within himself, was superhumanly steady, his little secret, his passport to everything.

He turned to survey the room. Had he somehow sensed that he'd see the police lieutenant interviewed? Was that why he'd dressed in the caftan, the symbol of his elemental self, then come here to this retreat within a retreat, one defensive ring inside another?

For Hitler there'd been the bunker, a place of mystery and power: that superior being, martyred by hordes of lesser men, barbarians at the gates. Only the warrior understood death.

To kill was to live, sustained by the victim's blood, the essence of human sacrifices. Virgins, thrown over Grecian cliffs, burned in Inca flames, their throats ceremoniously slit by priests. Blood drunk from golden goblets, to propitiate the gods.

Just as he had propitiated the gods. One god to celebrate sensation. One god to celebrate the natural superiority of those who could kill.

And, god of all gods, Mammon: the god of power.

**6:25 P.M.** It was a simple task. Trip the concealed latch, withdraw the tape from its hiding place. One tape of two now. After Wednesday night, two tapes.

Take the tape to the console. Insert the tape. Dim the lights with one touch, start the tape with another touch.

Simple tasks. Elemental tasks, exercises a child could learn.

Then sit in the carved chair. Then watch it begin: Meredith, about to die.

It was the only refuge. Only in the tape could he liberate himself.

But first he must control the uncontrollable: his palsied fingers, shaking so badly they could hardly trip the latch.


**6:30 P.M.** The interior of Cassiday's was dimly lit. The music was soft, the voices restrained, the laughter muted. At six-thirty on a raw February evening, at five dollars for a martini, the mating ritual of the yuppie was well advanced.

As his eyes adjusted to the low light, a forty-eight-year-old retina, slow to open, Price saw the detective sitting in a small booth along the back of the bar. All the other booths, Price noted, were occupied, two to a booth, Cassiday's inflexible policy after five. Had the detective—Hastings—flashed his badge? If he had, what were the probable consequences, himself connected to a policeman? A plus for his professional image? A minus?

Had he considered the point when he'd agreed to the meeting?

He nodded to the detective, made his way among the small, crowded tables. Hastings was rising, extending his hand. They shook hands, sat facing each other across a small table.

"Thank you for doing this, Doctor. I appreciate it."

"Are you making any progress?"

The other man hesitated briefly, obviously deciding how much he should say. Hastings was plainly a deliberate, methodical man, accustomed to think before he spoke. Without doubt, this mild, muscular detective with his calm eyes and orderly habits was well suited to the life he'd chosen. And his routine good looks would doubtless yield an active sex life, if the spirit was willing. Price glanced at the detective's left hand. There was no wedding band. If he was married, it was odds on that a man like Hastings would wear a wedding band. Loyalty, fidelity, security would be important to him.

"So far," Hastings admitted, "we haven't made much progress."

"Are you still proceeding on the theory that her lover may have done it?"

The detective considered the question, then spoke carefully. "As I said, whenever a woman's murdered, we look for a husband or a boyfriend. It's standard practice."

Standard practice—ah, yes. The catechism.

"But you had some particular reason for suspecting this man Meredith was involved with," Price pressed.

"I have some particular reason for wanting to talk to him, yes. But that's not to say I have any real grounds for suspecting him." As Hastings spoke, their waitress arrived. Price ordered a glass of Chardonnay and noted that the other man ordered a seltzer water. Was Hastings a teetotaler? A straight arrow? Was he on the wagon? Whose choice—his, or AA's? Time, perhaps, would tell. Part of the recovering alcoholic's credo always involved a random willingness to talk about the problem.

"You're looking for grounds," Price pressed. The message: Before they could proceed, it was necessary that they agree on terminology—his terminology.

In reply, Hastings shrugged. "I'm always looking for grounds. That's my job."

Reflecting on the answer, Price finally nodded. The reply was acceptable, a civil servant's concession.

The drinks arrived. As Hastings drew the check toward him,

Price sipped the Chardonnay, a mediocre vintage, entirely too cloying. He spoke crisply, concisely.

"I've given this matter considerable thought, Lieutenant. As I told you earlier today, there's an ethical question for me. And there're potential legal questions, too. If I told you that Meredith had been involved with an unsavory character, and if her family decided I was defaming her memory, therefore causing them grievous harm, they might decide to sue me. They probably wouldn't win. But I'd have to defend myself."

"I doubt that her father would sue."

"All it takes is one shyster lawyer who's willing to work on contingency. However—" Price sipped again at the Chardonnay, at the same time glancing at his watch. "However, the fact is, as I intimated on the phone, I'd certainly like to see her murderer caught. That goes without saying."

On cue, Hastings nodded. "Of course."

Price let a long moment pass while he ordered the sequence of his thoughts. When he spoke, it was in the measured cadence of his profession. "Meredith saw me nine times, as she may have told you. Her problem—her concern—was quite a common one. Which is to say, she seemed unable to sustain a long-term relationship with a man. Any man. Short term, she was in-ordinately successful with men. That's to say, she was a beautiful woman and men chased after her, as you can imagine. But relationships always turned out to be destructive for her. Some-times very destructive." He paused, raised the glass, finished the wine. Hastings signaled for a second round.

"For the past two years," Price continued, "she was involved in a relationship like that. It was a constrictive relationship. That's to say, the man she was involved with wanted her all to himself. Which isn't, of course, unusual. The man was rich. Very rich. He could pay for his pleasure, so to speak. However, perhaps six months ago, she began to feel that this man was repulsive. She couldn't stand to have him touch her. And, perhaps sensing her state of mind, the man began making unnatural demands on her. Turning up the heat, in other words."

"What kind of demands, Doctor?"

"Some of them—" Price measured the other man with a calculating look of thoughtful appraisal. Then: "Some of them have to do with, ah, what I'd call abbreviated snuff. Are you familiar with the term?"

With obvious effort, personally involved in spite of himself, Hastings said, "I certainly am. One of them—the man, usually—begins choking the woman while they're having intercourse. It's supposed to heighten the orgasm, just as you lose consciousness. Men do it with men, too. And women with women."

"I see," Price answered dryly, "that you've had, ah, professional exposure to the phenomenon."

"In Homicide," Hastings answered, his voice hard, "you get professionally exposed to everything."

The drinks arrived. As Price drank, he looked carefully at the other man. Was Hastings mocking him? Mimicking him, twisting the phrase and tossing it back? To decide, he probed. "I suppose you see everything in time. All kinds of depravity."

Hastings nodded. "All kinds. And there's always something new." He hesitated, then spoke quietly. "But when it happens to someone you know—" Silently the detective shook his head.

Signifying that they weren't contesting. The mimicked phrase, then, had been an aberration, nothing more, no challenge to Price's control of the dialogue. Signifying, therefore, that he could continue.

"Meredith hated it. And feared it, too. But, to her credit—" Price paused, to frame the thought more precisely. "To her credit, she admitted that perversion attracted her, too. Most people won't admit that." As he spoke, Price was aware that the other man was looking at him intently.

And now, speaking very softly, a man who'd lost a friend, the detective said, "Meredith was strangled. That was the cause of death."

"Ah—" Price nodded. "I wondered. I was going to ask." He hesitated. Then: "Was there, ah, any evidence of, ah, sexual activity?"

Now the detective was hesitating, before he finally said, "I shouldn't answer that, not really. But the truth is—yes, there was semen. And that's why I called you, Doctor. This lover of hers, she was scared of him. Scared that he'd kill her, I think."

"And you're looking for him."

"I certainly am."

"Without success."

"Without success."

"And you want me to help, give you a name." As he spoke Price glanced at his watch. Already seven o'clock. Dinner awaited. "Well—" He sighed regretfully, finished his wine, declined the offer of another round. "Well, I can't really help you, Lieutenant. I might not help you even if I *could* help you, for the reasons I've already stated. The truth is, though, that I don't *have* a name. So my conscience is clear."

"But she talked about him to you. She must've said something. Is he married? Rich? Poor? Young? Old? He's a pervert, that's obvious, a sexual deviate. Has he ever been arrested?" Earnestly now, the detective leaned urgently across the table. "*Think. Anything.*"

"The only thing I can tell you is that he's certainly rich."

"How rich?"

"Very rich, I suspect."

"Do you have any idea how old he is? Whether he's thin or fat, anything like that? You might not think it's important, Doctor, what you have to say. But sometimes we can add bits and pieces together. Like a jigsaw puzzle." Hastings spoke earnestly; his eyes were urgent.

Considering the point, Price pushed back his chair, ready to rise. "I'd have to listen to the tapes to see whether I could find anything. You talk about bits and pieces—that's what I'd have to do, go back over the tapes, listen for a phrase here, a nuance there. But—" He frowned thoughtfully. "But I somehow have the feeling that physically, he's attractive. Or, at least, not un-attractive. And if I had to choose between young and old, I'd probably say old. Why, I'm not really sure. And, above all, rich. As I said."

"Does he work, do anything?"

Price spread his hands. "I have no idea, Lieutenant. None at all."

"Those tapes—" Obviously Hastings was choosing his words. "I'd like to listen to them."

Price shook his head decisively. "No way, Lieutenant."

"I could get a court order."

"And I could hire a lawyer to resist. Which I most certainly would."

Quickly Hastings raised his hands, palms forward: a peaceable disclaimer. "Okay—just asking."

"I'm afraid I've got to go, Lieutenant." The psychiatrist began to rise.

Rising with him, Hastings said: "I've just got one more question, Doctor. It's, ah, personal."

Price raised an eyebrow. "Personal?"

"When Meredith and I talked, she—" Hastings paused carefully. "She said something about her early life. She—" Another pause. "She said she was abused when she was a little girl. And I'm wondering, did she say anything about it to you?"

"Sexually abused, you mean?"

"Yes."

Price studied the other man gravely, deciding. Then, perhaps regretfully, he shook his head. "Sorry, Lieutenant. I'm unable to respond to a question like that."

11:15 P.M. "She told me about it, told me her father molested her. But I don't think she told Price." In the darkened bedroom, Hastings's voice was awed.

"If she told him, though, he might not've admitted it to you," Ann offered. "From what you say, he doesn't sound very forthcoming."

"He's a typical tight-ass doctor. They're all the same, when you start asking them questions. But she depended on him. I *know* she did. I asked her why she didn't leave San Francisco, if she was into something she couldn't handle. And one of the reasons she gave for staying was that Price was here."

"You'll probably never know whether she told him, Frank. It doesn't sound like you ever will."

A pause. In the silence, lying on his back, he stared at the ceiling. As a car passed in the street beyond the window, its headlights made patterns move across the ceiling. When he was a boy, on Thirty-ninth Avenue, he'd lain like this, watching the shadows of the night move across the ceiling of his room and down the walls. Followed by other shadows—and other shadows, an endless procession. Until, finally, he fell asleep.

But before he fell asleep, he often heard the sound of his parents' voices, from the floor below. Sometimes he heard them arguing: short, bitter arguments, followed by silence. In their own way they'd both been proud people, his mother and his father. Neither would ever admit defeat, or even acknowledge a wound.

Until that afternoon in late September, when he'd come home to see the envelope on the kitchen table, leaning against the salt shaker. Unsealed, unaddressed. He'd opened it—and read that his father had left them. When he'd given the letter to his mother, she'd cried. It was the first time he'd ever seen her cry.

Of all his early memories, all the scattered images, the plain white envelope propped against the salt shaker was always the most vivid, the most persistent.

"I don't understand what you're concerned about," Ann said finally. "Do you wish she hadn't told you?"

"I don't know," he answered. "I just don't know. I—Christ—I just wish we could close the case, that's all."

"You will. I know you will." As she said it, speaking softly, he felt her touch his cheek, felt her move toward him, an invitation to intimacy.

"I shouldn't do this," he said. "I shouldn't bring my troubles home. It's a bad idea."

"You don't do it often, Frank. This is something special."

"Why should it bother me, that she told me about her father?"

"Maybe it's because of the responsibility. You already have so much responsibility, just doing your job, trying to—to insulate yourself from the pain you see, all the time. So when it's someone you know, it's worse. It's got to be worse."

"There's no family—no one who cares what happens to her body, not really."

"God, that's the saddest part of it all, really. She was so beautiful, so desirable. She drove men wild—every woman's dream. But—now—there's no one who really cares. You probably care more than anyone. And you hardly knew her."

As he listened to her, the image of Meredith's father came back across the years: Johnny Powell, a big, blustering bully. Then, a soundtrack overlay, today's telephone conversation replayed: the hallway phone, the confusing noises in the background, the bleary voice of Meredith's father.

"Maybe it's her father. Maybe that's what's really bothering me—that I've got to see him tomorrow."

She touched his cheek again, came closer. Her voice was husky, deepened by desire as she said softly, "Don't think about it now, darling. Not now."

# SATURDAY
# FEBRUARY 17

2:20 P.M. "Call me Johnny, Frank. Everyone in the block called me Johnny. Don't you remember?"

Aware of the effort, Hastings glanced at the other man, then spoke coldly. "All right. Johnny." He returned his gaze to the freeway: six lanes of traffic flowing north from the airport toward San Francisco.

Meeting the flight from Los Angeles, he'd had no difficulty recognizing Powell: a hulking wreck of a man, red faced, with a paunch so huge that it dwarfed his arms and legs and drew his shoulders and head forward, as if the whole body was needed to support it. His thick, graying hair was badly cut, his shapeless blue polyester jacket and mismatched trousers were wrinkled and stained. Close up, the face had the texture of badly kneaded dough; the flesh was a solid network of broken blood vessels. The eyes were moist and rheumy: faded blue, edged with mottled white. The large, shapeless lips were slack; the flesh beneath the jowls sagged pendulously. It was the face of a lifelong drinker, a man who had long ago surrendered.

"Where're we going now, Frank?" Powell's voice was permanently roughened: a panhandler's voice, thin and whining. The eyes were in constant, restless movement. Con man's eyes.

"We're going to the funeral home." He was aware that he was speaking curtly. "Then I'll take you to the hotel."

"Will we—" Powell coughed: a harsh, wet rattle, deep in his chest. "Will we—see her? Is that why we're going to the funeral home?"

"No, we won't see her. It's just that you have to sign some papers. If you—" He was forced to pause. "If you want her embalmed, that's a decision you have to make. It's a financial decision."

"Financial?"

"It costs extra, to have her embalmed." He looked at the other man, another sharp glance, without compassion. "Your wife and Kevin, they died. Haven't you been all through this?"

"Well—ah—no. Not like this. I mean, there was always—you know—Meredith. She took care of it. I—you know—I always did whatever I could. But plumbing—you know—the work's always spotty, when you're a plumber."

"I always thought plumbers made good money."

"Well, sure. When you work, you make good money. But I'm—you know—I'm sixty-seven years old. I got Social Security, and that's it, Frank. That's the whole story." Powell coughed again, deeper this time—a spasm that wracked his whole body. Then, recovering, noisily swallowing the phlegm, he began to speak.

But Hastings cut him off. "I'll vouch for the fact that she has assets, so there shouldn't be a problem."

"Ah—" Powell nodded, coughed again, nodded again. "Ah, that's good, Frank. I can't tell you how good it makes me feel, to know I'll be able to—you know—do something nice for Meredith. It—" He blinked, snuffled. "It means a lot to me, I'll tell you that."

Once more Hastings glanced briefly at John Powell, then returned his eyes to the traffic. He would wait in silence for what he knew would surely follow.

"By the way," Powell said, "since we're speaking of money, I was wondering, Frank, whether you could see your way clear to . . ."

**4:00 P.M.** Even when the weather was gray, Granville had discovered, enough people came to Golden Gate Park over the weekend to keep him in food through Tuesday.

And in the summer, even with the fog in, the food could last until Thursday, for him and Chum. Sometimes the food spoiled before they could eat it all.

He set his plastic trash bag on the grass and bent over the large green-painted steel barrel, yellow-stenciled CCSF. The barrel was lined with plastic. Things had gotten better since they'd started lining the green steel barrels. Cleaner, and better. And healthier, too. Healthier for him, and healthier for Chum. Only a few months ago, Chum had gotten sick a lot, thrown up a lot. Or was it a few years ago?

Beside the barrel, weighted down with a rock, neatly folded, someone had left a copy of the Sunday *Sentinel*. The Sunday papers, he knew, had been out only since noon. So someone had paid a dollar for the paper and then left it under a rock.

All his life, even when he was very small, he'd been able to read. They'd all been surprised, how well he could read.


**4:45 P.M.** Granville tucked the funnies under the edge of his sleeping bag and opened the main news section. They were the only parts of the paper he ever read: the funnies and the main news. And only on Sundays. He could get the daily paper. There wasn't a day that he couldn't get the daily paper. But it was too much, to read the paper every day. It took too much time.

On the top half of the front page there was nothing that he recognized, only names of places he didn't know, pictures of people he couldn't recognize. But at the bottom of the front page there was a picture of a dog. It was a small dog with large ears. And soft eyes, too—soft eyes, and a mouth that smiled. He looked at Chum, curled up beside him on top of the sleeping bag. Had Chum ever smiled? He couldn't remember.

He returned to the newspaper, and began reading the large

145

letters of the headline: HAVE DRUG LORDS PUT PRICE ON PRINCE'S HEAD?

Price on Prince's head? He looked at the picture again. What did it mean? If he read the story, took the time, he could find out. He knew he could find out, if he took the time. But already the leaden gray clouds of the sky overhead were darkening. In another hour the words would be invisible.

While he thought about it, he would turn to the second page.

Near the top of the second page—no, the third page—there was a picture of a woman. She was a very beautiful woman with blond hair. She was smiling directly into his eyes. Now she was smiling.

It was the same woman he'd seen in the park. Naked. Leaves matted in her hair, eyes open wide, staring at the sky. Insects crawling on her white skin. Then she hadn't been smiling.

But now she was smiling. At him. Just for him.

This, he knew, was a sign.

Today was Saturday, in the late afternoon. Two days ago—on Thursday morning, early, he'd found her. And every day, every hour—ever since—he'd thought about her. It was as if she'd come into his life through a door that was closed, but unlocked. Somehow she'd gotten tangled in his thoughts, even tangled in his dreams. When he wasn't thinking of Chum, he was thinking of her, the woman with the leaves in her beautiful blond hair.

Carefully he creased down the newspaper and settled himself against the base of the big pine tree that just fit his back. He turned the newspaper for the brightest light, then began to read:

POLICE SEEK CLUES IN MURDER OF MEREDITH POWELL.

"This is Canelli, Lieutenant."

Looking through the glass partition toward the squadroom, he saw Canelli standing at his desk, facing him. Like the sotto-soft pitch of his voice, Canelli's expression was broadly conspiratorial. "We've got a confessor, Lieutenant. The first one."

"Where is he?"

"He's the one at Segal's desk." Surreptitiously, Canelli moved his head. Seated at Segal's desk, Hastings saw a man who had probably fallen as far down as he was going to fall. A medium-size mongrel dog lay on the floor beside the man.

"That bum?"

Reacting to Hastings's obvious exasperation, Canelli's face immediately registered mild consternation. "Yessir. His name's Granville Foster."

"Is that dog on a leash?" At the question, grunting, Friedman shifted his bulk in the chair, giving himself a view of the squadroom.

"Yessir. It's—well—there's a piece of rope. Do you want me to—?"

"Have you talked to this guy?"

"Sort of. He's a little crazy, I guess. But, on the other hand, he seems to track pretty well, even though he's not very smart, that's for sure. But then I remembered that case three years ago, maybe, when it turned out that the guy who—"

"You did talk to him, then."

"Yessir."

"So what'd you think?"

"Well, it's like I said, Lieutenant—" Acutely ill at ease now, Canelli was squirming, shifting his weight from one foot to the other. "I was remembering that case three years ago, or whatever it was, when it turned out that the guy who found the victim was the perpetrator. So I thought I should—"

"This guy found her?"

"That's what he says, Lieutenant."

About to admonish Canelli for not getting to the point sooner, Hastings decided instead to simply sigh. "If he discovered her, then obviously we've got to hold on to him."

"Yessir." Canelli's voice registered contrition; his eyes were anxious. "That's why I wanted to—"

"I'm going to go out in the field pretty quick." He shot an inquiring look at Friedman, who nodded. "You report to Lieutenant Friedman."

"Yessir." A pause. Then, tentatively, Canelli said, "The way I figure this guy, I've got to let him keep the dog with him if we want to get anything. I just wanted to tell you."

In spite of himself, Hastings chuckled. "It's whatever you think, Canelli. I'll fill Lieutenant Friedman in. He's crazy about dogs."

"Yessir."

As Hastings cradled the phone, Friedman raised a long-suffering hand. "Don't say a word. I've got the picture." He glanced at his watch. "Listen, I've got to get some stuff ready for the DA on that Benefiel thing. So—" He pointed to the file folder he'd brought. "So let me tell you what I've got on Meredith Powell."

"Right." Hastings flipped his notepad to a fresh sheet.

"What I've got," Friedman said ruefully, "isn't a hell of a lot more than what we had on Friday. Beyond what you found at her flat, there really isn't much that the lab turned up. Nothing hidden, no surprises. And, yes, I made sure they did it right. There're lots of prints, of course, which they're classifying and trying to match up. The ME didn't have much to add, either, beyond what you eyeballed at the scene. She was asphyxiated because of strangulation—manual strangulation. Assuming she had a normal dinner at seven o'clock, and extrapolating on the body temperature, they figure she died about midnight, give or take. As for the car, there's a little more there, but it doesn't change much, doesn't elaborate much on your guesses.

However, there were smudges on the wheel and the door handles."

Hastings's interest sharpened. "Gloves?"

Friedman nodded. "Looks like it."

"Premeditation . . ."

"I've always figured it might be premeditation," Friedman answered.

"Oh?" It was a skeptically ironic question.

"Just a guess, of course."

"A guess. Yes."

"Anyhow," Friedman continued briskly, "there was also debris from the park that was found in the trunk. Along with—" He coughed delicately. "Along with some fecal matter and some urine, which we also knew about. So the way it looks to me, she was killed elsewhere and taken to the park, where she was dumped. The guy used her car, obviously. He wore gloves. He also probably wrapped the body. Maybe he'd already selected the spot. He took the body out of the trunk and put it on the ground. He rolled it out of its covering, whatever that was—a tarp, or plastic sheeting, maybe. He put the tarp back in the trunk. Then he got out of there. He got rid of the tarp and her clothes and her purse. Then—surprisingly—he drove her car to her garage and drove it inside, using her opener. Then he split. At least, that's one version, assuming that Lee Persse's story is credible."

"Why do you say 'surprisingly'?"

"Why wouldn't he just ditch the car?"

"Because," Hastings answered, "he figured that if he put the car back where it belonged, maybe she might not be missed for a while. Days, maybe. And even when she was found, there was a chance she wouldn't be identified."

"An outside chance," Friedman answered dubiously.

"But, nevertheless, a chance."

Friedman shrugged, glanced at his watch. "Listen, I'd better start working on that thing for the DA. However—" He shuffled his notes. "However, there's one more thing."

Hearing him say it, Hastings looked suspiciously at the other man. Yes, Friedman was doing it again: saving the snapper for his exit line, working his audience.

"Well," Hastings asked dryly, "what is it?"

"Her building," Friedman answered blandly. "I finally got something on the ownership. It's owned by a real estate holding company based in New York. The name of the company is Allegro." Still building the suspense, he paused. Hastings stoically refused to take the bait. Finally Friedman continued. "Allegro bought the building four years ago, from a local company. There're three units—three floors, I gather, plus garages on the ground floor. About two years ago Allegro decided to turn the building into condos. They sold two of the condos during the next year, but didn't sell the top-floor unit."

"Meredith's unit." In spite of himself, Hastings's voice registered taut anticipation.

Friedman nodded. "Meredith's unit. Allegro still owns it." Savoring the moment, Friedman began gathering up his papers as he said, "I can see that you're trying to visualize her checkbook. And the answer is that, no, she didn't write any rent checks to Allegro—or to anyone else, that I could see."

"Is Allegro cooperating?"

"They're about as cooperative as a Swiss banker dodging a court order," Friedman answered. "However, I've got an old friend who's an NYPD captain. He's promised to pound a few desks."

"Meredith was involved with someone at Allegro. He was paying the rent. He was doing it all through Allegro, so his wife wouldn't find out."

"That's the way it looks." Friedman spoke laconically.

"Does Allegro have any branches here? Any connections?"

"Not that I can find."

"Then maybe one of us should fly to New York."

Friedman raised a hand in protest. "Not in this weather do I fly to New York. Never. I used to fly bombers, if you recall. I know what can happen, in weather like this."

"Then maybe I'll go."

"Why don't you give my NYPD guy a chance?"

"Well . . ." Hastings frowned.

"Meanwhile, there's one last point about Allegro."

"What's that?"

"They own three other buildings in town." Friedman sailed a paper across the desk. "They're all commercial buildings. But you might find out something. Why don't you check them out? Meanwhile, later today I'll give my guy in New York another call, see what he says. Then fly to New York, if you want to go."

As Hastings scanned the addresses, he nodded. "Fine."


11:45 A.M. "The truth is," Jonathan Taylor said, "it's demeaning, to show my stuff in the same room with this shit." As he spoke, he flung out an arm, gesturing to the gallery's far wall. "It's self-debasement."

"I'm not saying it's *not* demeaning," Cass answered, keeping her voice low. "But for God's sake, Jonathan, be reasonable. You've got a *show*. You're thirty-six, and you've never had a show—not in any kind of a real art market, anyhow."

"That's not true." Fists propped indignantly on his hips, chin truculently outthrust, eyes snapping, Taylor turned to face her squarely. He was a short, muscular, bandy-legged man with a sharply etched face and a longshoreman's torso. He'd never been known to wear anything but work shoes, blue jeans, a sweatshirt, and a scarred leather jacket. His only vanity was his luxuriant head of thick brown hair, worn medium long and always carefully combed. "What about Tucson?"

She sighed wearily. "Sorry. I forgot about Tucson."

"If you're trying to inject a little irony into the discussion," he said heavily, "you're succeeding."

"Oh, Jesus, Jonathan, I didn't come here to argue. I came to help you hang your show."

"Nobody told me I'd be sharing a gallery with shit."

"Galleries are full of shit. You should know that by now. The *world's* full of shit. But don't forget, flowers grow in shit. Beautiful flowers."

His face quizzical, he studied her for a moment. Then, unpredictably, he smiled. "I'm the flower. Is that it?"

Her smile matched his. "Definitely, that's it."

"Well—" As if in fresh appraisal, he looked her over head to foot. "Well, if I'm a flower, then so are you. A very nicely packaged flower. If there were an artist's lounge in this so-called gallery, I'd take you there and ravish you."

She moved closer, smiled, arched her body toward him. "Hold the thought."

"Right."

The moment held between them, an erotic promise. Then Taylor sighed, turned to face the long blank wall that was his for the next three weeks. He sighed again. "The problem," he said, "what's really bugging me, if I'm honest with myself, is that I feel like a whore. I feel like I'm taking money to get into bed with Edwin Corwin. And I can't think of anything more repulsive."

"You're mixing your metaphors. It's not Corwin's money you're taking. It's *their* money. The great unwashed public's money. In fact, technically Corwin will be taking your money, part of it, if he sells anything of yours."

Sulking now, he stubbornly shook his head. "You know what I mean."

"I know that people like Edwin Corwin make the reviewers take notice. And reviewers make the public take notice. It's a fact of life, Jonathan. You may as well face it."

"Do you think he and Charles are screwing each other?"

Involuntarily she looked over her shoulder, dropped her voice. "Jonathan, for God's sake."

"Did you see them, the other night? I thought Charles was going to peel him a grape."

"If Charles peels Edwin's grape," Cass said, "it's no skin off your ass, to mix another metaphor. You've got to learn to lighten up, Jonathan."

He turned to look at her. "One of the reasons I'm in love with you," he said quietly, "is that you've never told me to lighten up."

For a moment she didn't respond. Now her eyes were somber; her voice was pitched to a low, solemn note. "I'm sorry, Jonathan. Truly. It won't happen again."

His voice, too, was solemn. "And that's the first time you've ever said you're sorry."

Her lips parted in a small, intimate smile. "That probably won't happen again, either."

They stood silently for a moment, face to face, smiling into each other's eyes. Then, sharply shaking his head, he said, "This is what happens when people like us get mixed up with people like Corwin. We're changed. We're corrupted."

"If you feel corrupted," she said, "then let's not hang the show. Let's go home and feed the dog and the cat and then get into bed. Remember, you promised to ravish me."

He smiled. "So I did."

"And, furthermore—" With her eyes on the entrance to the gallery, behind him, she broke off. Seeing her mouth tighten and her eyes harden, he turned to face the entrance. It was Charles. Dressed impeccably in a dark three-piece suit, stiff white collar, and gleaming black shoes, Charles went to one of the gallery's low benches. Sitting down and crossing his legs, adjusting his shirt cuffs and trouser creases, Charles looked at them each in turn. It was a deliberate scrutiny, coldly appraising. In his twenties, elegantly slim, he could have been either a gentleman's gentleman or a rising young banker. His face was a pale, sallow white. His eyes were dark, unfathomably expressionless. Against the pallor of his face, his small, shapeless mouth was unnaturally vivid, a rosebud red. His dark hair was lusterless, dark and lank, yet impeccably barbered. A large antique opal stickpin adorned his old school tie. When he spoke, his voice was thin. But, compensating, his manner was aloof, foppishly arrogant.

"For your opening, Jonathan, I hope you can find a clean sweatshirt." As he said it, Charles fingered the opal stickpin. Unlike his body, his fingers were short and stubby: sausage fingers, with nails bitten to the quick. Pointedly he spoke only to Taylor, ignoring Cass.

"Edwin asked me to mention your, ah, dress code, in fact. Artistic panache is one thing. But hygiene is something else."

"I'd be willing to bet, Charles, that I take more showers than you do. Whatcha say?" Taylor stepped aggressively forward, extending a muscular hand. "Whatcha say, Charles? Bet?"

Charles smiled: a small, pained smile. "I don't discuss my bathing habits, Jonathan. I'm surprised you do."

"I don't, normally. But you brought up the subject."

Shrugging elaborately, Charles consulted his watch. "I've got to meet Edwin."

"By the way, Charles, how'd your show go? Many commissions for skewered pigs?"

Charles shrugged again. "The reviews were mixed. Predictably mixed. But the good reviews came from the right reviewers. In conceptual art, that's all one hopes for."

"How about money?" Mockingly, Jonathan imitated the studied cadence of the other man's speech. "Does one hope for money?"

The small, smug smile returned. "Gentlemen don't discuss money."

"Oh—" Taylor smiled, then burlesqued a deep, ingratiating nod of abject apology. "Oh, I see. Excuse me." Then, mock-innocently, he asked, "By the way, Charles, how long've you been a gentleman? I keep forgetting."

Aware that he was growing angry, therefore losing control, the other man rose to his feet. "If you'll excuse me . . ." He half turned away.

"I haven't hurt your feelings, have I?" Taylor asked, mockingly anxious.

Charles refused to answer, but also refused to turn fully away, leaving the field of honor.

"I wouldn't want to hurt your feelings," Taylor persisted, "because I have another question to ask."

The other man held to his stiff, disdainful pose.

"What I wanted to know," Taylor said, "was whether you think it helped, dropping your last name. Are people impressed, would you say? Or amused? Which?"

"I have to meet Edwin. You'll have to excuse me."

Taylor waved airily. "You're excused, Charles. You're definitely excused."


**12:15 P.M.** The third building on Friedman's list was 2157-59 Hayes Street. The first building on the list had been a twelve-story office building, the second a small, upscale residential hotel. But 2157-59 Hayes was a two-story storefront, double frontage, with three apartments on the second floor. The building was at least seventy-five years old, probably older. Located only three blocks from the city's civic center, the Hayes Street building could have begun with a neighborhood hardware store on one side and dry goods store on the other side, with working-class tenants in the apartments above. Following World War II, Hayes Valley had declined, and in the sixties succumbed to a drug blight that overflowed the Haight Ashbury. But in the late seventies, with New York real estate money changing the San Francisco skyline and rapid transit bringing office workers into the city from the suburbs, Hayes Valley suddenly became trendy. Go-go speculators bought up leases, renovated the vintage Victorian buildings, and quadrupled rents. New-wave tenants opened upscale boutiques, restaurants, antique shops, and art galleries. Hayes Valley had arrived.

After parking the Honda in a loading zone and propping his police placard on the dashboard, Hastings switched off his beeper as he strode across the street. Flanked by an antiques store on one side and a small, elegantly decorated French restaurant on the other side, 2157-59 Hayes Street was an art gallery. The gold-leaf lettering on the plate glass was discreet: THE CORWIN GALLERY. The entire show window contained only one painting: a wall-filling abstract that was kin to the paintings in Meredith's flat.

**12:15 P.M.** As he bent to fit his key into the Fiat's passenger-side door, Charles saw it: an orange Honda station wagon, the same color and model he'd followed on Tuesday, from 450 Sutter to the Hall of Justice. The car was coming toward him. The driver, a man, was alone in the car. Signaling for traffic to go around, the man had stopped at a loading zone. Now he was backing the Honda into the loading zone.

At first straightening, involuntarily seeking a better view of the driver's face as he parked the Honda, Charles quickly crouched down again for concealment. The man got out of the car and began walking across the street toward the gallery.

The man he'd seen lunching with Meredith Powell.

The detective, interviewed on the TV news.

It was important, he knew, absolutely essential, that he remain calm, carefully registering his own responses, his second-to-second reactions. Dispassionately he must begin his calculations, factoring in this instant's turn of fortune's wheel.

But first, just as meticulously, he must search his psyche. Was it fear that had quickened the instant's beat of his heart? Or was it anticipation: the first sting of danger's flay on untested flesh, himself at the limits and beyond, finally tested, surely supreme?

12:25 P.M. Like Meredith's flat, the walls and ceiling of the gallery were painted a flat white, with track lighting on the ceiling, also painted white. The floor was thickly carpeted in beige wool. A high-style receptionist sat at a small desk. When Hastings decided to avoid her cool, politely questioning glance, pretending to browse casually, she immediately allowed her gaze to wander into the disinterested middle distance. To her practiced eye, Hastings had obviously failed to match the Corwin Gallery's preferred customer profile.

Movable partitions divided the large overall space into several smaller spaces. In one of the spaces, a salesman and his client were discussing a huge canvas painted entirely black, with a single thread of color in the center that represented the flesh and blood of an open wound. The customer was a tall blond woman, dramatically dressed in tight white silk pants, short leather boots, an overbulked designer leather jacket, and a flowing over-the-shoulder serape. Her blond hair was fashion-frizzed; her wide, petulant mouth was vivid crimson, her eyes were shadowed a deep blue-green. As she eyed the painting, she stood with shoulders aggressively squared under the layered leather jacket, one hip dramatically outthrust. It was a pose that suggested the cover of a rock music magazine.

Except for a tarpaulin that partitioned off a rear gallery, the other display spaces were deserted. Back in the reception area, avoiding the arch stare of the high-style receptionist, Hastings pretended to examine a piece of abstract iron-studded wooden sculpture. Should he immediately find a phone, call Friedman? Friedman would—

A man materialized in the hallway that led from the curtained-off rear gallery. He wore paint-daubed blue jeans and a gray sweatshirt. His vivid blue eyes were sharp-focused, constantly in restless movement. Taking no notice of Hastings, he strode directly to the receptionist's desk.

"Do you happen to know," the newcomer said, "whether I'm going to get any help hanging this show? An electrician, for instance, to hook up the lights?" His voice was don't-give-a-damn loud, heavily laced with both irony and exasperation.

"The guy should be here by one o'clock," the receptionist answered. "It's the lunch hour, you know."

"He was supposed to be here at ten o'clock."

She shook her sleek head good-humoredly. "That's not strictly true, Jonathan. I said I'd ask him to come at ten. But he wasn't sure he could make it."

"Will he bring light bulbs?"

"If he doesn't," she answered, subtly mocking him with sweetness, "we'll send him out for some, won't we?" Playful now, she smiled. This skirmish, Hastings realized, was part of a long-running event: this garrulous man who obviously enjoyed his role as irrepressible artist versus the super-cool receptionist.

Fists propped on hips, the stranger stared down at her. Then, unpredictably, he also smiled. It was a pixie smile that instantly transformed the face, whimsy erasing truculence.

"You know, Gloria, you were cut out for better things than this. Christ, you may as well be greeting customers in a high-priced whorehouse."

The playful smile widened. "I'm glad you said high priced. It shows you're perceptive. That's important in an artist, you know. Perception is a very big deal."

The artist snorted good-humoredly, casually waved, and turned back down the hallway. Deciding that, odds on, the talkative Jonathan offered a better chance for information than the ice-eyed receptionist, Hastings followed the artist, who was reaching out to pull back the tarpaulin that screened off the rear of the gallery.

"Excuse me."

Reacting quickly, tensed, the man turned to face Hastings, who held his gold shield in the palm of an outstretched hand. "My name is Hastings. Lieutenant Frank Hastings. I'd like to ask you some questions concerning an investigation we're conducting. Your name?"

As he studied the badge, the man's reactions were complex, mingling amusement, interest, skepticism, and quick-thinking speculation. Then, smiling quizzically, he raised his eyes to study Hastings's face before he finally said, "Jonathan Taylor. What's the trouble?"

"No trouble, exactly. I'm investigating the death of Meredith Powell."

"Ah—" Taylor nodded, grasped the tarpaulin, pulled it back. It was a spontaneous, forthcoming response, a good beginning. "Come in here. I'm hanging a show. We can talk."

"Thanks." Entering a large all-white gallery that opened on an elegant Romanesque rear garden, Hastings found himself facing a young woman. Dressed in jeans, sneakers, and a work shirt worn with the tail out, she had the black hair and the black eyes and the dark, dusky good looks of a South Seas beauty. Her body was excitingly proportioned; she carried herself like a Tahitian princess.

"This is Cass Tanguay." Taylor gestured to the woman, then gestured to Hastings. "Lieutenant Hastings, Cass. He's asking about Meredith Powell."

Listening to Taylor say it, watching the other man's face as he and the woman exchanged a significant glance, Hastings experienced the instant's quick lift of a hunter at first sight of game. Between Jonathan Taylor and Cass Tanguay and Meredith Powell, there was a connection.

The woman stepped forward, extended her hand. Her grip was firm, her gaze direct. Hastings returned the greeting with pleasure, released her hand with regret, then turned to the man. "You knew Meredith Powell."

Taylor nodded. "I didn't know her well. But I knew her."

"Do you know that she was murdered last Wednesday night?"

"I read about it in the paper. The Sunday paper, I think it was." As he spoke, Taylor looked around the gallery at the confusion of ladders, paintings propped against the plain white walls, sawhorses and tools. "I'm sorry. No chairs."

Dismissing the point, Hastings waved. "This won't take long."

"Here—" Cass Tanguay spread newspapers on a sawhorse. "Sit here."

"Thanks." Hastings did as she asked, waited for them to sit on another sawhorse and a small packing crate. Then, looking at each of them in turn, he said, "Tell me how you knew her. In what connection?"

"The Corwin connection," Taylor answered promptly. "What else?"

"Why do you say 'what else'?"

Instead of answering the question, Taylor looked at him sharply, appraisingly. "I guess you're not, ah, plugged into the local art scene."

"I guess not," he answered dryly.

"The reason I asked," Taylor said, "Edwin Corwin is the great high priest of art in San Francisco, or so he deludes himself into thinking. This is his gallery—" With a mocking flourish, Taylor raised both hands outstretched to the ceiling, perhaps to the heavens beyond. "We're surrounded by the Corwin aura. It envelops us. It's a *presence*."

"Okay—" Hastings nodded patiently, ready to wait out the amiable flow of Taylor's rhetoric. But then the Edwin Corwin name began a deep reecho in the depths of his consciousness, followed by random fragments of memory.

One of the great American fortunes.

Court battles, custody trials.

Edwin Corwin, poor little rich boy.

The original robber baron, August Corwin, had been the equal of the Astors, or the Rockefellers, or the Vanderbilts. But in recent years ancestral blood had thinned, the branches of the family tree had begun to rot. And Edwin Corwin had been the result.

And then, quickly, a more immediate image came clear: the

Corwin mansion on Jackson Street, in Pacific Heights. Big, elaborate parties. Extravaganzas. Major production numbers. And, in the wee hours of a morning long ago, a girl, dressed like a Roman slave. Drugged out. ODed. Dead.

Hushed up. Big money, high-priced lawyers, deals made behind closed doors. One law for the rich, one law for the poor.

"Are we talking about *the* Edwin Corwin?" Hastings asked. "The multimillionaire?"

"That's him," Taylor answered, cheerfully derisive. "That Edwin. He's crazy, but he's rich."

"And you met Meredith Powell through Edwin Corwin."

"Right."

"Was Meredith an artist?"

"No."

"Interested in art?"

Taylor smiled. "I don't know whether she was interested in art. But Corwin was definitely interested in Meredith Powell. Or, at least, as interested as he gets in women."

"Women as opposed to men, you mean?"

"No," Taylor answered, "I mean anyone, man or woman, as opposed to himself."

"Ah—" Hastings nodded. "He's egocentric, then."

"Edwin Corwin has got to be the most self-absorbed person I've ever known," Taylor answered. "And I speak from firsthand knowledge. I mean, *I'm* self-absorbed. But Edwin is possessed by himself. Absolutely possessed."

"You said he was crazy. What'd you mean?"

"What do I mean?" Considering the question, Taylor paused, frowning thoughtfully. "Well, for openers, Edwin is self-delusional. Do you know anything about his history?"

"I've read about him, like everyone else."

"Well, then, you know that the family tree narrowed down to Edwin and his mother and his aunt. There was his grandmother, too. Lady Macbeth. But she died at age ninety-five, not too long ago. While she was alive, the old woman and her two daughters spent all their time in court, fighting over the Corwin fortune. Now it's just the two daughters—and Edwin. And, of course, the legal battles go on. Edwin's fifty years old now, give or take. He inherited a fortune when he was eighteen, and another fortune when he was twenty-five, something like that. But he was totally fucked up long before he was eighteen. His mother saw to that. Apparently he was kicked out of several schools for corrupting the morals of his tender young classmates." Taylor paused, let his eyes wander reflectively away. "He was probably a pitiful spectacle, one of those poor little rich kids trying to buy friendship. And, in fact, he's still at it—still buying people, or trying to. And he's still a pitiful spectacle, really. He comes on like Caligula. But sometimes you get a glimpse of the confused little kid peeking out."

"How's he buying people now?"

"The art world—especially modern art, so called—is riddled with trends and fads, sad to say. And people like Edwin have enough money to set a trend. He's got galleries in San Francisco and Dallas and Santa Fe and New York. And he's just opened one in Los Angeles. So if he decides an artist is hot, then he's hot—at least for a while. All of which means there're dozens of artists standing in line to kiss Edwin's ass. And the incredible thing is, he does all this on pin money. Apparently his grandfather, the male chauvinist pig, put it in his will that when Edwin reached thirty or whatever, he could make the final decisions on the investment of the Corwin billions. As distinguished, you understand, from the measly millions he got when he turned eighteen. Whereupon Edwin apparently fell in with some wacky financier, so called, who talked him into taking a flyer on a couple of really far-out schemes. Like cornering the world silver market, or buying control of Belize, his own private country, things like that. And the result was that he lost maybe half the whole fortune. Which can happen, of course, if you gamble with million-dollar poker chips. So the result was that his mother and his aunt got worried enough to quit fighting between themselves and go to court and restrain him. Meaning that he can't touch any principal. Meaning, in turn, that he's limited to maybe a million dollars in income a year. Or maybe it's only a half million. Anyhow—" Taylor gesticulated. "Anyhow, he's on a budget. Just like the rest of us."

"Are his galleries successful?"

"That depends on how you define success, I suppose. Actually, Edwin's eye isn't terrible. It's just not nearly as good as he thinks it is. But, of course, no one's about to tell him. Not even the critics, a lot of them. They just seem to go with the flow. Maybe they like being invited to his parties."

"So—" Hastings gestured to Taylor's paintings, all of them mind-stretching abstracts. "So now is it your turn?"

As if he'd been pinpricked, Taylor grimaced. "My turn to kiss Edwin's ass, you mean?"

Hastings decided not to reply.

"I guess it is my turn." Taylor spoke softly, ruefully. "Of course, I believe that I'm the exception, the only one of Edwin's protégés with real talent. Which is a little like thinking you're not really going to die, I guess."

Cass Tanguay shifted, gestured impatiently. "Give yourself a break, for God's sake."

As Taylor looked at her silently, his expressive face revealed a complex play of contradictory emotions. Watching, Hastings could clearly see affection flash between them. But it was an affection complicated by both competition and artistic tension: two willful, forceful people, in contest.

In contest, and in love.

A moment of tight, decisive silence passed. Then, letting it go, Taylor snorted, turned to Hastings. "So what's this all about, Lieutenant? The newspaper account wasn't very specific. How'd Meredith die?"

"She was found murdered in Golden Gate Park. We think she was actually killed somewhere else, and we're trying to get some idea of her movements Wednesday night between, say, eight o'clock Wednesday and two A.M. on Thursday morning."

Taylor promptly shook his head, shrugged, spread his hands. "I can't help you there, Lieutenant. I've seen Meredith Powell exactly twice, both times at one of Edwin's orgies."

"Orgies?"

Taylor's muscle-knotted lumberjack's face broke into a quick grin. "I exaggerate. Orgies aren't exactly Edwin's style. He's too anal to let the program get out of hand. Call them mass erotic homages to Edwin." Satisfied with the phrase, he nodded puckishly.

"Who was Meredith with?" Hastings asked.

"At the party?" Taylor asked. "Or, rather, homage?"

Aware that time was passing, Hastings answered cryptically, in departmental officialese: "Yes, sir."

"She was with Edwin, of course. She was one of his conquests, I assumed. Or, at least, one of his handmaidens."

"Handmaidens?"

"Sure. If Edwin wanted something—a goblet of wine, for instance, that was her function. She was there to gratify Edwin's every whim—or, at least, his public whims. His private whims, of course, are a matter of avid speculation."

"Are we still talking about Meredith Powell?"

"We're talking about Meredith Powell and others."

"You say Corwin is about fifty."

"About."

"Describe him, will you?"

"He looks like one of those neurotic, tyrannical ballet masters. He's real skinny, no more than a hundred fifty pounds, if that. He's got one of those deeply lined faces. You know—a road map of all his assorted neuroses. It's a real narrow, cruel face. Deep, intense eyes. Small mouth that never smiles. He combs his hair forward, like Napoleon. And, God, he acts like Napoleon, too. His whole thing is manipulating people, cutting them down. He's a practicing sadist."

"What color is his hair?"

"Gray. Or, rather, graying. Edwin would never deign to color his hair."

"Thick hair?"

"No. Sparse."

"How tall is he?"

"Not tall. Five eight, maybe. He's actually a shrimp, when I think about it. Like Napoleon. Or like a retired jockey. Take your pick. Why?" Interested now, Taylor leaned forward. "Why're you asking?"

"There's a man we want to question. We think he's average height, average weight, maybe a hundred seventy. Twenty-five or thirty. He's white. Dark hair, probably thick."

"Does he know Edwin, hang around with Edwin?"

"We're not sure. Why?"

Taylor shrugged. "Because that description could fit a psycho named Charles."

"Charles? Charles who?"

Grimacing, Taylor shrugged, shook his head. "Just Charles. He's a conceptual artist."

Hastings frowned. "A conceptual artist?"

"You know—like Christo. Which is where Charles probably got the idea of just using Charles. He's a bona fide, certified creep. And his art is creepy, too. It's too bad you weren't here a month ago. Edwin gave Charles a show in the small gallery in front—" Taylor waved a hand. "He painted the whole room black, and the floor, too. There was just a dais in the center of the gallery, draped in black velvet. There was an open casket on the dais. It was lined in white satin. A pig was lying in the casket. With an ornamental dagger stuck in its chest. The pig wore a red cardinal's hat, trimmed in gold."

Hastings swallowed. "You're kidding."

"Actually"—Taylor sighed—"it was pretty effective. But then the pig started to stink. Apparently it wasn't embalmed; an artistic oversight."

"And Charles knows Edwin. Is that what you said?"

Grimacing again, Taylor answered, "There're lots of rumors circulating about the relationship between Charles and Edwin. You can take your pick. Some say they're lovers. Or bisexual, and lovers sometimes. Some say Charles is Edwin's procurer. In any case, Charles is Edwin's gofer, his alter ego, whatever. Incidentally, you didn't miss Charles by more than a few minutes. He could still be in the gallery, for all I know. He manages the place for Edwin."

Instantly Hastings rose. "Give me a description. What's he look like? What's he wearing? What kind of car does he drive?"

Eyes snapping avidly, Taylor spoke quickly, tersely. "He's about thirty, I'd say. It's hard to tell. He's always dressed in dark suits, double breasted. Always a white shirt, formal tie, black shoes, always shined. He looks exactly like a funeral director. Real pale, pasty face; dark eyes. Dark hair, too. Straight, dark hair. He never smiles. He definitely pulled the wings off flies when he was little. Still does, probably."

"Do you know where he lives?"

"Hell, no. But Gloria probably does, at the reception desk. She might not tell you, but she probably knows."

"What kind of a car does he drive?"

"It's a blue Fiat convertible. Good-looking car," Taylor admitted grudgingly.

The three of them were standing now, closely facing each other, sharing the sudden, muted excitement. Hastings took out a card, handed it to Taylor.

"If you think of anything else, call me. Leave a message, if I'm not there."

"Right."

"And don't mention this. To anyone. Is that clear?"

"That's clear."

1:10 P.M. Outside the phone booth, two teenage girls were waiting, both of them staring at him coldly, one of them holding up a quarter. Pretending to talk on the phone, Charles turned his back on them. The booth was across the street from the gallery, and four doors west. The Honda was parked three doors east of the gallery. The Fiat was parked on Gough Street, safe from discovery. He would wait until—

Behind the gallery's plate-glass window a figure materialized, coalesced, became a man—a big man—the detective, opening the door, walking briskly to the Honda. This was a man with a purpose, clearly revealed in the pattern of his movements, the set of his head, the swing of his arms. The man got into the Honda, pulled out of the parking place, a loading zone. As the Honda drew abreast of him, Charles turned away, avoiding the stares of the girls. Then he slipped two dimes into the slot, dialed the gallery's number.

"The Corwin Gallery."

"Gloria."

"Hi." It was her customary flat, disinterested greeting. Long ago he should have demanded that Edwin fire her.

He hadn't planned his opening question, a mistake. Was he beginning to make mistakes?

"I—ah—I wondered, has anyone been asking for me?"

"As a matter of fact, Charles," she answered, "someone *was* looking for you."

Clearly, he could hear the pleasure in her voice, the smug, sadistic satisfaction. His respiration, he knew, was quickening. Palms wet, shirt sweat-sticky at the armpits. Breath too short, voice too tight. "Well? Who was it?"

"It was a policeman." Her voice silky, venom-syruped. "A cop. Homicide, in fact."

"H—" His throat closed, the body master of the mind. He swallowed, cleared his throat. "Homicide?"

"His name is Hastings. *Lieutenant* Hastings."

"What'd he—" Once more the words died. "What'd he want?"

"He wanted to talk to you. I told him he just missed you. He asked for your address and phone."

"Did you—did you give them to him?"

"I figured I should." A pause. In the silence he could visualize her face: the small, smug smile, the eyes slyly slanted. "After all, he's the law." Another pause. Then, mock-innocently: "That was right, wasn't it?"

"The law. Yes. Sure. But I—" As his voice caught again, he realized that he had no choice. He must break the connection, free himself from her venom.


1:20 P.M. As Hastings pulled away from the curb and entered the stream of Hayes Street traffic, he was visualizing Friedman's face when he heard the news. In Friedman's lexicon of favorite targets, politicians and fat cats, unspecified, shared top billing. Even the outside chance that they could tie a can on Edwin Corwin would make Friedman's day.


1:25 P.M. At the other end of the line, Luis answered the phone on the second ring.

"Yes. This is Charles. Let me speak to Mr. Corwin."

"Mr. Corwin is upstairs, sir."

"All right." He broke the connection, consulted a slip of paper taken from his wallet, dialed the pay phone again. On the fourth ring, the call was completed.

"Hello."

"Edwin."

A pause. On the static-sizzling line, tension cracked. Tension, and the emanations of sudden fear.

But fear could galvanize. Terror paralyzed, but fear could be salvation's goad, the forest primeval, bloody in tooth and claw.

These random images, these strange, unpredictable flashes. He'd never experienced them before, not like this.

"Yes?" Edwin's voice was wan. Were images flashing for Edwin, too? "Yes? Wh—" Edwin's voice had clogged in his throat.

At the thought, Charles felt himself sustained. Strengthened. Ready. As Edwin mewled, he triumphed. Tooth and claw. Jungle law. Universal. They'd already established that, he and Edwin. He was the hunter, the executioner. Edwin was the high priest.

"I'm talking from a phone booth. And I want you to listen. I want you to listen very carefully. Do you understand?"

"Y-yes. I understand."

"The man we talked about, he's a policeman. A lieutenant. And he's been at the the gallery."

"Oh, no. *No.*"

"Yes. He didn't ask about you. But he asked about me. That's all I know. But I think we should—"

"How did he . . . ?"

"*Listen.* Just listen. I don't want to talk too long."

"Y-yes. I see."

"I think I should leave. I think that's best. I've been thinking about it. He spent a half hour, at least, at the gallery. It gave me time to think, to plan. And I think I should fly to Los Angeles and then go to Europe. Portugal, maybe. On a buying trip, I'll say. Primitives."

"But they—do they—?"

"As far as I know, they don't connect us, you and me. I don't think you're involved. But we can't—"

"M-maybe I should go, too. Maybe we should both—"

"No. That's wrong. Absolutely wrong. If we both go—disappear, suddenly—they'll make the connection. You understand that, don't you?"

As he heard himself say it, heard his own voice, heard the strength, he realized that he was smiling. Edwin was quaking, he was smiling. How loud was the crash when the mighty fell.

"Yes. I understand."

"Good. Now, here's what you've got to do. You've got to get me some money. There's still time to get to the bank. Get fifty thousand in—" He hesitated. "It'll have to be in cash."

"But that much money in cash. I can't get it, not so soon."

"You don't have a choice, Edwin. Gloria gave the police my address. Everything. I can't even go home. I'm phoning from a pay phone. Do you understand?"

"Yes—I understand." It was a cowed, craven response. Edwin Corwin, no longer the master, now the slave; ecstasy incarnate.

"We'll meet tonight at the Legion of Honor, the north side. Drive the Jag, so I'll recognize you."

"Th-the north side?"

"Where we shot that video last year, with Parker. Drive up and park in front of the courtyard. I've just been out there, driven the route. We'll meet there at nine o'clock."

"But I—"

"Nine o'clock, Edwin. Be there, with the money. Don't send anyone. Come yourself. Do you understand?"

"Yes."

"Nine o'clock."

"Yes."

"Are the videotapes safe? Hidden?"

"Yes," Corwin answered. "Certainly."

"Well, you've got to destroy them."

"Destroy them? But—"

"If the police ever find them, they'll have the whole thing laid out for them. Don't you understand that?"

"Well, yes. But—"

"I want to ask you something, Edwin. Before I hang up, I want to ask you something. And I want you to tell me the truth."

"Wh-what is it?"

"Am I on those tapes? I know you're on them. But am I on them?"

A silence. And with the silence came certainty: the raw, chilling certainty.

Yes, he was on the tapes.


2:35 P.M. "Okay," Friedman said, "we're all set. Culligan has two men staking out Corwin's mansion, and Sawyer and Allingham are staking out Charles's place."

"Where's Charles live?" Hastings asked.

"It's a loft on Bryant Street. The building was a warehouse, converted into lofts for artists."

"Has either of them been spotted?"

"Culligan's pretty sure Corwin's inside his house. And even if he isn't, assuming that he's guilty, I can't imagine him running, somehow. But Charles isn't home, and he hasn't been seen after he left the gallery."

"Are you getting warrants?"

"I don't think we've got grounds to search Corwin's place," Friedman said. "I mean—" He spread his hands. "I mean, what've we got? A sorehead artist saw Corwin and Meredith together at a couple of parties. Tell that to a judge, and we'd use up a year's credibility. Minimum."

"If we can tie Corwin to Allegro, though—tie him to the ownership of her condo . . ."

"That, obviously, is something else. Meanwhile, though—" Frustrated, Friedman sharply shook his head. "Meanwhile, I'm having a hell of a time getting a line on Charles."

"Why?"

"For one thing, I can't find out his last name, if you can

173

believe that. And without a last name, no judge in the world is going to issue a search warrant. It's also impossible to check out his car, obviously, without a last name."

"It's a blue Fiat convertible. How many can there be in San Francisco?"

"Except that the color doesn't scan, for the computer."

Hastings nodded. "I know that."

"I've got a computer guy checking Fiats registered to owners with the given name Charles. And, obviously, he's running Fiats registered to Charles's address. Incidentally, how'd you get Charles's address and phone, without a last name?"

"I got it from the gallery. He manages the place, apparently."

"Ah—" Friedman nodded. Then: "Did Canelli tell you about that confessor?"

"Canelli said you let the guy go. He didn't say why."

"Well," Friedman said, "it didn't take a genius to see that Granville was bonkers. He's the homeless guy who found the body. Nice old guy, lives in Golden Gate Park with his faithful dog Chum. Crazy, but nice. Harmless, too, obviously. As near as I could figure it, he began to identify with her. Or maybe he wanted to see himself on TV. Or, more likely, it was a combination, plus the chance to live in a nice warm prison cell for the rest of his life. Anyhow, I listened to him for a while and petted his dog—who growled at me. And then I explained to Granville that if he confessed to murder, he'd go to prison for a long, long time—without Chum. And that was that. A half hour later he and Chum were on their way back to Golden Gate Park."

"So what about Corwin and Charles? What's next?"

"Obviously," Friedman said, "the best-case scenario would be to find Charles, ask him a few questions, run him by that kid—" He glanced at his notes. "Lee Persse, who was parked outside the victim's building Wednesday night. Then, when Charles confesses, we talk to Corwin. Who, in the meantime, we've tied to ownership of Meredith's building and the ownership of the paintings and the art in her apartment. No sweat."

"Except that Charles has disappeared."

"Except that Charles has disappeared. Correct."

"So?"

"So," Friedman said, moving forward in his chair, ready to rise. "So, while we're waiting, let's see what Edwin Corwin has to say about his relationship to Meredith Powell."

"You and me?" Hastings pretended disbelief. "Out in the field? You?"

"I save myself for the big fish. Exclusively."

3:20 P.M. Grimacing, Hastings turned the windshield wipers to full speed. Rain was falling in sheets, whipped by the wind. Overhead, the sky was a solid, leaden gray.

"We should've picked up a couple of slickers," Friedman said.

Switching on the headlights, Hastings made no response.

"You didn't have anything to do with that girl who died at one of Corwin's parties, did you?" Friedman asked.

"No."

"So you've never met Corwin, never been inside his house."

"No."

"Well," Friedman said wryly, "you've got a surprise in store."

"How do you mean?"

"I mean the guy's downright bizarre. And so's his house. You'll see."

Hastings turned left from Octavia into Jackson and began looking for a parking place. In the twin crescents left by the windshield wipers, he saw both curbs lined solidly with cars. No loading zones, no passenger zones. Just cars.

"Culligan probably has the last parking place," Friedman said, peering through the rain. "Do you see him?"

"No."

"Jesus, what weather. They're flooded in Marin County. They've called out the—" He interrupted himself. "There's a fireplug." Friedman pointed across the street, then pointed to a three-story mansion set on a double lot. It was a brick-and-stone imitation of an English Tudor country estate: slate roofs, towering chimneys, lead-paned windows. "And there's the house. Good. We won't get soaked."

"From the outside, there's nothing bizarre about it."

"Just wait."


**3:25 P.M.** As Friedman pressed the small illuminated button set into the stone frame of the door, Hastings stepped back, saying "Why don't you go first? You know him."

Friedman's round, bland face registered mild amusement. "I wouldn't say I know him. However, I—"

The carved oak door swung open. A small man dressed in a white jacket stood in the open doorway. His features were classic Chicano: olive skin, black eyes, black hair. With his shield in his hand, Friedman stated their business. "We'd like to see Mr. Corwin," he finished, using his bulk to intimidate the small brown man.

With his eyes fixed on the shield, the houseman spoke in a soft, reluctant voice, transparently lying. "He isn't here. Sorry." As if to close it, he put an uneasy hand on the door.

"Well, then—" Friedman stepped forward. "We'll wait."

"But—"

"It's okay. We won't be any trouble."

Finally the houseman looked up, with great effort meeting Friedman's gaze. The houseman's soft brown eyes were timid, his voice hesitant. "Please. I—I don't think I'm supposed—"

"Don't worry," Friedman said, crossing the threshold. "I'll take full responsibility. It's no problem."

"But—"

Once inside the entryway, with Hastings beside him, Friedman confronted the houseman squarely: two hundred forty pounds and a gold shield bulking over a blinking, twitching hundred forty pounds. Friedman spoke slowly, heavily, investing the standard opening question with the full force of the law. "What's your name?"

"It—it's Luis. My name is Luis Raiz."

"Well, Luis, we're both officers, Lieutenant Hastings and myself. We're not just policemen. We give the orders to other detectives. Do you understand?"

With great effort, Raiz still managed to meet Friedman's flat, relentless stare. "Lieutenants. Yes. I know."

"And we're here—both of us—because we're investigating the murder of a woman named Meredith Powell. *Comprende?*"

"*Sí*—" Raiz gulped. "Yes. Yes, sir." At his sides, Raiz's small, nervous hands were clenching and unclenching.

"We think Mr. Corwin can help us, give us some information we need. So it's very important that we talk to Mr. Corwin."

Raiz nodded. "Yes . . ."

"So, because it's important that we talk to Mr. Corwin—very important, to our investigation—anyone who keeps us from seeing Mr. Corwin is actually breaking the law. It's called obstructing justice." Friedman paused, waited while his victim squirmed. Then he said quietly, "And people can go to jail, Luis, for obstructing justice. They can go to jail for a long, long time."

"But I—I can't—" Raiz drew back miserably. As if to look for a way out, his eyes slid aside. On his forehead, sweat glistened.

Friedman shifted his attack expertly. Pitching his voice to a confidential note, he asked quietly, "Did you know her, Luis? Did you know Meredith Powell?"

"I—" Raiz licked his lips. "I saw her, yes."

"Here? In this house?"

The houseman silently nodded.

"How many times did you see her, Luis?"

"I—I saw her many times."

"She was—" Friedman paused delicately. "She was with Mr. Corwin. Here. Is that what you're saying?"

"Y-yes, sir, that's what I'm saying."

Smiling encouragement, Friedman stepped back. Now his bulk was teddy bear friendly, no longer menacing. "Okay," Friedman said, "you've been helpful. You've got nothing to worry about. At least, not so far. Do you understand?"

Slowly, tentatively, Raiz nodded, plainly suspicious of this casual gift of hope. "I understand. Yes."

"Okay—" Now, briskly, Friedman moved to his left, away from the front door. "Now, Luis, we're going to sit down, Lieutenant Hastings and I"— he gestured to a large room off the entry hall—"and we're going to wait for Mr. Corwin to show up. We're going to wait for as long as it takes for him to show up. And we've got men outside, waiting. They're on stakeout. You understand about stakeouts, don't you?"

"Oh, yes—" Still speaking softly, hesitantly, Raiz said, "Cops and robbers. Stakeout. Yes."

Friedman nodded solemnly. "That's right, Luis. Cops and robbers. Exactly."


3:30 P.M. It was happening again—happening still. Always. The same sensations registering the same voices, the same nameless phantasms of recollection.

Voices from downstairs. His mother's voice. His father's voice, dimly remembered. Lawyers' voices, from behind closed doors. Overheard voices. Bedroom voices: his mother's voice, and the voices of strange men overlaying hers. First he'd been a child, crouched in the hallway darkness. And now he was a child grown into a man, still listening in hallways, unconsciously pressed against the balustrades, clinging, trying to make himself even smaller.

Hearing the sound of their voices, from just below.

After all the voices, a lifetime of listening, it had finally come down to one voice: Luis Raiz, betraying him.

**3:32 P.M.** Hastings watched Luis Raiz leave the room, then turned his attention to the mansion's decor as he circled the room with baffled eyes. Like the building's exterior, the interior was imitation Tudor: rough-hewn beams, natural wooden paneling and trim, slate floors, roughly troweled white plaster walls, a majestic stone fireplace crowned by a heraldic coat of arms. The leaded windows were small; the panes were imperfect, distorting the outside view.

Except for a huge iron-studded plank-top table in the center of the room and the benches on either side of the massive fireplace hearth, the room was unfurnished. A huge circular wrought-iron candelabra was suspended by chains from exposed ceiling beams in the center of the room, but interior light came from many small concealed spotlights set into the beams. The spotlights illuminated the paintings and collages that covered the walls and the statuary that rested on individual display pedestals.

Like the paintings at Meredith Powell's flat and the Corwin Gallery, most of the canvases were overscale abstracts. But these paintings, Hastings sensed, were subtly different. With Friedman standing by, Hastings stepped closer to one of the paintings. The background was a textured blue-black, with color clustered irregularly at the center. From a distance, the colored portion was abstract. But seen close up, the cluster of color was actually an intricate collection of nude figures, animal and human, pornographically intertwined.

Hastings glanced at Friedman, shrugged in response to the other man's small, knowing smile, then turned again to face the wall. A huge three-dimensional wall sculpture hung beside the painting. The sculpture was a surreal representation of a human eyeball that had been torn from its socket, sinews and nerves and blood vessels dangling, the white of the eye a network of red lines. In the pupil of the eye, Hastings saw the figure of a beautiful nude woman. One of her eyes was missing, leaving a bloody socket.

"Kinky," Hastings said.

"Definitely kinky." Friedman sat on one of the rough wooden benches.

"So what now?"

"I figure he's probably here," Friedman said. "All we've got to do is wait."

"I don't see why both of us should wait."

Friedman considered the point, then said, "Let's give it a half hour, see what happens. If Charles gets collared somewhere, Communications'll beep us."

"Is the rest of the house like this?"

"I only saw a couple of rooms—this one and another one, if I remember. Plus the hallway, which looks like it's a medieval castle, for God's sake. You know: suits of armor, crossed swords. And, of course, a few shrunken heads."

"Are you kidding?"

"I'm half kidding."

"Shrunken heads are African."

"Not if you stir them in a witches' stew."

"We should've gotten a bio on this guy."

"I ordered one."

"Did you check any priors? What about that girl who died at one of his parties?"

"I don't know about priors on him. And I can't remember the girl's name, to run it."

"Christ—" Hastings shook his head. "This is crazy. We can't get a search warrant on Charles because we don't have a last name. And we can't run Corwin because we can't remember a victim's name. What good are million-dollar computers?"

"Patience," Friedman said. "We'll get her name. I've pulled out all the stops, gone to afterburners."

"What's that supposed to mean?" Hastings asked sourly.

"It means," Friedman answered solemnly, "that I posted a notice in the bathrooms. Ten bucks, for anyone who remembers the girl's name."

**4:15 P.M.** With the storm raging outside the second-story window, the bedroom was in half darkness. Standing before the full-length mirror, Corwin carefully studied his reflection. Yes, the image was satisfactory, a convincing representation of the casually dressed Ivy Leaguer: tweed jacket, button-down white oxford shirt, flannel trousers, loafers. Even the socks fitted: wool argyles, an evocation of his earliest childhood returned to fashion favor.

He turned from his reflection, sat at the desk, took the straw, bent over the two lines of cocaine on the sheet of dark paper. Yes, for this performance, two lines would be required. One line for courage, one line for inspiration.

Quickly he inhaled. One line, and the other line. He leaned back in the chair, let his eyes close, felt the rush begin. Heard the cymbals. Saw the light that made the shadows glow. At Andover, he'd gotten a part in the junior play, one of his most vivid memories. On opening night, alone on the stage, utterly alone, just himself and the multicolored lights rendering the audience invisible, he'd become a second person, released. Reality had fallen away, leaving him omnipotent. It had been a magical moment. His first moment of pure magic, and his last.

He opened his eyes, drew a long, deep breath. His eyes were fixed on the telephone, close to his hand. He should call a lawyer. He knew he should call a lawyer. But then the nightmares would begin: voices of lawyers, shredding his soul. Faces of judges: monsters, dangling from their fingers the strings that controlled his life. Lawyers—judges—his mother—his aunt. All of them, dangling the strings. Leaving him with nothing. From earliest memory, nothing.

He was walking to the bedroom door, unlocking it, opening it, stepping out into the hallway. From downstairs, he could hear their voices: the two detectives questioning Luis, who had been summoned back into their presence.

This time there was no glare of lights. And no one to prompt him, give him the lines. There was just the sound of cymbals, sizzling softly: his own thoughts, slowly frying.

4:17 P.M. As Raiz left the room, Hastings frowned at his watch. "This is dumb. We're not outwaiting him. He's outwaiting us."

Impassive, Friedman made no response.

"I'm going to at least call Communications," Hastings said, "find out whether they've got anything on Charles."

"If they had anything, they'd beep us."

"These walls are rock. Maybe the signal can't—"

In the archway that opened on the central reception hall, a man appeared. His body was improbably slim: not athletically slim, but desiccated. The graying hair was thin, combed forward over a balding scalp. The deep-set eyes were manic, perpetually fix-focused. The face, too, was desiccated, etched with lines deeper than aging. It was a ravaged aristocrat's face, destroyed from within.

Rising, Friedman stepped forward. "Mr. Corwin."

The man nodded. Friedman made the introductions, then fell silent. The three men remained motionless for a moment, looking at each other in turn, making their separate assessments. Finally Corwin came into the room, leaned against the huge central table, gesturing for the two detectives to take their seats on the benches that flanked the fireplace.

"I'm sorry you had to wait," Corwin said. "Luis had orders not to disturb me."

"Ah—" Friedman nodded. "Yes, we were wondering."

"Wondering?"

"We had a feeling that you were here. From the way Luis acted."

"I see." Corwin's lips stirred in a thin, humorless smile that left the eyes eerily empty. "Very perceptive." The smile faded instantly.

"Thank you." Friedman smiled, nodded genially. Then, aware that he was unable to remain seated, eyes raised, while Corwin stood at his ease, arms folded, looking down at them, Friedman rose, stepped to the fireplace, leaned easily against the eight-foot mantelpiece. Also rising to stand beside the fireplace, Hastings knowingly noted the smile. With a member of the privileged class within range, Friedman was adjusting his sights, fixing the cross-hairs on his victim.

"The reason we've come," Friedman began, "is to ask about Meredith Powell. You knew her, we understand."

Corwin spoke very softly. "She was murdered. Thursday, wasn't it?"

"You did know her, then."

Still leaning against the edge of the table, arms folded, legs crossed at the ankles, Corwin nodded. "She's been here often. Meredith was beautiful, one of those natural beauties."

"You say she's been here," Hastings said. "Have you ever been to her place?"

Corwin nodded. "Yes. Twice, I think. She lived on Hyde Street, right at the top of the hill. It was a wonderful view, I remember. Really spectacular."

"When were you there?" Friedman asked. "How long ago?"

Corwin shook his head. "I'm sorry. I can't remember." He smiled.

"Just approximately. A week? A month? A year?"

Corwin shrugged languidly. "Months, certainly. Not weeks, anyhow. And not a year, I wouldn't think."

"When was the last time she was here?"

"I'm not sure," Corwin answered. "It was at a party. I'm in

the art business, as you may know. Every month or so I give a party for my artists and their friends." Once more his face registered a counterfeit smile, instantly gone. "They're mob scenes, I'm afraid. The neighbors seem to think so, anyhow."

"Several years ago," Friedman said, "we met, you and I. It was after one of your parties. When a girl died."

"Ah . . ." Broadly regretful, Corwin shook his head. "Yes. It—I'll never forget that, as long as I live. Someone brought heroin to the party. It was terrible. Absolutely terrible."

"What was the victim's name?" Friedman asked. "Do you remember?"

"It was Tina Betts," Corwin answered promptly. "She was only nineteen. Someone brought her to the party."

"You'd never seen Tina Betts before that time, if I remember."

"That's correct. She came with someone. An artist named Esterbrook, if I recall correctly."

Friedman nodded, exchanged a quick glance with Hastings. The time had come to turn up the heat.

"Getting back to Meredith Powell, Mr. Corwin, can you give us any reason why she was murdered?"

As if he were puzzled, Corwin frowned. "I'm afraid I don't understand what you mean."

"What we're doing," Friedman said, "is checking out everyone who knew her. 'Known associates' is the official phrase. You knew her, obviously. Do you have any idea why someone would want to kill her?"

"None at all."

"Was she involved with drugs, for instance? Did she hang around with people you'd consider dangerous?"

"Not that I was aware of, certainly. I really didn't know that much about her friends, I'm afraid. I was simply—" Corwin paused, searching for the phrase. "I was simply an admirer." Another pause, another search for the appropriate phrase. Then: "Someone as beautiful as Meredith deserved to be admired."

"Like you'd admire a work of art . . ." As he said it, Hastings allowed his gaze to wander to the gouged-out eye, with its ganglia dangling down the wall.

Ignoring the direction of Hastings's glance, Corwin nodded appreciatively, smiled. "Exactly."

"What about Meredith Powell's life-style?" Friedman asked.

Corwin frowned. "Her life-style?"

"I'd calculate," Friedman said, "that she needed at least a hundred thousand dollars a year to live the way she lived, assuming she was paying rent and making car payments. But she apparently didn't work. And we don't believe she had a whole lot of money in the bank, or in stocks and bonds. Not enough, anyhow, to produce that kind of income. So—" Friedman spread his hands. "So we think someone was paying her bills. Have you any idea who it might've been, Mr. Corwin?"

"No, I'm afraid I don't, Lieutenant. Sorry."

"You say she's been here for your parties. Did she come with someone?"

"At first she did. But then I invited her. As I said, Meredith was so beautiful, she was like a—a spectacle."

"So she came as your date," Friedman pressed.

Corwin lifted himself to sit on the table, legs dangling, arms braced wide on the ancient planks. He spoke judiciously. "You might say that. Except that, typically, I ask several women to come to my parties as my guests."

"You're not married, I gather."

Amused, Corwin shook his head. "No, Lieutenant, I'm not married." His manner was both condescending and playful, as if he were teasing the two detectives, gently chiding them for the question. "I tried marriage once, a long time ago. It didn't work. I've never had the desire to try it again."

As if to join in the other man's quizzical little game, Friedman smiled. "You're very candid, Mr. Corwin. We appreciate that."

Corwin gracefully inclined his narrow head: dry, yellowing skin stretched across the aging bones of the skull. "As you've doubtless suspected, Lieutenant, I'm a spectator, I'm afraid. A dedicated spectator. Provocative art, beautiful women, anything that's unique—I collect them all. Some would say I'm a voyeur, I suppose, a collector of new experiences, new sensations." He shrugged. "And I can't disagree." He focused his avid eyes on Friedman. "It must be the same with you, in your work."

"I'm afraid I don't understand."

"I was thinking of murder," Corwin said. "After all, murder is the ultimate human experience, wouldn't you say?"

"The difference between us," Friedman answered, "is that you're a spectator. With me, it's business."

"Ah—" Corwin nodded appreciatively. "Yes."

Watching them, Hastings realized that he was witnessing the opening moves in a contest of equals, each man probing the other's defense.

"I'm still trying to decide on the true nature of your relationship with the victim." Friedman said it tentatively, as if to ask Corwin for help. "She's been here several times, and you've been to her place a couple of times. Now—" Pretending to search laboriously for the right words, the right phrases, Friedman paused. "Now, I understand why she came here. She was a beautiful woman, and you wanted her for your parties. An adornment, you might say. Is that it, pretty much?"

Smiling fatuous encouragement, Corwin nodded. "That's it exactly, Lieutenant. Excellent."

"And when you went to her place—" Friedman delicately let the question go unfinished.

Corwin's answering smile was playfully elfin. "I went with the thought that"—he shrugged, twisted his lips in a lascivious smile—"that, who knows, there might be a happy ending."

"That she might go to bed with you." Friedman's smile, too, was playfully lascivious. Watching the two men leer at each other, Hastings experienced a momentary rush of anger. It was Meredith they were talking about.

In reply, Corwin smiled, shrugged, recrossed his feet at the ankles, dangling the sporty loafers, the with-it argyle socks. Watching the two men smiling at each other, swapping locker-room innuendoes, Friedman leaning against the massive baronial fireplace, Corwin sitting on the huge oak-and-studded-iron table, Hastings felt reality suddenly shift. What was the meaning of this strange encounter, played against the bizarre backdrop of surreal modern art displayed in a room meant for a medieval castle? What were they doing here, the three of them?

"But it didn't work out," Friedman prompted, his voice genial, his full lips curving in a small, knowing smile. Hastings recognized that mannerism, recognized that smile. Friedman was about to spring a carefully prepared trap.

"No," Corwin answered, also genially. "It didn't work out. She was kind but firm."

"But you continued to invite her to your parties."

Corwin nodded urbanely. "Of course."

As if he were reviewing the ground they'd covered, Friedman nodded thoughtfully, allowed his eyes to wander across the room until they fixed on one of the statues, a candy-striped abstract representation of two women making love. Friedman held the pose, letting the silence lengthen, letting the tension slowly build. Finally he turned again to face Corwin.

"Tell me about Allegro, Mr. Corwin." He spoke casually, almost negligently.

The effect was electric. Instantly Corwin's head snapped up, his eyes came into sharp, hard focus. "Allegro?"

Still casual, Friedman nodded. "Allegro."

"But I—" Corwin levered himself down from his seat on the tabletop to stand facing Friedman. His face was a mask, an inscrutable network of countless lines and creases drawn in on itself. "I don't understand what Allegro's got to do with this."

"Allegro owns the building you've got your gallery in," Friedman said. "Isn't that true?"

"I—ah—yes." Corwin's lips parted; a small pink tongue moistened thin, dry lips. "Yes, that's true. But—"

"Allegro also owns the building on Hyde Street where Meredith lived." Friedman's eyes were very still, fixed on his victim.

As if he were incapable of wrenching his eyes away, Corwin stood motionless, staring at Friedman. The silence lengthened, the tension heightened. Finally, speaking in a low, ragged monotone, eyes still fixated by Friedman's cold, dispassionate stare, Corwin said, "I—I knew that—knew Allegro owns the building on Hyde Street. That's—ah—" He broke off, suddenly dropped his eyes. Transparently, Corwin was struggling to think ahead, anticipate the interrogation's next turn, guilt entangled in the tightening coils of truth. Both detectives scrupulously avoided each other's eyes, afraid their excitement would show. Edwin Corwin, multimillionaire, child of the nation's headlines, self-admitted voyeur, was making the amateur criminal's most predictable mistake. Rather than remain silent, waiting for his lawyer, Edwin Corwin would now begin to lie. Beginning, predictably, with deceptive bits of truth.

"That's—ah—true, that Allegro owns both buildings. And others, too—other buildings, in San Francisco."

Deftly setting out another snare, Friedman spoke affably. "And New York, too. And other cities."

Corwin nodded eagerly. But, instantly, caution shadowed his eyes. "Y-yes, that's right. It's—ah—Allegro, it's actually my family's business. One of my family's businesses."

Still affable, Friedman said, "I imagine the rents are substantial, for Twenty-one Fifty-two Hyde Street."

"Well—" Once more Corwin licked his lips. "Well, I suppose they are. But that's not my affair. I—naturally—I don't collect the rents."

"Do you pay rent on the Hayes Street building—your gallery?"

"Yes." As if he were reassured by the conversation's turn, Corwin nodded. "It's a paper transaction. I pay Allegro rent, they pay me dividends." Corwin's attempt at a smile was grotesque, a sudden, spasmodic realignment of the lines and creases. "Fortunately, the dividends exceed the rent."

"And what about Meredith, Mr. Corwin? Did she pay the rent?" Friedman's voice was silky-soft.

Instantly the caricature of a smile disappeared. The narrow shoulders jerked upward, counterfeiting an indifferent shrug. "I suppose she did. As I said, it's not my function to—"

Hastings interrupted. "No, Mr. Corwin, she didn't pay rent." Like Friedman, he spoke quietly, gently.

"Well—" Corwin spread his hands. The fingers were trembling. He dropped his arms quickly, then refolded them across his narrow chest. "Well, that's between Meredith and Allegro. She—"

"We're checking out Allegro's records right now, Mr. Corwin. And what'll you bet we'll discover that Meredith lived rent-free?"

"Are you—" Corwin's throat closed, forcing him to break off. Then, in a half-choked voice: "Are you—you accusing me? Because if you are, I'm certainly not going to—"

"Accusing you?" Eyebrows blandly arched, Friedman raised both hands, an innocent disclaimer. "What would I accuse you of?" Holding the innocuous pose, he let a maestro's beat pass. Then: "Of Meredith's murder? Is that what you were going to say?"

At bay now, yet trying to conceal it, Corwin fell silent. His gaze slid toward the open archway, and escape.

"Well," Friedman said, "there's no point in pursuing the question of rent. Either she paid it or she didn't. It's a matter of record." He let another beat pass. Then, in a different voice, all business now, he said, "What about Charles, Mr. Corwin? Tell us about Charles."

Once more the small tongue protruded to lick lips thinned by silent desperation. The slack flesh of Corwin's throat was corded. For the first time, Hastings saw sweat glistening on the suspect's forehead and scalp.

"Charles?"

Friedman nodded gravely. "Yes. Charles. He's your right-hand man, we understand. Did he know Meredith?"

"I—I—" Once more Corwin's throat closed. Then, with great effort, he said, "I can't tell you anything about him, about Charles."

Friedman pretended surprise. "Why would you say that?"

"Because you—you're insinuating that Charles—that he had something to do with—with Meredith's murder."

The two detectives exchanged a long, significant glance. Then Friedman looked out into the entry hall before he asked politely, "Would you mind if Lieutenant Hastings and I take a few minutes to talk before we go on, Mr. Corwin? It won't take long."

Corwin nodded numbly. Looking around him as he walked out into the entry hall, Friedman led the way to a small stone cloister that featured a plaster statue of the Virgin Mary. The statue had been painted comic-book garish.

"So what'd you think?" Friedman asked softly. "Should we read him his rights? The book says we've got to do it when suspicion first enters our minds."

"Then let's do it," Hastings said.

"You're sure?"

"I'm sure."

Friedman glanced back speculatively in the direction of the gallery room they'd just left. "Why hasn't he done the lawyer dodge? I'd expect them to be here in a platoon front by now. What's he think he's doing?"

"If we charge him, sure as hell the lawyers *will* be here."

"That doesn't answer my question."

"Maybe it's ego," Hastings said. "The guy's supposed to be an egomaniac. A kinky, complicated egomaniac. Maybe it didn't occur to him that he couldn't do a number on us."

"So how do you see it?" Friedman pressed, still checking

over his shoulder. "How about if we give him his rights, but we don't charge him?"

"If we give him his rights, then we've got to charge him." Hastings frowned. "Don't we?"

"Let's assume we don't." Friedman spoke quickly, impatiently. "We aren't lawyers. We give him his rights, we're covered. We squeeze him a little more, then we get out. We keep the place staked out, and we get a couple of illegal listening devices. We do the same for Charles's place, obviously. By now we should have a license number for Charles's Fiat. We hope something develops between now and tomorrow morning, at which time we see the DA and fill him in. Right?"

"Sounds good," Hastings said, adding, "He mentioned her murder, did you notice?"

"I sure did. In my experience that could mean something."

"Or nothing."

"True." As he spoke, Friedman began walking across the entry hall to the gallery room. At first glance, the room looked empty. But then, blocked from view by the central table, they saw him: Edwin Corwin, seated on the fireplace hearth. He sat with head bowed, shoulders folded forward, knees pressed tightly together, hands desperately clasped between his thin thighs. Standing motionless, the two detectives momentarily studied the small, huddled figure, then exchanged long, searching looks. Was this the arrogant patrician they'd left only minutes before, the baron of this bizarre castle, the master manipulator of lesser mortals?

Holding Friedman's eye, Hastings nodded covertly. The message: At this delicate moment, perhaps with success or failure in the balance, it was Friedman, Homicide's senior co-lieutenant, who must take the lead, make the next moment-to-moment decisions. Accepting, Friedman nodded. As if they were stalking some small, skittish animal, neither detective made a sound.

The tableau held for more than a minute. Outside, the wind was driving rain against the room's small, lead-paned windows. As Hastings listened to the whine of the wind, still with his eyes fixed on the suspect, fragmentary images flashed before his inner eye: *Millionaire Playboy Held in Sex Slaying*, the headline read. And *Edwin Corwin Charged with Murder*.

And, yes, the images included himself, facing the TV mini-cams, answering questions. Lots of questions, lots of cameras.

In the lengthening silence, no one moved, no one spoke. Yet, palpably, the thread that connected the three of them was slowly, inexorably tightening.

Then, in another room, a telephone warbled. The sound ceased after the third ringing. Slowly Corwin raised his head. His eyes were haunted. The mask of his face was frozen, utterly expressionless. His voice was a dull, dead monotone.

"That could be Charles."

Involuntarily Hastings made a vestigial move in the direction of the ringing. But a quick glance from Friedman arrested the impulse.

"He's frightened," Corwin said. "Charles is frightened. And he's dangerous. He's very dangerous." He broke off, blinked, swallowed painfully. "And I'm frightened, too. Because I know why you left the room. You wanted to decide what to do next, how to handle this. You've got the scent. So there'll be more policemen. And search warrants, too. And the reporters, they'll find the scent. They probably have the scent right now. They'll be next, ringing the doorbell. Then there'll be lawyers. Courtrooms. A trial."

Still remaining motionless, the two detectives made no response, gave no hint that they were more than mildly interested as Corwin's disembodied monologue continued.

"When I realized that I was frightened—really frightened, for the first time in many years—I knew I had to sit down, here. I had to feel these stones. So I just sat down. And as soon as I did, there was a flash of déjà vu. It was probably from childhood, when I'd sat beside a fireplace like this." He broke off again, let his eyes wander away as the silence lengthened. Then, reflectively: "Sometimes I think that the feeding frenzy is the most provocative of all images. It goes right through the animal kingdom. Sharks—rodents—lawyers—reporters—they're all the same. Let them smell blood, and they go wild." Sadly he shook his head. "All my life, they've fed off me and my family. For some families, it's poverty, or disease, or maybe madness. But for me—my family and me—it's always been the lawyers and the reporters."

Once more Corwin lapsed into silence as he sat with his body pressed against the ancient stone of the great fireplace. Then he began speaking again, this time infinitely regretful.

"That's what frightened me," he said. "That's why I had to sit down here. Because I was so frightened of what'll happen—the police, and the lawyers and the reporters. I'm frightened of Charles, too. So—" Another silence, this one the last. "So that's why I'm going to tell you where to find Charles. Because he killed her, you see. And I'm afraid he'll kill me."


6:00 P.M. "The question is," Hastings said, "how solid is Corwin? If Charles calls him between now and nine o'clock, and Corwin warns him off, where are we?"

"I don't think he'd warn Charles. I think he wants Charles caught. Badly."

Not replying, Hastings stared out through the rain-streaked windshield. They were sitting in an unmarked car facing the entrance to the long, graceful curve of the circular driveway that led up to the Palace of the Legion of Honor. Located in Lincoln Park, set in a grove of cypress and towering Monterey pines, the Legion of Honor Museum was an exact replica of its namesake in Paris.

"So how're we going to handle it?" Friedman asked.

"I'll handle this end," Hastings said. "You should go back to the Hall, for communications."

"Or maybe I should go back to Corwin's. What'd you think?"

"I think you should go to the Hall, to coordinate. We've got three stakeouts going, after all. Four, counting the two guys at Meredith's flat."

"Translated into manpower, and then into money," Friedman said ruefully, "we're talking about some pretty big bucks here. If we don't get something from all this, we're going to be in deep shit at the next departmental review."

"Maybe you should get approval from one of the deputy chiefs. Hallahan, maybe."

Friedman grimaced. "No, thanks."

"Just a thought."

"I understand."

Hastings lapsed into glum silence before Friedman spoke. "Basically, I'd say the terrain is with us. You drive Corwin's Jaguar up to the steps and just wait. Charles arrives in the elusive blue Fiat. Or, more like it, the car he got after he ditched the Fiat. We block both ends of the driveway, and we've got him. I figure we should post about ten men with shotguns behind the pillars of the building. God knows, there're plenty of places to hide."

"There're plenty of places for Charles to hide, too, though, if he decides to come on foot."

"True." Friedman let a beat pass, then said, "Well, make it twenty men altogether, ten men in the trees, what the hell. Deployed by—when—eight o'clock?"

"Fine." Nodding absently, Hastings was surveying the terrain painstakingly. Except for the driveway and the front portico of the museum, there were no lights. Like Golden Gate Park, Lincoln Park after the sun set was a dark, dangerous place.

"I don't think I should drive the Jaguar," Hastings said. "I'm a lot bigger than Corwin."

"Those lights along the driveway are pretty dim, though. Unless you're silhouetted, he won't see you until it's too late. However—" Friedman reached for the cruiser's microphone.

"However, that's up to you. I'll stick with the big picture—out of the rain." He keyed the microphone and called for a squad car to pick him up and take him to the Hall of Justice.

**6:15 P.M.** "And will that be on Visa?" the clerk asked.

"Yes. Visa." Charles took the card from his wallet, slid it across the counter. The clerk took the impression, handed back the charge card, folded the rental contract, slipped it into its Avis folder. With a small flourish, she handed over the folder and the car keys. "If you have any problems," the clerk said, "anything you need, just give us a call. We'll answer twenty-four hours a day."

"Yes. Thank you." Charles took the keys, slipped the folder into an inside pocket, and picked up the plastic shopping bag he'd put on the floor beside the counter. The bag was filled with everything he'd taken from the Fiat: a flashlight, maps, an auto club membership, repair bills, a tire gauge—and the .38-caliber revolver that Edwin had loaned him the night Meredith Powell had died. Two hours ago, at a sporting goods store on Clement Street, he'd bought a box of .38 cartridges, which weighed heavily in an inside pocket of his jacket, distorting the drape. It was a cashmere jacket, bought less than a month ago, when he and Edwin had gone shopping on Grant Avenue. The bill for the jacket and two shirts and a pair of coordinating slacks had come to more than fifteen hundred dollars—for Edwin, pin money.

**7:00 P.M.** "Will there be anything else?" the clerk asked, smiling. "A scarf? A sweater?"

"No, thanks." Charles took the parcel, thanked the clerk, and left the department store by the main entrance. He would go to a gas station men's room, take the sack inside, and change into the jeans, dark jacket, sneakers, and the black watch cap he'd bought at a surplus store. Then, dressed for the part, a predator on the prowl, he would drive to Clement Street, where he would park the rented Tempo. There would be an hour left, to make his plans.

7:35 P.M. Except for a low-intensity baby spotlight focused on the platform, the chamber was in darkness. Soon he would go to the ceremonial carved wooden chair with the electronic console placed on a small table beside it. He would press the button that lowered the screen over the platform. He would depress the switch that activated the projector. The videotape would begin: two figures, he and Meredith Powell, both of them beginning the passage that would end in oblivion.

Oblivion? Was that the word?

A lifetime came down to days, then to hours, then minutes, finally to seconds. Time compressed, stopped on zero. Then time crossed over: exploding fragments propelled at random through infinity.

Lost on earth, would he be lost in space, wandering through infinity, oblivious to oblivion?

With luck, oblivious to oblivion.

Were there memories that he could take?

He stood in front of the window, staring out into the night. The house was silent, empty. There was no moon, no stars. Low scudding clouds obscured the twin towers of the Golden Gate Bridge. Soon the rain would begin again.

When he'd been a small boy, left alone in a large house that was empty except for servants, he'd made up stories. Fantasies, drenched in blood. The fantasies had often been more real to him than the sights and sounds of ordinary life. Once, imagining himself a masked avenger, he'd taken a knife from the kitchen. In darkness, he'd gone to his mother's room. He'd entered her huge wardrobe closet. Still in total darkness he'd begun slashing at her clothing, imagining they were dragons. Then reality had twisted, turned, fell away. Suddenly the dragons were real: phantasms pressing close, cloth transmuted into flesh, into horrible scales and glowing eyes and monstrous claws, dripping blood.

He'd never known how they'd found him, never known who took him to the hospital. His next clear recollection had been morning light coming into his window—and the nurse in white, sitting on a chair beside his bed. She'd been reading a magazine. When she realized that he was awake she'd smiled, and nodded, and then gone back to her magazine. Later, the doctor had told him that they were trying to locate his mother in Switzerland.

Now, tonight, staring out into the stormy night, his fantasies were more mundane, more matter-of-fact, more serviceable.

In tonight's fantasy, Charles would drive into the curving driveway that led to the broad, pillared arcade of the Legion of Honor Museum. Holding the revolver, Charles would walk slowly to the Jaguar. Every nerve would be stretched impossibly taut; every demon would be shrieking. In the darkness, with rain falling, the figure behind the wheel would be indistinct. Sensing danger, Charles would hesitate. And at that moment, out of the darkness, the police would spring at him. The revolver would come up. Police guns would roar. Charles would fall, dead.

Later he would give the police a statement. Charles, he would say, was a deviate, a psychotic, a sex maniac. He'd been terrified of Charles, he'd tell the police. For more than two years, ever since he'd been forced to participate in the ritual that had ended Tina Betts's life, he'd lived a life of terror.

As if he'd lived through the scene he'd imagined, Charles's death scene, he suddenly felt drained, utterly exhausted.

It was necessary, therefore, that he go to the carved chair, and lower the screen, and begin the show.

Because if the police ever returned and questioned him again, seriously, as a suspect, then he must surely destroy the two tapes. Even though they were concealed, ignominiously concealed, it would nevertheless be possible for the police to discover them.

And that could never happen. Ever.

Even with Charles dead, unable to incriminate him, the tapes would reach beyond the grave.

8:50 P.M. "I'll tell you, Lieutenant—" Dolefully Canelli peered out into the darkness. "I don't think we've got much of an edge here. I mean, if he comes by the road, then we're okay. But if he comes through the trees, well, hell, it's kind of a toss-up, it seems to me, whether he'll see us before we see him. I mean, Jeez, this is like jungle warfare or something."

Drumming on the car's dash with impatient fingers, Hastings said, "It'd take a hundred men to seal off this place, Canelli. You know that just as well as I do." Frowning, Hastings raised the microphone he held in his right hand, clicked the TRANSMIT switch. "Phil, are you ready?"

"I'm wet, Lieutenant. But I'm ready."

"It shouldn't be too much longer. Remember, I want everyone in your section looking into the trees, not at the road or the driveway. If he comes by car, we'll see him. But if he comes through the trees, that's up to you."

"Right."

"Pass the word."

"Right."

Hastings changed channels, spoke again into the microphone. "Sections, give me a radio check, please."

In succession, four unmarked cars and two patrol sections acknowledged the call. As they checked in, Canelli counted the sections on his fingers, nodded to Hastings.

"All right," Hastings said, still speaking into the microphone. "I'm switching frequencies, but Canelli'll monitor this frequency on his hand-held while I'm talking to Communications. Don't transmit on this frequency unless you actually see him, see something suspicious. And remember, Thompson'll be driving the Jaguar. If the shit hits the fan, he's going to block the driveway and drop down beneath the dash. We'll be covering him. Don't forget: I want absolute radio silence unless you spot him, no popping off. Acknowledge."

In succession, six voices acknowledged the order. Hastings nodded for Canelli to take over, then switched to Communications. "This is Lieutenant Hastings. Give me Lieutenant Friedman, please. He's at the Hall." Waiting for the connection, Hastings glanced at his watch: 8:56. In four more minutes, the Jaguar would appear, driving toward them on the badly lit road that connected Clement Street to the Legion of Honor. The road was narrow, and ran through Lincoln Park for almost a mile. Thompson had been instructed to switch off his headlights as he turned from the road into the circular driveway that led to the museum.

"Friedman" came the voice on the radio.

"We're all set here," Hastings said. "Anything on our rich friend?"

"Negative," Friedman answered laconically. "But our guys are sure looking. And they're listening, too."

The listening devices, then, were in place at the Corwin mansion.

"Good. Who's in charge, out there?"

"Marsten."

To himself, Hastings grimaced. From the first hour they'd worked together, he'd never liked Marsten. And Marsten, he knew, had never liked him.

As if he'd sensed what Hastings was thinking, Friedman said, "I've been thinking about going out to Jackson Street."

"Good idea."

"How long're you going to stay at it, out there?"

"It's supposed to come down at nine. I thought I'd give it until nine-thirty."

"If you shoot a blank, then the Jag goes back to Jackson Street. Right?"

"Right," Hastings answered.

"Who's driving it?"

"Thompson."

"Okay. Tell Thompson to contact me on surveillance channel three before he actually drives into the garage. Clear?"

"That's clear. Channel three," Hastings said.

"Right. I'm leaving now for Jackson Street. Keep in touch. And good luck."

"Thanks."


**8:56 P.M.** Underfoot, wet leaves and small fallen branches clutched at his feet. Overhead, wind and rain lashed at the restlessly blowing tree limbs. Close by, surrounding him on every side, tree trunks had turned the night deadly dangerous. Each of the trees, each bush, could hide a man with a gun.

As he'd done just moments before, Charles stopped, stood perfectly still, listening, looking. Above the sound of the wind-whipped branches and the drumming of the rain, he could hear nothing. But he could see the streetlights of the Legion of Honor Drive, to his right, and the curve of lights that traced the circular driveway, straight ahead.

Would Edwin come?

Had the police found Edwin, connected him to Meredith Powell?

At the thought, he realized that his hand had sought the cold steel touch of the revolver thrust into his belt. Edwin's revolver.

And Edwin's money. And Edwin's videotapes, hidden somewhere in the house, in the chamber.

When they'd first done it—stumbled into it, breathless as two small boys, desperately clutching and gouging, he'd suspected the camera was rolling. Right to the end, until they'd discovered she was dead, the sudden cadaver that had once been an art student named Tina Betts, he'd suspected the camera was rolling. And then, even while he still stood breathless, chest heaving, looking down at the dead girl, he'd realized that the video could change his life. He and Edwin were equals, because of the tape. Never again would he beg. Never again would—

From his right, down the narrow Legion of Honor Drive, a car was coming, one single car, a set of headlights, intermittently flashing between tree trunks. If it was Edwin, he was on time. Edwin, who was never on time, was on time now.

Was it an omen?

Was it really the Jaguar, now drawing close to the circular driveway? Was it . . . ?

The lights deflected; the car turned into the driveway. It was a sedan, possibly the Jaguar. Through the rain and the rising ground fog, positive identification was impossible. Therefore, one cautious step at a time, he must approach the car. Now the sedan had come to a stop; the lights had been switched off.

Edwin, waiting.

Fifty thousand dollars, waiting. The first payment on a debt that would never end.


**9:05 P.M.** Canelli's voice was hushed, a half-whisper: "Maybe you should've gotten Corwin himself to drive that Jag, Lieutenant."

"If there's shooting, and he caught one . . ."

"Yeah, that's true." Canelli sat silently for a moment, staring at the entrance to the driveway. Then: "Jeez, I hope he didn't drive by and see our cars, or something, and just keep driving."

"If he was driving the blue Fiat," Hastings answered shortly, "he didn't drive by."

"Well, that's true. But I mean, if he—you know—ditched the Fiat, or something, and if he saw us, then . . ." He shrugged, shook his head.

Hastings decided not to reply. On stakeout, Canelli apparently felt obligated to keep the conversation going, regardless of its effect, or content.

Headlights were approaching from Clement Street, the first

car since Thompson had arrived in the Jaguar. Watching the headlights come closer, both men stiffened slightly, sitting straighter in their seats. They'd checked out a short-barreled shotgun, which rested on the seat between them. When they left their car, Canelli would handle the shotgun; Hastings would take the walkie-talkie.

The approaching car was slowing, probably to turn into the driveway. Was it the Fiat? With the headlights bright in their eyes, it was impossible to know. Hastings's hand unconsciously moved to the door handle; Canelli touched the shotgun.

Now the car turned. It was a large American sedan, a Buick, or an Oldsmobile. With the pale light from a streetlight briefly illuminating the car's interior, Hastings saw two figures, probably a woman and a man.

Charles, with a woman he'd recruited—a woman and a car?

Approaching the Jaguar, the car was slowing. Hastings checked the walkie-talkie's frequency, keyed the mike, and then quickly released it, verifying that, yes, the channel was open. The car drew even with the Jaguar—then continued, disappearing from Hastings's field of vision. He keyed the mike again, spoke into the microphone. "Phil?"

The patrol sergeant's voice was hardly audible. "Check." He was speaking softly, afraid of being heard.

"What'd you think? Can you see?"

"Hold on."

Ten seconds passed. Twenty seconds. Finally Phil Toll said, "They look like neckers, Lieutenant. It's hard to tell, the light's so bad. They're past the Jag, heading for the exit."

"Did you see the guy's face?"

"Not really. He looked young, though. The woman looked like she was a blonde. This goddamn rain, you can't see anything."

"Gord," Hastings said.

"Yessir." In one of the four unmarked units assigned to the stakeout, Gordon Rayfield's voice came through clearly. At that moment, Hastings saw the large American car emerge from the far end of the driveway and turn into the Legion of Honor Drive, going back the way it had come.

"Follow them, Gord. It could be him, with a woman. Go to Communications. What's your designation?

"Inspectors Fifty-five."

"Roger. Inspectors Fifty-five. I'll get you backup, for a rolling tail. I might want a traffic stop."

"Yessir."

"Be careful."

"Always," Rayfield answered cheerfully. "Here we go." Ahead, without headlights, Rayfield was making a U-turn as the unidentified car continued at a steady pace, leaving the scene. Hastings spoke again into the radio. "Do you think the driver could tell it was Thompson in the Jag?"

"I don't know, Lieutenant," Phil Toll answered. "He had to pass on the right side." A pause. Then: "Do I have to guess?"

"Yes."

"Then I'd say he didn't see Thompson clearly."

"What'd you think, Thompson? Was he craning his neck, to see you?"

"I don't know, Lieutenant. I figured I should be looking the other way, so all he could see was the back of my head."

"Okay." Hastings sighed, clicked off the radio, checked the time: twelve minutes after nine. And still the rain came down, bouncing on the pavement, hammering the roof of the car.

9:07 P.M. A foot at a time, an inch at a time, Charles advanced. Ahead, through the trees, the pale crescent of streetlamps revealed the Jaguar, certainly Edwin's. And, behind the wheel, he could see the indistinct outline of a man's head.

Edwin's head?

Carefully, cautiously, cowboys and Indians, he moved another long step forward. Beneath his forward foot, a branch cracked, cowboys and Indians. But the sound of the wind and the rain would deaden the sound.

Cowboys and Indians . . .

Had he ever played cowboys and Indians when he was a boy? Had he ever played hide-and-seek, or gone fishing, or wrestled with other boys?

Had Edwin ever played cowboys and Indians?

Did it all go back to childhood, a tracery of despair? Everything? Always? Had he been—?

Ahead, beside the trunk of a huge Monterey pine, there was a hint of alien movement, a thickening of the darkness. Was it an animal? A man, close beside the massive tree?

A policeman, standing guard?

If he went to the right, even a single step, he could—

The figure moved. It was a man, crouched down beside the tree. Protruding from the crouching figure at an angle, a tubular object reflected the pale light from the stormy sky.

It was a gun barrel. A rifle or a shotgun.

Involuntarily he had stepped back: one quick, reckless step. But now he must stand perfectly still, until he could master the terrible hammering of his heart, the sudden spasmodic shortness of breath, the knees trembling. He must not move. Because it was movement that would betray him. People moved. Not trees. Not the underbrush. Only people. Only animals, and people.

If there was one man with a gun, surely a policeman, then there must be more men. All of them watching. Waiting. Guns ready. Eyes peering into the darkness.

Without moving his feet, he turned to the right, then to the left, staring into the raging dark of the night, wind still howling, rain still falling. Except for the swaying of branches in the wind, there was no movement.

Slowly, deliberately, he turned. One step. And another step. And another. Ahead, through the trees, the lights of Clement Street were closer. Another step closer. And another. In the car, the Ford Tempo, he would be safe. Driving, he would be safe.

Away from the men with rifles, waiting, watching.

Away from the Jaguar—and whoever sat behind the wheel, the Judas goat.

9:15 P.M. On the screen, Charles was moving to the right, about to disappear, as completely as he might disappear from the earth, stepping directly into oblivion.

Primitive tribes still believed it, believed one could step off the edge of the earth.

In less than a minute, it would be finished. The stage would be empty, even though the video camera had continued, focused on the inanimate stage: the draperies, the candles, the low catafalque, the sculpture, all of it so synchronous, so perfectly balanced. Even the plastic sheeting in which Meredith was wrapped draped gracefully over Charles, bent beneath his burden as— yes—they finally disappeared, Charles and Meredith, both of them gone off the screen, entering a new dimension, fallen off the earth.

As he clicked off the VCR he was conscious of a malaise, a debilitating deadness of the spirit.

He would miss her.

Only now, this moment, had he realized how much he would miss her.

If art was the constant quest for perfection, then death was surely its seal. Memory must enshrine before the flesh could decay.

Thus she would always remain for him: perfection incarnate, confirmed forever on the tapes he could never destroy.

It was an oath he must swear, inviolate. If the tapes went, then must he follow.

Therefore, he rose slowly, went to the small room that housed the props, and switched on the fluorescent lights. For tonight's program, a contingency, the stage must be set, the camera readied. Then the mind must be prepared.

**9:24 P.M.** Beneath the dash a green light glowed as the dispatcher's voice broke into the dispirited silence of Hastings's command cruiser. "Inspectors Eleven."

Hastings raised the microphone. "Inspectors Eleven."

"I have a patch-through from Inspectors Fifty-five for you. Hold on." A moment of static-filled silence followed. Then: "Lieutenant?"

"What've you got, Rayfield?"

"We stopped that car for an intersection violation. The name of the driver's Roger Sobel, age eighteen, car registered to his father. We checked out the kid and the car. They're both clean."

Hastings sighed. "Okay. Let him go."

"Shall we come back there?"

"No. We're going to close it down here."

"Roger." The green light went off—then came on again. "Inspectors Eleven, I have a message for you." It was Communications, back on.

"Go ahead."

"Lieutenant Friedman reports that he's in transit to Jackson Street. Do you copy?"

"I copy. Thanks." He clicked off the microphone, sat silently for a moment, staring at another set of headlights, coming up the gentle hill from Clement Street. It was a white pickup truck that passed the museum driveway without slowing down.

"Well," Canelli said amiably, "it looks like another busted stakeout, Lieutenant. Jeez—" Looking out the window, Canelli shook his head. "I bet those guys out there in those goddamn trees won't mind taking a hot shower. Neither will I, come to think about it. This dampness gets to you."

Without replying, Hastings spoke into the walkie-talkie. "That's it for tonight, I guess. Sorry about the weather. When you leave the area, be discreet. Conceivably, he could be hiding somewhere close by, watching. So get out slow and easy, one at a time. If you're on special assignment for this one, return to the Hall, check in your weapons, and sign out. Canelli and I are going to follow the Jaguar out of here. Do you copy that, Thompson?"

"Yessir. You want me to go back to the Corwin place?"

"Right. Have you got Corwin's garage-door opener?"

"Yessir."

"Okay. When you get within hand-held radio range, call Lieutenant Friedman on surveillance channel three. He—" Struck by a sudden thought, Hastings broke off. Then: "Listen, Thompson, when you get within, say, two blocks of the Corwin place, park the car. I'm going to swap places with you. I want to drive the Jaguar into Corwin's garage. Got it?"

"Got it."

"Okay." And to the detail at large: "Okay, guys. That's it. Thanks a lot. And remember, slow and easy leaving here." He gave the radio to Canelli and started the cruiser's engine.

"Hey," Canelli said, smiling appreciatively and nodding. "Pretty clever, Lieutenant. You get the opener, you get inside Corwin's place without a warrant. Implied permission, right?" He nodded again, then asked, "Want me to come with you?"

Hastings shook his head. "I don't think so, Canelli. You're right about implied permission—hopefully. But only one can ride on that ticket, it seems to me." As he spoke, the Jaguar began to move forward. He put the cruiser in gear, ready to follow. "Here we go."


9:27 P.M. Charles brought the Tempo to a stop, switched off the lights, sat motionless for a moment, his eyes unfocused, his thoughts incandescent, a blaze of wild, helpless confusion. All around him, surrounding him, he could sense the city pulsating: the predators stalking their prey. Sirens screamed, the audible signal of the hunt, waves of savage sound. But radio waves could stalk him silently: dispatchers at police headquarters, policemen in their squad cars.

The gangland word was "squealer."

The police—the lieutenant—had found Edwin, discovered the secret of their meeting place, the time and the place. Edwin, then, had squealed on him, offered his car to lure him, entrap him. Edwin would go free. He could die.

Or Edwin could die—while he went free.


**9:45 P.M.** With the chamber locked behind him, with his robe draped over the carved chair, his throne, safe behind the massive oak door, Corwin was descending the staircase from the third floor to the second. Dressed again in tweeds and flannels and oxford cloth, back in costume, he was about to make his entrance. But would the lines come? When he stepped onstage, faced the lights, would the lines come?

Yes, the lines must surely come, had always come. Change the scenery, touch up the makeup, and the lines would surely come.

At the second-floor landing, he paused. With Luis off, the house was deserted. Only the two front rooms were lighted; the rest of the house was dark. Outside, the police were stationed, watching. At the Palace of the Legion of Honor, Charles could be in custody.

Or Charles could be dead, lying in the rain.

Or Charles could have escaped.

The difference, for him, could be profound.

Yet, incredibly, he experienced no anxiety. Here, now, he was apart from it all. And apart from himself, too. Lost, somehow, in random images that returned from the past, wayward fragments, long forgotten.

*Poor Little Prince.*

It was a headline he'd once seen, with his picture beneath it: a small boy in a stiff white collar, with large, bewildered eyes. He hadn't been able to read the words, but he'd torn out the picture. Then he'd wandered through the house, looking for someone to read the words. Finally he'd found a gardener, an immigrant Portuguese. Together, he and the gardener had puzzled out the headline and part of the story beneath the picture.

"By God," the gardener had said, shaking his head in wonderment, "you're famous. Such a little boy, so famous."

**9:47 P.M.** With his hand resting on the butt of the revolver—Edwin's revolver—and the key to the service door in his hand—Edwin's key, taken the night Meredith died—he was slowly advancing toward the small iron gate that led to the service entrance in the rear of the mansion. If the service door was bolted from the inside, he would fail. If it was unbolted, he would succeed. On such random chances rested great enterprises. For want of a nail, the horseshoe was thrown. Napoleon's Waterloo. And Edwin's, tonight.

With his hand resting now on the gate, he realized that he was standing motionless. Was he defying them, whoever might be watching? Had they followed him, stalked him through the stormy darkness?

Yes, he was defying them. Because even if they arrested him he would prevail. Just as Edwin was invulnerable, so would he be.

Because he would have the tapes. And with the tapes, Edwin's destiny became his destiny. The money, the lawyers, even the headlines—it was share and share alike. Beginning now.

Beginning this moment, as he pressed the gate's latch and stepped forward.

**9:47 P.M.** Parked on Jackson Street, Friedman sat behind the wheel of his cruiser with a walkie-talkie on the seat beside him. A few minutes ago, as he was driving from the Hall of Justice to the Corwin mansion, the rain had slackened, then subsided. Overhead, the dark clouds were ragged, edged with moonlight. As he looked at his watch, calculating the time of Hastings's arrival in the Jaguar, the walkie-talkie sputtered to life.

"Lieutenant." It was a hushed voice, excitement suppressed.

He picked up the walkie-talkie. "Friedman."

"There's someone approaching the scene." It was MacLean, his voice low, tight. "You can't see him, I don't think, from your angle."

"What's he look like, Mickey?"

"Medium build, that's about all I can see. He's white, though. Five ten, maybe. Slim. A hundred seventy, maybe."

Hastings had used the same words, the same phrases, to describe Charles.

"How's he dressed?"

"Jeans, dark jacket, dark watch cap. You know—dressed like a burglar."

Conscious of his own rising excitement, a tightness at the throat inappropriate to the voice of calm command, Friedman allowed a deliberate beat to pass before he said, "What's he doing now?"

"There's a little gate at the sidewalk here that leads down to the service entrance, I guess it is. He's unlatched the gate."

"Is there a back way out?"

"No, sir. Once he goes down there, that areaway, then that's it. He's got to either go inside the house or else come back out. I checked it out, Lieutenant. Personally."

And now, still the calm voice of authority, he must make a decision. A second-to-second decision. Up or down. Right or wrong. Winner take all. Was a lieutenant's pay enough now?

"All right. If he goes inside—" Friedman drew a long, fateful breath. Had he stayed in the office, his natural habitat, this problem wouldn't exist—not for him, at least. "All right, if he goes inside, let him go. Don't stop him, if he goes inside. Clear?"

"Yessir, that's clear."

"But if he comes back out—doesn't go inside—then collar him. Give a shout, for reinforcements. And collar him."

"Yessir. He's—" MacLean's voice trailed off, diminished by indecision. "I can't quite see, but—wait. Just—" A pause. Then, decisively: "He went inside, Lieutenant. Opened the door, and went inside."

"Ah—good." Was it satisfaction that had made him say it? Yes—a gambler's satisfaction. Win or lose, minute by minute, the stakes were rising. Soon Hastings, in the Jaguar, would—

In the rearview mirror, he saw headlights. Was it Hastings?

"Listen, Mickey, I've got to change channels. Marsten's got the net. Channel three."

"Got it," MacLean answered. The other three positions acknowledged the command change. Friedman switched channels quickly as the headlights drew abreast of him—

Corwin's Jaguar, with Hastings at the wheel.

Friedman raised the walkie-talkie, signaling that they must talk. Then he raised one finger, saw Hastings raise one finger in response. He watched the Jaguar pull to the curb, stop within fifty feet of the Corwin driveway. Moments later he heard Hastings's voice on channel one.

"Pete?"

"Yeah."

"Anything?"

"There might be." Briefly Friedman described the situation. Hastings's response was a speculative grunt.

"So they might both be in there," Hastings said.

"It sounds a little better than fifty-fifty. Corwin's there, for sure. Unless there's a secret tunnel, he's in there. And this guy in the stocking cap sounds enough like Charles that I decided to let him go in."

"Why'd you do that?" Hastings asked. "I'm just curious."

"Call it intuition," Friedman answered. "Or maybe wishful thinking. I thought—you know—maybe the pot would start to boil, with the two of them in there together, especially if Charles figures Corwin set him up. And if that happens—if they start arguing—maybe we can hear something, get lucky. I've got two of those new directional mikes that're supposed to pick up a pin dropping in Cleveland. Inadmissible, of course. But useful, maybe."

"If I can get inside, you won't need the mikes, and I'm admissible."

"If you get inside, in the car, they'll hear the garage door opening, sure as hell. Those things rumble."

"I know . . ."

"Maybe I can force the lock, raise it by hand," Friedman said. "I've done that on my garage door when the electricity's off. I've got some tools. What'd you think?"

"Go ahead. I'd better stay in the car, out of sight."

"Right. Keep your eye on me. You take over the net. Channel three. Four positions total. Marsten's coordinating. Canelli's here, too."

"Roger. Good luck with the door. D'you want to go inside with me if it opens?"

"I'd better stay out here," Friedman answered, "on the radio. Besides, we could be on thin ice if more than one person returns the car."

"The DA strikes again."


9:52 P.M. Slowly, cautiously, Charles pushed open the small door that led from the utility rooms to the baronial entry hall. An inch at a time, he closed the door behind him, then stood motionless, listening. The mansion's interior lighting was wired into small control consoles in every room, so that light levels could be adjusted to the occasion and to Edwin's mood. Now, tonight, the lighting was dim, throwing the hallway into shadows so deep that men could crouch in the corners and beneath the curve of the central staircase, unseen. There was no sound.

Unconsciously he'd drawn the revolver from his belt. Edwin's revolver, a talisman. The revolver was Edwin's property, an extension of the man, as had he been.

Until now he'd been Edwin's captive. Until a few hours ago, when he'd heard the mewling quaver in Edwin's voice, and sensed the fear that had rotted through Edwin's arrogance to the craven depths of Edwin's soul.

Leaving him the master now.

From above, he heard the sound of soft, furtive movement: the scrape of a shoe on wood, nothing more. The sound had come from the staircase, curving above him. Quickly, soundlessly, he stepped into the shadows beneath the staircase.

"Charles?"

Edwin's voice, from overhead.

In the single word he could hear the same tremor he'd heard earlier, on the phone.

Holding the revolver, he stepped out from the shadow into the dim light that suffused the entry hall. It was a celestial suffusion, that light. Price tag: thousands of dollars.

Thousands for the downstairs lighting, thousands for the chamber, the center of it all. The center of himself, drawing him back.

No, not the chamber.

It was the money that compelled him. Edwin's money, the essence of Edwin.

Edwin's money—Edwin's tapes.

One more step, one final step, and he saw the small, slight figure standing on the second-floor landing. Edwin Corwin, dressed to please his ancestors, the aging preppie.

Signifying, beyond all doubt, that he'd gone over to the police. "Copped a plea" was the phrase. Made a deal.

Holding the revolver at waist height, he began to ascend the staircase, one slow, deliberate step at a time. As he went up, he began to speak.

"I came in through the side door, Edwin. I looked in the

garage. Your Jaguar isn't there." A brief, silky pause. He was in control now. He could see it in Edwin's face: the fear, confirming the surrender. Confirming, therefore, his control. Complete control. "You're here. But the Jag isn't."

"I—I can—"

"You let them drive the Jaguar out there. They were waiting for me, at the museum. They knew exactly where to wait. They would've killed me out there. If I'd driven a car, they'd have killed me. Was that your arrangement? Your deal?"

"They—they came here earlier. They knew everything. And they—they forced me to do it, give them the car." Corwin's voice was hoarse; his eyes followed the gun, helplessly fixated.

"They didn't force you to do it, Edwin." They were standing on the broad, deep landing now, facing each other. "Don't lie to me. Never, never lie to me." He was satisfied with his voice: low, quiet, completely controlled. His gestures, too, were controlled, utterly responsive to his will. When he moved the gun, he saw the other man's eyes follow the movement: snake's eyes, hypnotized, following the movement of the flute.

Snakes could strike; snakes could paralyze.

Snakes could kill.

"I'm going away, Edwin. You knew that. I told you that, on the phone."

"Y-yes. I—"

"And I need money, to go away. I need a lot of money."

"I—I know. But I don't have that much. I can't—"

"I'll take what you have, and I'll tell you where to send the rest, Edwin. And if you don't send the money, then I promise I'll send Hastings a letter. I'll tell him what happened. I'll tell him everything. I'll tell him you killed her and hired me to dispose of the body. I'll—"

"But that's not true. Th-this was like the last time. Tina. I gave her to you, unconscious. You killed her. You—"

"I want money, Edwin. Money now, money later." He let a

beat pass. Then, the reason he'd come, risking it all: "And I want the tapes." He spoke very softly.

As if he couldn't comprehend it, mouth pursed by sudden puzzlement, eyes helplessly blinking, still staring at the gun, Corwin said, "The tapes? But—"

"They're my insurance, Edwin." Feeling the consummate control, the power, he spoke softly, intimately. "They make me as good as you, those tapes. They connect us." A pause. "You can see that, can't you? Tina Betts and Meredith Powell, they connect us."

"No—" Doggedly Corwin began to shake his head dumbly. "No. You—you can't—"

"We're going upstairs, Edwin. We're going to get the tapes. Then we're going to—"

"No." It was a desperate monosyllable. "No."

"Oh, yes, Edwin." Slowly, his ultimate performance, conceptual art conceptualized, his quintessential concept, he raised the revolver to eye level, watched his victim's eyes enlarge, watched the mouth fall open, watched the throat constrict. All the clichés were coming into perfect alignment, in perfect balance, transcending the elements of the whole, his improvised masterpiece.

"Oh, yes," he repeated, still speaking very softly. "You had your turn. So now, you see, it's my turn."


9:57 P.M. Amused, Hastings watched Friedman sitting on the wet concrete driveway, working at the garage-door lock. Friedman wore a regulation blue nylon foul-weather parka over his habitual ill-fitting three-piece suit. Plainly Friedman found both the work and the position beneath his status.

But, moments later, the large double door began slowly, cautiously, rolling up as Friedman bent double to the task. As the door came up a light went on inside the garage. Without switching on the headlights, Hastings started the Jaguar's engine and swung the big car into the middle of the street, lined up to enter the garage. As he came even with the garage door, Hastings lowered his window, saying softly "Did the door make much noise?"

"I don't think so," Friedman answered softly. "You sure you want to go in alone? The training manuals don't advise it, you know."

"I'm just going to listen, try to hear what they're saying."

"Be careful."

"Always."

**9:58 P.M.** At the door of the chamber, Corwin turned. His face was colorless, his eyes desperate. He spoke with great difficulty.

"Those tapes are safe now. They're hidden where they'll never be found. If you take them, and if the police arrest you, then—" Startled, he broke off, listening, staring apprehensively toward the staircase and the floors below. "What was that?"

In response, Charles smirked, raised the revolver. "That's unworthy of you, Edwin. Really. What'll you do, distract my attention, then wrestle the gun away? You're old, Edwin—out of shape. Badly out of shape."

"But—" A pink tongue tip circled colorless, withered lips. "But I heard something. I really did. It—it could be the police. They could be watching the house."

"If the police were watching, I'd've seen them. They'd've stopped me, when I came in. It was a gamble, for me. But I want those tapes. I'll be asking you for money, Edwin. Lots of money, as the years go by. And those tapes are my insurance."

Standing with his back pressed against the locked door to the chamber, Corwin shook his head. "N-no. I—I won't give up the tapes. I'll give you money. I've got about ten thousand, I think, in the house. I'll give you that. But I won't—"

Charles raised the revolver, gently pressed the muzzle into

216

the sagging flesh beneath the other man's jaw. "Do you believe that I'll shoot, Edwin?"

"I—I can't—"

"You don't think I'll shoot, do you?" Charles spoke very softly. His obsidian eyes, black beneath the dark brows, were utterly empty. Against the pallor of his face, his mouth was prim. "Well—" He withdrew the muzzle from beneath Corwin's chin, moved the revolver a foot from his victim, then brought the barrel crashing into Corwin's left temple. Corwin sagged, opened his mouth wide. Quickly Charles clapped his left hand over Corwin's mouth, banged Corwin's head against the thick wood door. "Well, you're right, Edwin. I won't shoot. It would be senseless, to shoot you. But I know you, Edwin. I know you very well. You must remember, Edwin, that we're connected, you and I. You understand that, don't you?" Now his voice was mock-solicitous, as if he were gently prompting a favored student, hinting at the correct answer to a difficult problem. "We have caused two women to die, you and I. We did it to set ourselves apart, accomplish something utterly unique." A short, reflective pause. Then: "When two people share something like that, there're no secrets left. That's how I know—" He raised the revolver again, for another blow. "That's how I know that if I hit you again— draw blood again, watch it run down inside your lovely white collar, which you wore to impress the police—if I hit you again, I know it'll destroy you, Edwin. Don't you agree?"

Eyes streaming, tears mingling with the blood, mouth gone wild, Corwin began to shake his head numbly. "No, Charles. Don't. W-we can't. We've got to—"

As the blood-smeared blue steel of the gun barrel struck again, he screamed. Almost instantly the sound was smothered by Charles's bloody hand.


9:59 P.M. Gun in one hand, penlight held in his mouth, Hastings used his left hand to experimentally turn the knob of the door that opened off the utility room. As the door yielded, he heard a scream, instantly muffled. Reflexively he pulled the door open quickly, stepped into the large central hallway. Should he activate his walkie-talkie, request assistance? Should he leave the premises, join Friedman, then knock on the front door, demand entrance, citing the scream as their authority?

Moving silently, he stepped into the deep shadow beneath the freestanding curve of the central staircase. Motionless, intently listening, he returned the penlight to his pocket, making sure the clip was engaged. He looked down at the walkie-talkie, secure in its holster at his belt. Should he switch the radio to TRANSMIT, then key the mike three times, signifying that Friedman must monitor his open radio, in case of emergency? Should he—

Voices came from above. A frightened voice and a menacing voice.

Corwin and Charles?

Charles and Luis Raiz, the valet? Charles and a live-in bodyguard, exchanging threats?

Were they armed?

Armed and dangerous?

Life-or-death questions. Make the right guess, and he would sleep in Ann's arms tonight, secure.

Make the wrong guess, and the ambulance would roll. The ambulance and the coroner's wagon.

Without fully realizing that he'd made the decision, he was moving out from the sheltering shadow of the staircase. Now he was at the bottommost step, his head raised, listening.

And now, one slow, deliberate step at a time, he was ascending the stairs.


10:03 P.M. As the door to the chamber swung inward, Charles jammed the revolver into the small of Corwin's back, propelling the other man inside. The chamber was in semidarkness. On the low platform, props had been placed in the camera's field: a sacrificial Mayan stone sculpture and an authentic medieval rack. Studded leather restraints and straps were artfully draped across the rack. Thrusting the revolver in his belt, Charles braced himself, laid violent hands on Corwin, threw the other man across the platform. Another heave, and Corwin sprawled spread-eagled on the rough oak rack.

"The tapes, Edwin." Slowly he drew back his hand. "You can't stand pain. Remember?" Openhanded, with all his strength, he slapped Corwin's face. The hand came away bloody. He wiped his palm deliberately on the gentleman's tweed sports jacket. Then, holding Corwin with his left hand, a slack, sobbing dead weight, he used his right hand to take a long brass-studded black leather strap from the assortment draped over the rack, part of the composition. A quick, vicious turn of the strap around Corwin's scrawny neck, a twist of the strap around the rack, and the picture was perfect: Edwin Corwin, bloodied, the wild-eyed actor in one of his own videos, the master forever the slave.

With his face within inches of Corwin's, he whispered, "Should I turn on the camera, Edwin? Would you like that?"


10:05 P.M. At the head of the stairs, the only light came from a huge stained-glass window set into the mansion's south wall. Hastings moved into the deep shadow of a massive newel post. He faced two hallways, both dark. From the hallway to his left came the sound of voices. Holding his revolver in his right hand, he dropped his left hand to the walkie-talkie holstered at his belt. He pressed the TRANSMIT button three times. He heard the white-sound cycle, followed by an answering three clear-air signals. Yes, Friedman was still there, still with him, on channel one. Without that assurance, that essential connection, he could not continue. Years ago, the go-go rookie, he might have eagerly sought this chance: the headlong hero, making his own luck.

Now, in his forties, Ann came into his thoughts. Already he'd missed dinner. Midnight was the next time frame. At midnight she would turn out her bedside light and settle herself for sleep. Against her flesh, the silk of her nightgown would rustle.

Outside, on surveillance, a dozen men waited, watched— wondered.

Inside, to his left, the sound of the voices continued, softer now. But angrier, therefore more dangerous.


10:06 P.M. The revolver forgotten, thrust in his belt beneath the housebreaker's dark-blue jacket, Charles used both hands to draw the leather strap tighter. With their faces only inches apart in the dim light, he saw Corwin's eyes begin to bulge. The desperate fingers clawing at the leather strapping were weakening. With his mouth open wide, his tongue bulging, Edwin's breath was rattling in his throat. Soon the eyes would begin to glaze; the fingers and feet would begin to twitch.

For Tina Betts and Meredith Powell, death had followed: that pure, perfect ecstasy.

Relaxing his fingers, he allowed the strap to loosen. First came the instant's convulsion, then the long, sobbing intake of breath. Focus came back to the bulging eyes—focus, and life.

"Well, Edwin . . ." He was pleased with his voice, so low, so satisfactorily sibilant, so perfectly matched to the moment. "This is your last chance. Your very last chance."

As Corwin's fingers tore at the strap, Charles relaxed the pressure, let the strap fall away. On his knees, on all fours, scrabbling, the elegant prince reduced to the animal, Edwin was moving across the floor—moving toward the walk-in closet where the props were kept.

The props, and most certainly the tapes.

**10:07 P.M.** Standing beside the half-open oak door, back to the wall with the door to his left, revolver raised to shoulder height, the approved stance, Hastings held his breath, listening. Clearly one man was threatening the other man: logically Charles, with his young man's voice, the silky-spoken sadist threatening Edwin Corwin. Terrorizing Edwin Corwin.

Charles—getting the job done, breaking down the older man. Hastings's job.

Exhaling cautiously, he inched toward the door frame. And now, conscious that the knot of fear was there, at the center of himself, he pivoted his body until he could look into the room. At first he saw nothing in the dim light. But then there was movement: two men, emerging from a large closet.

Hastings moved his jacket back to expose the walkie-talkie, so Friedman could hear better. Then, using his left hand, he pushed the massive oak door fully open.

"Okay, you two. Just hold it right—"

The taller figure—Charles—sprang clear. With the movement, objects clattered on the floor: two videotapes.

*"Hold it. Freeze, right there."*

The smaller figure—Corwin—fell instantly to his knees, a desperate, prayerful pose, surrender. But Charles's right hand was in motion. Was there a gun? Seconds were gone; only milliseconds remained. Knees bent, revolver raised to eye level, trained on the suspect's torso, Hastings saw the glint of light on steel at waist level, saw Charles's hand touch the steel.

*"No. Freeze. Don't—"*

As the hand closed on the glint of steel, Hastings fired: three shots, rapid-fire, double action. As the reverberating crash of the shots died, he heard the voices. Cowering against the wall, Corwin was screaming. On his knees, struggling to rise, Charles was gasping raggedly for breath, eyes glazed as he struggled to reach the revolver that had fallen from his hand. With his own gun trained on the fallen man's head, Hastings stepped forward,

221

lifted the revolver by its trigger guard, dropped it carefully in his jacket pocket.

10:25 P.M. Knees cracking, Friedman grunted as he straightened to stand looking down at Charles.

"Looks like one in the upper thigh and two in the stomach. His pulse isn't bad, though. You okay?"

Hastings shrugged. "It never gets any easier."

"Have you got his gun?" Friedman pointed to the bulge in Hastings's pocket.

Hastings nodded. "I didn't want it lying around, since I didn't cuff Corwin. And I didn't want to unload it, because of prints."

"Did he get off any rounds?"

"No."

"His gun's loaded, then."

"It's loaded, but it's uncocked. It's a revolver."

"What about you? How many rounds did you get off?"

"Three."

The two lieutenants stood close to the fallen man. Friedman gestured to Canelli and Marsten, standing close by. "I want to talk to Lieutenant Hastings out in the hallway," Friedman said, addressing Canelli. "When the lab guys come, tell them we've got the suspect's gun, waiting for an evidence bag."

"Yessir."

Friedman pointed to the two boxed videotapes, lying on the floor beside Charles. "According to Lieutenant Hastings, these could be important. Very, very important. I want you to make sure they aren't screwed up, Canelli. I want you to walk them from here to the lab, then to the evidence room. I want you to carry the receipts close to your heart. Otherwise, it's your ass. Right?"

Brow furrowed earnestly, Canelli nodded gravely. "Right."

"Okay—" Friedman nodded, followed Hastings out into the

hallway, now brightly lit. As the two men moved to the staircase railing, looking down, they saw four ambulance stewards mounting the staircase. Two of the stewards carried a collapsible gurney; two carried medical kits. Friedman gestured them toward the crime scene, then turned to Hastings.

"Which room's Corwin's?" Friedman asked.

"There—" Hastings pointed to a door at the head of the stairs.

"Did he go directly from the crime scene to his room?"

Hastings nodded. "And he hasn't budged. MacLean's with him, inside."

Obviously relieved, Friedman nodded. "That was my next question."

Hastings made no response.

"So what now?" Friedman asked. "What's the plan?"

"I thought *you* had the plan. I've been busy."

"The plan," Friedman said, "probably depends on those videotapes. It's pretty obvious what Corwin and Charles were doing in that room. And it's pretty obvious how Meredith Powell fitted in. It's also pretty obvious that Corwin and Charles are at each other's throats. So if those movies actually tell all, then we can sit back and rake in the chips. If we keep them separated, maybe tell them little white lies, we can't lose."

"What about tonight?" Hastings asked. "Now. Do we take Corwin into custody?"

Signifying that he'd been expecting the question, Friedman nodded heavily. Then, signifying that the question was troublesome, he shook his head. "I don't know—" Thoughtfully chewing at a pendulous lower lip, Friedman ventured, "Corwin's cooperated. He turned Charles."

Hastings nodded tentative agreement.

"And if we keep the place staked out," Friedman said, "Corwin's not going anywhere."

Nodding once more, Hastings said, "I think we should play those tapes for the DA in the morning, and let him take it from there, let him decide whether to arrest Corwin. I don't want to get in that box again—arresting a rich, well-connected suspect without a go-ahead from the DA."

"On that point," Friedman answered, "I concur. But what about this—" He gestured toward the crime scene. "What if we decide to leave Corwin here tonight and he destroys evidence?"

"We photograph the place, and fingerprint it, and take everything movable downtown. We seal the room. We keep the place staked out. If he breaks the seal, he's culpable. If the place's staked out, there's no way he can remove anything from the premises."

"Hmmm . . ." Dubious, Friedman considered.

"I don't see us treating him like a murder suspect," Hastings said. "Not now, at least. After all, he gave us Charles. Or tried to, anyhow. And Charles was beating up on him. *Really* beating up on him. So to me, Corwin looks like he could be a victim. And if it turns out he *is* a victim, and he's telling us the truth, and we lock him up, we'd be in deep shit."

"He *might* be a victim," Friedman said. "Let's see what Charles says, when he can talk."

"There's no question Corwin was playing sex games," Hastings said. "But murder, that's something else."

"Hmmm."

"So what about tonight?" Hastings pressed. "Do we leave him here, or jail him?"

At the last phrase, Friedman grimaced. "Jail Edwin Corwin . . ." Then he smiled: a pixie-tilted troublemaker's smile. "It's tempting, no question."

Impatiently, Hastings gestured. "Come on, Pete. It's late. Decide."

"Okay," Friedman said, "I'll go along."

As he spoke, the ambulance stewards came out into the hallway, wheeling the gurney. Against a green blanket, eyes half closed, Charles's face was deathly white.

"How is he?" Friedman asked.

"Deep shock. Lost a lot of blood." The steward shrugged. "Fifty-fifty, I'd say."

Watching the four men maneuver the gurney down the stairs, Friedman spoke reflectively. "Fifty-fifty. In this business, that's about it. Fifty-fifty."


**1:25 A.M.** They'd crisscrossed the door with yellow "Crime Scene" tapes and posted an official seal, signed by Friedman. Solemnly, they'd warned him not to break the seal. Then, following a detective who carried two plastic bags, one containing the video cassettes, the other containing his revolver, the two lieutenants had bade him a grim good night, warned him not to leave the premises, descended the staircase. They would return at mid-morning, they'd said—with the district attorney.

Ever since the afternoon, even with more cocaine—an instant's eternity of cocaine—he'd been conscious that something never born was about to die. Hour by hour—minute by minute now—the images compounded, came clearer: faces of strangers. Faces of lawyers, faces of judges. And his mother's face, always in shadow.

And his father's face, always a blank.

Sights and sounds—faces and forgetfulness. Finally fading, gone so long.

Ending always with the two faces, each so pale: flesh transmuted into marble, spinning disembodied through the void.

A measurable time ago—a minute, or an hour—he'd tried to break the yellow tape that sealed the door. But the tape had not yielded—or he had not prevailed, strength drained away. Therefore, holding fast to the railing of the staircase, he'd descended to the second floor, and then to the first floor, then to the kitchen and the knives he knew were there. He'd selected a knife, tested its edge, made his judgment. Allowing him, therefore, to begin his passage up the stairs, to the door of the chamber.

But, instead, he'd taken the wrong turn, found himself in the utility rooms, headed for the garage.

He'd known, of course, how it had happened. Thinking of Meredith Powell, he'd allowed her to guide his footfalls. Even though he'd walked quietly, slightly, lightly, she'd been perceptive. She'd preempted him, usurped the mind-body connection, propelled him into the dark, dim reaches of the utility rooms, bound for the garage, knife in hand. But, recovering, he'd retraced his steps, asserted an essential mind-body integrity.

Allowing him, therefore, to free himself from her insidious manipulation as he climbed the stairs to the third floor.

Allowing him to carefully, delicately, insert the knife between the door and the frame—and begin to cut the yellow tape.

Slightly, lightly . . .

Yes: slightly, lightly.

As, yes, the door was swinging inward.

Slightly, lightly.

Allowing him to enter the chamber.

Allowing him to close the door, lock the door, bolt the door.

Allowing him to avoid the blood—Charles's blood.

Allowing him, therefore, to reach the console, switch on the light, switch on the video camera. Yes, the camera was running. And, yes, the tape magazine was full. They'd operated the camera, determined that the film was blank. Then they'd decided to leave both the camera and the film, a pivotal decision.

Allowing him, therefore, to go to the closet and select the knife he knew was waiting: a French dueling dagger, a collector's item, once having belonged to Louis the Fourteenth, an authenticated antique.

He laid aside the kitchen knife, a banality. Now, dagger in hand, he was moving onto the platform.

Where—yes—she waited.

Ready to serve him as he mounted the platform, let the silken robe slip away as he knelt, he on one side of the stone statuary, she kneeling on the far side, her smooth, pale marble flesh a complement to the texture of the rough, porous stone.

But if she faced the camera, then he was turned away. Would she move, as he moved? Yes, the angles were changing. So that now, dagger drawing closer, face upturned to the camera, the creation could commence, his ultimate statement.

As, yes, the pale blade, a liquid gleam of steel, came close to the flesh, his hand and forearm resting palm upturned on the stone.

The touch of the steel was cold, but the momentary sting that followed was its antidote, the sensation he'd always known would come.

He placed the knife on the floor beside the statue, to let the camera study the pattern of blood on polished steel. The dark, rich flow of the blood against the stone, the ultimate conception finally consummated, was wonderfully warm. Allowing him to close his eyes and rest his head against the rough stone.

His masterpiece.

# WEDNESDAY
# FEBRUARY 21

11:30 A.M. As the limousine pulled away from the curb and took up its position behind the hearse, Hastings was aware that, beside him, John Powell was sobbing.

When he'd dressed for Meredith's funeral, he'd resolved not to pander to whatever emotions Powell might choose to display. During the short, canned service at the funeral home, they hadn't spoken. When their shoulders had touched as they sat side by side in the first pew, Hastings had moved sharply away. As the minister droned on, random fragments of memory had returned: Meredith smiling at him in the hallway of 450 Sutter Street . . . Meredith, the focus of so many avid male eyes, preceding him to a table at the restaurant . . . Meredith, eight years old, following him and Kevin . . .

. . . Meredith, with the dirt and the dead leaves tangled in her tawny blond hair.

And, an image so searing that it distorted itself, Meredith in bed, a child, crushed beneath the bulk of a monstrous weight: her father, thrusting his obscene flesh into her. The image was—

"—going to live?" Powell was asking, his voice thick.

Aware of the effort it cost, Hastings turned to him. "What?"

"Charles, that crazy artist, is he going to live?"

"Yes, he'll live."

228

"And the one that committed suicide—Edwin Corwin, the rich one—did he leave a note, or anything?"

Briefly Hastings considered the question. Then, returning his gaze to the front, seeing only the hearse in the windshield of the limousine, he said cryptically: "No, there wasn't any note. There was a videotape, but no note."

They rode for a time in silence. Then, blowing his nose and thrusting the wet handkerchief into the pocket of the blue suit they'd rented with a SFPD payment voucher, Powell said, "There was a lot of people there, wasn't there, Frank?" A pause. Then, when it was plain that Hastings chose not to reply, Powell ventured: "She must've had lots of friends, all those people. Hundreds of friends, it looked like. Wouldn't you say?"

Deliberately allowing a long moment of silence to pass before he finally turned again to face the other man, both of them confined in the elegant interior of the funeral home's limousine, Hastings said, "Those were curiosity seekers, that's all they were. People read about things in the papers, see things on TV, they want to see for themselves. Then—" A brief, merciless silence. "Then they crawl back under their rocks."


12:35 P.M. Walking beside Hastings from the graveside toward the limousine, Powell sighed heavily. "Well, Frank, I see what you mean, all right. There sure wasn't many who really cared about her, it looked like. That kid from the apartment building, that boy, and those two artists you said they were, they were all that had manners enough to—you know—pay their respects." As he spoke, Powell sighed again, looked up into the leaden sky. "God, it's going to rain again, sure as shit."

They approached the limousine and the driver in his dark suit moved to the rear of the Cadillac to open the door. As Powell stooped, about to enter the limousine, Hastings spoke. "Just a minute, Mr. Powell. Just hold it, a minute."

Powell straightened, turned to face Hastings, who gestured for the driver to get back inside the limousine, out of earshot. "Frank. Please." Powell's slack mouth twisted in an obscenity of a fatuous smile. "Please. It's Johnny, remember? Everyone calls me Johnny."

Nodding silently, Hastings waited for the driver to get inside the car, door closed, window rolled up. As he waited, he took an envelope from his pocket, held the envelope out to the other man. As Powell took the envelope, frowning, Hastings spoke very softly. "That's your return ticket—*Johnny*." Accenting the last word, he allowed himself the luxury of letting the bitterness come through—and the fury, and the frustration. "This driver will take you to your hotel, and then you're on your own. I don't care what you do after that—*Johnny*. Maybe you can cash in your ticket, and buy some booze with it—*Johnny*."

"Frank—" Powell spoke piteously, guilelessly. "Frank, you—"

"But before you go—*Johnny*—there's something I want to tell you. There's something I want to tell you, and I don't want you ever to forget it—*Johnny*. Do you understand?"

"Frank, I—" Now uncertainty tugged at the fleshy, florid ruin of the other man's face. And, following the random twitching of uncertainty, fear began to cloud the watery eyes. "Frank, I—"

"I want you to know—*Johnny*—that I know your dirty little secret. Meredith told me—*Johnny*. She didn't really want to tell me, because she was so ashamed. But it hurt too much, I guess, for her to keep it to herself anymore. She was thirty-six years old, and I think maybe she only told me and her doctor, her psychiatrist, what you did to her. That's because she didn't have any friends, not really. Ruined people, you see—people who can't put any value on themselves—they don't have friends. They—"

"Frank, I—I honest to God, I don't know what you're talking about. I—"

"I'm talking about child abuse—*Johnny*. I'm talking about incest. And I'm telling you—*Johnny*—that if you hadn't raped Meredith, all those years ago, she'd be alive right now. She'd be alive, and she'd be smiling—*Johnny*. She'd have a husband, and children, and she'd be smiling."

He turned away and began walking across the cemetery—away from the limousine, away from the open grave.